SUMMER BREEZE

Eve did not like the extra little hop her heart gave at the mention of Brad's new love. She had thought that she was over him. Later, when she was alone, she would assess her reaction. For the time being, she decided that she simply did not like the idea of the man who had promised to remember her forever finding some-one else. She did not want a relationship with him, but she had not anticipated that Brad would bond with someone else so quickly.

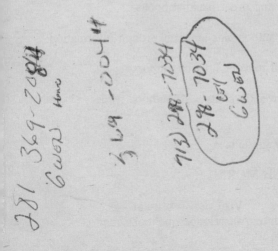

Summer Breeze

COURTNI WRIGHT

ARABESQUE
BET
BOOKS™

BET Publications, LLC
http://www.bet.com
http://www.arabesquebooks.com

Chapter One

Eve Turner carefully folded the heavy wool sweaters that she hoped she would not have to wear for a long time and placed them in the bottom of her suitcase. She had already given her wool skirts and slacks to her sister for safekeeping, knowing that she would not need them for at least a year. She had purchased a few soft cotton sweaters that should provide sufficient protection from the cool island evenings.

Her sister, Helen, sat cross-legged on the bed watching her. Helen alternated between periods of sulking over her big sister's imminent move and jubilation at the increase in the size and quality of her wardrobe. Eve had given her so many items that she had long admired and begged to wear that Helen would have to rearrange her closet and drawers to fit all of them into the already cramped space in her bedroom in the condo they shared. She would wait until Eve left before allowing her wardrobe to spread to her sister's room.

"I don't know why you have to move so far away. There are schools everywhere. You don't have to move to Bermuda." Helen sulked as she admired the pearl buttons on the cream-colored soft wool cardigan.

"We've already discussed this at least a hundred times," Eve replied gently but with a voice tinged with impatience.

Shrugging, Helen replied, "I know we have, but I still don't understand why you couldn't have moved to Florida or Arizona. They're just as far, but, at least, they're in the States. Bermuda's an island, for goodness' sakes! You'll be isolated from everyone, even me."

"I've told you the money was better there than anywhere else," Eve stated slowly as if speaking with a dear but irritating child. "The school system really wants to build up its English curriculum, especially the American literature courses. I'll serve as a resource teacher for the entire system. I'm psyched. I wish you'd stop whining about it. Since I graduated from high school, we haven't always lived together, you know. I remember when we didn't see much of each other at all."

"That was when you were a college freshman and I was a high school senior. We were both so busy then, but I missed you just the same. I had the pressure of advanced placement courses and college essays, and you had freshman-adjustment issues. We talked to each other on the phone almost every day. Bermuda's just so far away. I know that this is a good opportunity for you, but I won't be able to borrow anything from you or ask your advice anymore. It's another country, for Pete's sake." Helen pouted, adding the black wool and silk blend pullover to her bulging pile of goodies.

Chuckling, Eve replied, "You won't have to borrow anything. I've given you all the things you usually borrow, plus all the stuff I wouldn't let you use. As for the advice, which you never listen to anyway, you can always phone me."

"It's not the same thing at all," Helen insisted with a sniff.

"Just pretend that one of us is away at college again. It's just like that. Besides, you're planning to visit for vacation," Eve reminded her sister gently.

"One lousy week!" Helen exclaimed with frustration.

Stopping her packing for a minute, Eve commented, "Look, you're the one who decided to be a well-paid investment banker. You could have decided to teach and have summers off and the thrill of serving others without the financial reward."

"No, thanks," Helen responded, waving her hand. "I watched Mom pore over stacks of papers to grade every night. She worked all the time for little money and even less appreciation. That wasn't the life for me. I was surprised that you decided to teach."

"You know she loved it," Eve protested. "She's still friends with a number of her students. As a matter of fact, their annual reunion is coming up soon. Besides, I enjoy being a part of helping kids learn. When I no longer enjoy it, I'll do something else."

Fingering a scarf that Eve quickly snatched from her greedy fingers, Helen said, "No, you won't ever leave teaching. It's in your blood. You're like Mom and I'm like Dad. Making money was his favorite activity. I just hope you won't forget that Maryland is your home and not Bermuda. Teaching there is fine for the year, but I don't want you to fall in love with one of those handsome island men and forget to come home."

Eve laughed. "I'm going there to teach, not look for a man. Besides, you know that I've just ended a long-term relationship with Brad and don't want another one. I want a change from our always gray winters and our humid summers. I can't see myself living there forever, but I'll enjoy the year to the fullest. I'm afraid to relocate permanently. I think I'd run out of things to do."

"I wouldn't. I could lie on the beach doing nothing all day, especially if I had one of those hot Bermudian men to bring me drinks and rub suntan lotion on my back," Helen said dreamily.

Smiling at her younger sister's vision of life, Eve replied, "I'm sure Bermuda becomes just as boring as Maryland. The only difference is that the weather's perfect there and far from it here."

"You'll miss the changing seasons," Helen insisted.

"And the snow, sleet, and pollen . . . not to mention the air pollution."

"I'm sure there's something negative about Bermuda, too. Every place has something wrong with it."

"I'll let you know if the pounding of the waves on the shore or the splendid sunsets and sunrises on the water cause me discomfort," Eve said with a snap of her suitcase.

"When's Brad coming?" Helen asked as she carried the heavy bag to the door to join the others.

"At six tomorrow morning," Eve replied, tugging another slightly smaller duffel bag to the pile.

"That's the strangest thing I've ever heard," Helen muttered as she walked from the door of the condo she shared with her sister to the kitchen.

"What is?"

"You and Brad. You broke up with him, but he's taking you to the airport. He even transported those back-breaking boxes of yours to UPS. You've helped each other through high school, undergrad, and graduate school, but neither of you could hang in there a little longer and work out your differences. I don't understand that kind of relationship."

"We're still friends," Eve explained. "I told you that

we had discussed ending the romantic side of our relationship long before I accepted the job in Bermuda. He's too busy with the last of his pediatric residency right now to give a woman the attention she needs, especially me. We talked on the phone all the time, but he couldn't squeeze in an evening now and then for more than that. He's always at the hospital. He's taking me to the airport on his way home from working the night shift. His generosity will save me the anxiety of a cab ride. You know I don't like taxis."

"I still say it's a strange relationship. Neither of you was heartbroken over the breakup, although Brad looked a little down when it first happened. He's in your life as much now as before. It's just weird to me," Helen insisted, handing her sister a can of soda and popping a top for herself, too.

"I guess it is hard for people to understand," Eve mused, sipping her soda. "We still care for each other as much as ever. We're simply not ready for the work of a relationship. Maybe one day after I've lived a little and he has gone into private practice, we'll be able to make it work. For now, we need our space."

"You'll have all the space you could ever need with that much ocean between you. I just hope you're not making a mistake. Brad's a great guy," Helen added with a roll of her eyes.

"I'm not, and I know he's a great guy. He's the best friend anyone could ever have. He's just missing a little something on the romance quotient. What's that saying? 'Absence makes the heart grow fonder.'"

"Or it makes people forget," Helen retorted, collecting their trash and walking to the trash can.

Shrugging her shoulders, Eve said, "If we forget the good times we've shared, it means that we really didn't have a solid relationship between us. A few birthday cards and Christmas gifts isn't enough for me . . . or for him. I don't know if we'll ever get back together romantically, but I do know that our friendship will endure despite the distance."

"I hope you're right. Good friends are hard to find," Helen replied as she picked up a book and started reading.

The Turner sisters were close not only in age but in admiration for each other. They had amicably shared a condo since they first started earning a living. Eve was a year older than Helen, which made for an almost twinlike sibling relationship. Helen had chosen the same college and grad school so that she could be near her big sister. Eve's teaching assignment in Bermuda would mark one of the few times that the two would be apart, and Helen did not like it.

Helen understood that Eve needed more in her life. She had watched her sister grow impatient with teaching in the same school, a going-nowhere relationship with Brad, and living in Silver Spring, Maryland. She needed to live alone and away from family and old friends. Like many people who live in one place all their lives, Eve needed to get away from the people she loved so that she could really appreciate them for the contributions they made to her life. Helen would miss her terribly and was glad that the teaching position would only last a year, but she did not try to stop Eve from going. Her sister's promise to return did not squelch Helen's fear that the island and its people would cast an irresistible spell on Eve.

Although she knew her sister's fears and had tried to assuage them, nothing Eve had said since April, when she made up her mind to leave, until now would make Helen feel better. Eve knew that it was futile to try to put Helen's worries to rest when she was nervous about the changes that moving to Bermuda would make in her own life. For the first time in their lives, something larger than the Potomac River would separate the sisters. They were so close that it took an ocean to put space between them.

Eve would miss home, her friends, and her family, but she had to make the journey. She had to see what another place had to offer. She had to expand her horizons. Eve had to get away and find adventure and maybe love.

Unlike some of her friends who had moved to exotic locales in search of love, Eve was not on that mission. She had been content in her relationship with Brad, although it had long ago settled into a comfortable stage without much fire and passion. They were compatible and relaxed together, but the sparks had stopped flying. Their romantic relationship had ended long before she officially called it off. If the opportunity to teach in Bermuda had not arisen, Eve would have hired an employment agency to find her a position in another state. She was ready and had to stretch her wings.

Reluctantly, Brad had agreed that the relationship was over and that, during her year in Bermuda, they would date other people. He hoped that Eve would come to her senses about their relationship if he did not pressure her too much. He knew that he could not stop her and only hoped that she would return to him of her own free will. Living alone in another country might prove to Eve that home and their old comfortable relationship had their good points. Brad hoped, too, that she would miss him. Everyone said that they were two peas in a pod.

Eve often thought that their similarities contributed to her desire to meet new people. She wanted surprise and excitement in her life, not more of the same old comfortable predictability. Taking the one-year teaching job in Bermuda would give her a change of locale and the newness that she needed. Without looking for him, she might find the man of her dreams.

Eve glanced at Helen, who was pretending to be interested in the newest romance novel by her favorite author. Although Helen did not agree, Eve felt that the sisters needed a break from each other, too. Although they each had separate friends, they always came home to share their deepest secrets and concerns. Since childhood, each had been the other's best friend and staunchest ally. They understood and trusted each other completely, realizing that the best possible advice would come from the one person who loved them the most despite idiosyncrasies and temperament. However, that complete faith often prevented them from seeking the closeness of other people. Neither Eve nor Helen was guarded with friends, but each knew that serious or private matters were better discussed with the trusted sibling.

Watching her sister try to read her novel, Eve thought about the good and bad times they had shared. She would miss listening to Helen's stories over dinner, but she knew that frequent phone calls would help to ease the loneliness of being separated. Besides, Eve had decided that she needed to make the change, and there was no going back now. She had officially requested and received a one-year sabbatical leave.

"Have you finished packing?" Helen asked, tossing the book onto the coffee table.

"Almost."

"Do you want any help?"

"No, I just have makeup and other last-minute stuff to toss into the bag in the morning," Eve replied with a gentle smile at the strained expression on her sister's face.

"Oh. Well, I guess I'll go to bed then." Helen sighed. "Don't forget to call Mom and Dad before you turn in."

"I won't."

"Night. Wake me before you leave in the morning," Helen requested with sadness in her voice.

"Okay."

Eve sat in the silence of their condo long after she could hear Helen's gentle snores through her open bedroom door. Family photos covered the tops of all the tables, reminding her of the physical similarity that existed between Helen and herself. Close in age and appearance, they had often been mistaken for each other as children. Like twins, they had tried to confuse people by dressing alike. As adults, new friends often misidentified them. Their tall, thin, athletic, well-proportioned figures looked equally at home in shorts, slacks, or evening gowns. Their brown eyes laughed with the same sense of fun, and their beautiful warm complexions required no makeup. They enjoyed the same foods, music, and people. They wore the same size clothing and were practically identical except in their sleeping habits. Eve was an insomniac whereas Helen could sleep standing up.

Helen's ability to fall asleep always amazed Eve, who had tried everything from soothing tapes to warm milk. Helen always fell asleep within minutes of lying down. No worries, fears, or concerns ever caused her to lie awake nights. She never tossed, turned, or fought with her sheets. Helen never awoke with deep circles under her eyes from a restless night. When Helen entered her bedroom, she put aside all troubles and focused on sleeping, her favorite activity. Even that night on the wake of their separation, Eve knew that Helen would sleep soundly.

To the contrary, Eve knew that she would hardly

sleep a wink that night. Unlike her sister, she would rise in the morning with bags under her eyes and a bad case of "bed head" from tossing and turning. The rush of emotions that surged through her body at the thought of leaving home and family for life on an island would keep her awake all night.

Straightening the books and magazines on the coffee table and turning out the living room light, Eve softly crept past her sister's dark room. Peering into the darkness, she could barely make out the outline of her sister's body as she lay on her side with her left arm under her head. Although Eve would keep her word and awaken Helen before leaving at six, she knew that her sister would not remember her departure. Helen was instantly awake during the week as soon as the alarm sounded, but, on the weekends she liked to sleep as late as possible. She would often get up, eat a bowl of cereal, and return to bed only to awaken a few hours later without memory of the trip to the kitchen.

Turning on her bedside light, Eve surveyed her room one last time before climbing into bed. She had already placed her suitcases in the hall near the door, leaving only her carry-on bag sitting forlornly on the blanket chest at the foot of her bed. Her traveling outfit, consisting of a soft print skirt, a light blue T-shirt, and white strap sandals, lay on the chair under the window. Her dresser looked empty since she had packed the photos of her family and Brad; Eve could not leave home without them.

Before turning out the light, Eve phoned her parents. She left a message on their voice mail telling them that she would call as soon as she arrived at her new home. It was after midnight, and they had already turned in for the night. The next day, she would be too rushed to phone. She would not see them until winter break if she decided to fly home or until summer when she had satisfied the conditions of her contract and returned to the States.

Eve lay in the total darkness of her familiar room. Unlike her sister, who slept with her door open to allow the cat to enter, Eve had closed the room and now could hear only the hum of her radio. She felt alone but secure. In twenty-four hours, she would sleep in a new bedroom with unfamiliar sounds and smells surrounding her.

Adjusting her pillow again, Eve could not help wondering if she was doing the right thing. She had broken off her relationship to a perfectly wonderful but somewhat boring man and requested a sabbatical from a good job. She had packed her belongings for an unknown land. Only now did she wonder what she would do if Bermuda offered no more excitement than Maryland. Perhaps the locale was not at fault; perhaps the ennui resided within her. She would soon find out the truth.

Turning away from the clock's glowing face, Eve tried to push the thoughts of morning and Bermuda from her mind. She did not want to think of the pink beaches, the handsome men, the gentle summer breezes, and the clear blue water. She wanted to sleep so that she could awaken ready for the trip in the morning. However, the thoughts returned almost as quickly as she shoved them away. Bermuda was the land of adventure and new beginnings, her home for the next year, and the opportunity for happiness. Eve was ready.

The alarm jarred her from a fitful sleep at five-thirty. Quickly, Eve made her bed and rushed into the bathroom for a shower. She would grab something for breakfast at the airport while waiting for her flight's departure. The new check-in rules gave her plenty of time to eat a leisurely breakfast and relax before the flight. She might even try phoning her parents although they usually slept late.

Stepping into the hall, Eve heard her sister's deep breathing. Although Helen would never remember, Eve would wake her for a final good-bye before leaving their condo. Brad, though not usually punctual, might already be waiting at the curb to drive her to the airport.

Looking lovingly into her sister's face, Eve saw that Helen looked very much as she had as a child. Her beautiful face was still unlined and her lips curved into a sweet smile as she blew puffs of breath into the air. Eve would miss her terribly and hoped that Helen would be able to visit despite the demands of her job as an investment banker. Helen had often spoken of becoming self-employed. Perhaps having the condo to herself and plenty of space to spread out would give her the push she needed to do it.

"Bye, little sister," Eve said softly after gently shaking Helen awake. "I'll call you as soon as I arrive in Bermuda."

Sleepily, Helen replied, "I'll miss you."

"Me too. I love you," Eve said, planting a kiss on her sister's cheek.

"I love you, too." Helen yawned and settled into the heavy breathing again.

Leaving a little good-bye note on the dresser, Eve softly left the room. The condo looked elegant and peaceful in the early morning gray that preceded sunrise. Their cat slept on the cushion in front of the patio doors. He did not lift his head as she unlocked the front door and stepped into the quiet hall.

"You didn't get much sleep, did you?" Brad asked as he loaded Eve's bags into the trunk of his car.

"No. Do I look awful?" Eve asked, checking her reflection in the car window.

"Not to me. Never to me," Brad replied gently.

"You old charmer." Eve laughed as she climbed into the passenger seat.

"You can still change your mind, you know, or insist on arriving later," Brad stated, heading the car toward the airport.

Shaking her head, Eve replied, "No, I can't. I want to do this. Besides, I like the idea of having some portion of the summer to get to know the island before plunging into the classroom."

"Then it's done," Brad said sadly.

"Yes, but you can come visit any time you want," Eve said, patting his hand softly.

"I know."

"You're so busy at the hospital that you won't miss me much, if at all," Eve said as they pulled into the light traffic.

"Only every minute of every hour."

"Come on, Brad. You know that our relationship had changed into something more platonic than romantic. You'll find someone else if you'll only give yourself the chance," Eve said, a little irritated by his attempt to make her feel sorry for leaving him.

"I know it's my fault that things didn't work out between us, but I'll change," Brad insisted. "I can become a lover again. Change your plans, and I'll show you."

"No," Ever replied firmly. "We've already had this discussion. We're great friends. Let's just be thankful for that."

They drove the rest of the distance to the airport in silence. Although Brad had understood her need to end their relationship, he had not wanted to change their status. He enjoyed knowing that one woman always cared for him and understood him. He was comfortable in the sameness that Eve had found stifling. They en-

joyed all of the same things. They had fun together. Deep
inside, Brad had hoped that she would change her mind
and not leave. Now, however, as they approached the
airport turnoff, he had to admit that Eve was really
going to Bermuda and leaving him behind.

As Brad nosed the car into the passenger drop-off
lane, Eve suddenly felt a surge of anxiety and the electricity of anticipation. She felt charged with incredible
energy and the desire to get under way. A new life and
an incredible adventure awaited her if only for a year.
Knowing that the Bermuda school system might offer
her a permanent position if her exchange year was successful, she wanted to do her best not only for the students but for the opportunity to remain on the island.
Eve was not certain that she wanted to relocate permanently, but she wanted to keep all of her options open.

Brad tipped the skycap who loaded Eve's bags onto
the conveyor belt and watched as she checked in. Her
eyes were wide with childlike wonder, and her hands
fluttered with energy waiting to be spent. He could not
share her breathless excitement and only felt as if his
insides had been rubbed raw. He wanted to hold her
and make her stay, but he could not. Brad had known
Eve long enough to know that she had to take this journey; she would resent his interference if he coerced her
into changing her plans. Besides, the year apart might
rekindle the sparks of romance between them.

"This is it!" Eve stated with outstretched arms that
pulled him close.

"Yeah. I could park and join you inside if you'd
like," Brad replied as he forced himself to release the
woman he had loved so well and allowed to slip away.

"No, it's too expensive. You've done enough already.
Besides, you can't go through the metal detector without a ticket," Eve said, shouldering her carry-on bag.

"Okay." Brad sighed. "Have a good flight and call me as soon as you can."

"I will," Eve said, impatient to be away from his sad face.

"I'll still be here when you come home. I love you."

"I love you, too, always." Eve stepped through the automatic doors and into the press of people.

A whiff of Eve's perfume lingered in the warm car as Brad drove away. Eve was starting a new chapter in her life as she firmly closed the door on the one they had shared. Mingling with the early morning traffic, he hoped that she would learn the lesson that his heart had taught him too late.

Chapter Two

As Eve stepped from the airport, the sunshine embraced her. The gentle island breeze disturbed the hem of her skirt and drew attention to her shapely legs. After long hours in the roar of the jet, she gazed at the crystal-blue sky with eager anticipation. Although she had slept little the previous night, she was wide-awake and excited about living in Bermuda, adding personal touches to the cottage the school system had provided, exploring the city, and settling into her home for the next year.

Since receiving the job offer, Eve had concentrated on teaching the last of her classes, finishing the paperwork that accompanied the end of the school year, and saying good-bye to her colleagues. She had deliberately pushed the excitement of relocation from her mind. Now, with the past behind her, she was free to concentrate on the beauty of the island.

She had not visited Bermuda since the day of the interview. Eve had loved the colors and sights of the island and hoped that the superintendent of schools would offer her a position. Although it would be only a year, Eve knew that she would be incredibly happy in this paradise. She had happily packed her few belongings, a tissue box and photo of her parents, said good-bye to her colleagues, and left without looking back. She would not miss the ice and snow of Maryland.

Since receiving the contract, Eve had marveled that prospects for an adventure of a lifetime had come from a fruitless search for a used car to replace her ancient vehicle. She had not been on a job search. Although in need of a change, she had not planned to make one this drastic.

Eve had thought that she had made a good impression at the interview. However, she had kept her fingers crossed until the letter arrived. As she opened it, a photo of a lovely little cottage had fluttered to the floor. According to the letter, the cottage on the lovely stretch of beach was simply one of the many perks that accompanied the teaching position.

Dragging her luggage toward the waiting line of taxis, Eve was again struck by the uniqueness of the island. People seemed happy, relaxed, and unhurried in a manner unknown back home in the Washington, D.C., suburbs. They smiled at each other or offered greetings. Men wore the fabled Bermuda shorts that Eve had thought were only a tourist attraction item. Straw hats and shopping bags were everywhere. As the cabby loaded her luggage into the trunk, Eve knew that she was somewhere special and unique.

Eve stared out the window and chatted with the driver as the cab moved through the heavy traffic around the airport. With the exception of island breezes and palm trees, Bermuda was like any other bustling city. However, as soon as they reached the city of Hamilton's limits, the scenery changed. White houses clustered in small communities or stood alone on the seaside. The soaring silhouettes of lonely seagulls replaced the song of city birds.

"How much farther?" Eve asked as the cab climbed yet another hillside.

"Not much. The village is just around the corner." The driver smiled into the rearview mirror. Eve had become accustomed to the English accent that marked him as a Bermudian.

"I've never seen the town," Eve commented. "Is it very small?"

"That depends on perspective," the cabby replied with a chuckle. "It'll undoubtedly look small to you, but it's about on par with all the other little settlements around here. It's smaller than some and larger than others. The population is mostly doctors, teachers, professors, and businesspeople who have settled here from other countries."

"Oh, that's too bad. I wanted to get the real flavor of the island," Eve said.

Chuckling again, the driver said, "You will. It's all around you. All you have to do is visit any outdoor market or stroll through the streets. You'll only sleep here. Your life will be among the people if that's what you want. The best way to live Bermuda is to make friends of the people. We'll show you a good time."

"I'll remember that," Eve promised as she returned to watching the sights pass outside the window.

Although the temperature was very warm, the ocean breeze constantly moved the air, creating a freshness that Eve seldom felt during the humid summer months in the Washington, D.C., area. The blue of the sky appeared deeper and clearer, too, as if the world of automobile pollution and industrial waste was far away. Blossoms on the familiar hibiscus were even larger and the color was more vivid than those at home. Eve felt her old tensions fading away and wondered if everyone fell beneath the spell of the Bermuda weather so quickly. She already felt at home and not in the least nervous about living alone.

The driver continued his running commentary on the history and climate of the island until he finally stopped the cab in front of an incredibly cute little cottage with a breathtaking view of the ocean. Window boxes and flowerpots overflowed with cheerful flowers that bloomed in mad profusion along the walk and nestled under the front windows. Heavily laden flower boxes adorned the upstairs windows. Grass, sand, and flower seemed to cohabit easily in this paradise.

Eve surveyed her new home as he unloaded her bags inside the property's white picket fence. Despite the beauty of the scenery, she felt strangely alone when the only person she knew on the island drove away. She was alone with only her cell phone as the connection to the familiar world that she had left behind.

As she opened the unlocked front door, Eve discovered that the school system had decorated the cottage's living room in bright floral-print upholstery. Although not fancy, the house projected a feeling of charm and serenity, closely resembling photos from home decorating magazines. Exploring its layout, she smiled at the sight of the charming dining room with its white-painted furniture that opened into the galley kitchen. Someone had stocked the pantry and refrigerator with enough food to last Eve for at least a week. Upstairs, she found two nicely decorated bedrooms with lace curtains at the windows and vases of fresh flowers on the dressers. The school board's staff had taken care of the personal touches that made her feel at home.

Dragging her bags inside, Eve remembered the cabby's instructions to obtain a bicycle for errands as often as possible. Searching the grounds, she found a bright red one neatly tucked away in a storage room at the back of the house. Now, in addition to her perfect little house with its fully stocked kitchen, Eve had transportation for exploring the island.

Struggling to carry the heavy bags and the trunk, Eve found the thought of unpacking to be something that she did not want to face. The scenery and ocean beckoned. She looked at the bags, smiled, and decided to leave them for another day. She made the obligatory phone calls home and then slipped into a pair of jeans and worn tennis shoes. She shoved her house keys into the pocket and dashed down the steps. Throwing her leg over the bike's bar, she pedaled down the road to explore her new hometown.

Although Eve was tired from the flight and anxiety of moving, she pedaled briskly along the quiet roads. She passed through clusters of houses that melded with sparsely inhabited areas of mostly sand and seagulls. Seeing a roadside stand that sold fresh juices, she bought a bottle and lay down on one of the few grassy patches amid the sand to watch the gulls gliding on the summer breeze.

"Mind if I join you?" a friendly voice asked in a sexy island accent.

"Not at all," Eve replied without looking away from the water. "Beautiful view, isn't it?"

Surveying the seascape, the man responded, "I suppose it is. I rarely have time to notice it."

Turning toward him with an expression of disbelief on her lovely face, Eve asked, "How can anyone not see the beauty here? It's breathtaking."

"I've lived here most of my life. I guess I don't see it anymore. I'm David Scott, by the way," the man stated with outstretched hand.

"Eve Turner," she replied and added, "I can't imagine ever not experiencing this place and all of its beauty every day. It's so clean and pure. Nothing at all like back home."

"Where's home?" David asked as he sipped his juice.

Smiling, Eve said, "Maryland. Don't misunderstand me; Maryland's a beautiful state with lush farmland and exciting cities. But after a while, it becomes too heavy. Life is too fast, too hectic, and too demanding. There isn't much time to experience yourself in a place like that. The heat from the political world of D.C. seems to enfold the suburbs and cut off the air. I prefer the peace and tranquillity of this lovely island."

"You must be new here. You haven't felt the isolation of island living. It gets lonely here in the off-season," David stated cynically.

Eve exclaimed incredulously, "How could that happen with all the water sports and marine life here? I think it would be exciting to watch the birds in all seasons."

"I'd like to have this conversation with you again after you've watched a winter storm push the gulls ashore. You'll think differently," David said as he twirled his empty juice bottle.

"Fine. We'll meet here in February. You'll see that I'm just as enthusiastic about the island then as I am now," Eve challenged.

Shrugging his massive shoulders, David said, "You'll return for another vacation and fall in love with the island all over again. It's not the same thing as living here."

"I'm not on vacation," Eve retorted with a touch of anger in her voice. "I've come to teach for a year. I can't imagine not loving this beautiful island."

Looking her over closely, David replied, "Stop by the university after the first real hurricane scare and tell me that. That's when tourists . . . and temporary residents ... usually start making their airline reservations, leaving us locals to ride out the season."

Changing the subject before she could forget her manners, Eve asked, "What do you do at the university?"

"I'm a math professor, head of the department actually," David said as he studied Eve from head to toe as if seeing her for the first time.

"Why aren't you in the classroom? Summer school hasn't started?" Eve asked more from politeness than real interest.

"It's intercessional, that one week of freedom between second semester and the summer session." David turned his attention to the view of the ocean, dismissing Eve as if she were of little significance.

"Well, don't let me keep you from enjoying your few hours of freedom. It's been nice meeting you." Eve rose and brushed the grass and sand from her jeans.

Without taking his eyes from the vista, David asked, "If you're not busy tonight, I'd like to take you to dinner, show you a few of the sights that only the locals see."

Shocked by the invitation that accompanied the aloof manner, Eve countered, "I'd like that, but are you sure that you want to give up your free time to show me around? After all, according to you, I'll leave when the times get rough."

Rising, David said, "I'm sorry I said that. It's just that I've known so many people who've come here for the island's beauty, enjoyed it without giving back, and left as soon as the climate changed. For some of us, this is home. It's insulting to those of us who really care for this bit of land in the ocean when people use us as a stopover on the way to the next adventure."

Climbing onto her bike, Eve said, "I can't promise

that I'll stay longer than the year since my family lives in the States, but I will work hard to become a productive participant in the community while I'm here. That's the best I can do; that's my adventure."

"Sounds good to me." David chuckled, offering his hand in a gesture of friendship. "Now how about that dinner? I know some great places that tourists never see. I'll pick you up at eight, if that's okay."

"Great. I'm living in the Peterson cottage on Paradise Cove Road," Eve said as she turned her bike toward home.

"I know exactly where that is. I'll see you then." David smiled.

Eve could feel David's eyes on her back as she pedaled toward the cottage. When he smiled, he was so handsome that her heart fluttered a bit at the thought of him. Despite his initial grumpiness, David possessed one of those magnetic personalities that attracted people to him. He was not the pretty boy kind of handsome but the type that even men would recognize as acceptable. His eyes sparkled beguilingly and his lips curved at the corners in a very kissable way. She liked the way his wonderful baritone voice reflected the pride he felt in his island home. Eve was impressed by their first meeting. Already she could tell that David was someone she would enjoy knowing.

Pedaling quickly, Eve rushed past the spectacular scenery in her effort to reach home. She had so much to do and so little time before he arrived. She needed to put away her stuff or at least push the bags into the closet so that he would not think that she was a complete slob. Although she had only just arrived, Eve wanted her new home to look as if she intended to stay for a while. The last thing she wanted was for David to get the wrong impression of her intentions.

As she pushed her bike through the little white picket fence, Eve stopped briefly to admire the garden. All of the flowers seemed to be trying to outdo one another as they basked in the brightness of the sun. Nowhere had she seen such a vivid display of color. Not even the garden shops at home could compare with the profusion of color that lined the walkway, cascaded from the window boxes, and spilled from the containers on the porch.

Even the houseplants that bloomed freely on every table in the little cottage seemed to produce more vivid colors and a larger profusion of blooms than the ones at home. Simple African violets produced blooms twice the size of her sister's prized plants. Her mother would be envious of the size of the philodendron leaves that tumbled from the wandering vine in the kitchen. Eve was notorious for her "brown" thumb and hoped that she would be able to maintain the plants in perfect condition. The strength of the sun and the moisture in the air seemed to make failure an impossibility.

Rushing upstairs, Eve kicked off her shoes and threw open the bedroom window. Although the day was hot, the sweetness of the breeze rushed in to expel the stale closed-up smell that had threatened to invade the little cottage since her departure. It was a house that needed to be a part of nature, not closed off from it. Eve would have to rethink her usual habits and leave the windows open when she went off on errands. Unlike in the big city, Eve felt that she would not have to double-bolt the window when she was away.

Although Eve had left the fall and winter half of her wardrobe in the condo she shared with her sister, she quickly filled the large closet with the items, both casual and work, that she had brought with her. Colorful

T-shirts, tops, and skirts made her closet as bright as the cottage's flower gardens. Her extensive collection of sandals and tennis shoes quickly filled the shelves.

Throwing the few sweaters she had brought with her into the dresser drawers, Eve darted into the bathroom. As with the rest of the master bedroom, someone had painted it a neutral linen color trimmed in a pale green with a yellow floral boarder at the ceiling line. White lace curtains billowed in the breeze and a matching shower curtain screened off the claw-foot tub and shower combination. The glistening simplicity of the white tile made the small bathroom appear larger. A single white orchid in a large white ceramic pot added ornamentation to the countertop.

Eve found the uncluttered elegance of the little cottage a welcome break from the heavily decorated condo she shared with Helen. She would have liked to use the simple approach there, too, but her sister preferred bold, bright decorations and lots of them. She had long suspected that Helen had an artist's soul and love of color. Eve had, however, refused to allow Helen's infusion of color to infiltrate her bedroom, which she had decorated in muted shades of cream and peach.

Wrapping herself in one of the fluffy white towels reminiscent of the clouds that hung over the island, Eve quickly applied a touch of blush to her cheeks. Already she could see the beginnings of a healthy glow where the sun had begun to remove the classroom pallor that dulled her complexion during the school year. At least this school year she would not have to cover herself in heavy sweaters, gloves, and face creams to protect her skin from the blistering cold wind. Eve was aware of the damage that the sun could wreak on her complexion. She had brought light creams with sunscreen at her sister's insistence. Helen had instructed Eve to take care of her skin or else she would look like a dried-up old leaf upon her return.

Ignoring the few pairs of panty hose she had packed on Helen's insistence, Eve slipped into an apricot-colored panty and bra set. Her one indulgence since college had been pretty lingerie that made her feel feminine even when covered in heavy wool sweaters and skirts. Easing her feet into strappy sandals, she chuckled at the mauve polish that Helen had painted on her toenails the previous night, saying that Eve could not take naked toes to an island paradise. Pulling on the mauve-and-blue-print skirt and the mauve silk blouse, Eve thought she looked presentable for a first date with a man she had casually met while enjoying the view of the sea and a refreshing bottle of juice.

Already Eve missed her pushy younger sister and would phone her before going to bed with details of her first day in her new home. Usually when Eve dressed for a date, Helen would sit cross-legged on Eve's bed waiting for her big sister to model her outfit selection. And just as often, Helen would send Eve back to the closet to look for another combination with more punch. Helen's theory of dating required that a woman pull out all the stops on the first few dates. She believed that the first impressions were truly the lasting ones and that a woman needed to dress to kill, accentuate every curve, and cast an unbreakable spell on the first date. Her theory never failed, and Helen was never dateless. Eve, on the other hand, often resisted and, on occasion, spent evenings reading rather than dancing. If the evening went well, Eve would have plenty to share with her sister. Even if it did not, she would paint word pictures of the island so that Helen would be able to experience its beauty with her.

Eve was not the impetuous type and never would have accepted a date from a man she had met so casually if she had been at home. However, she did not know any women on the island who would invite her to a cookout populated by single men. Unless she wanted to spend the summer and school year alone, Eve had to break with her reserved habits and accept dates from strangers. Besides, David Scott seemed perfectly respectable. He had voluntarily shared information about his teaching job at the university. His conversation had not been especially lively, but he had definitely sounded like a dedicated teacher. Eve was sure that she would learn more over dinner. Even if he proved to be the silent type, on an island with abundant fresh seafood, she would eat well.

Taking one last quick look at her reflection in the full-length mirror, Eve decided to verify David's story. After all, she did not know anything about him that he had not told her. With luck, the university's Web site would provide the sense of security that she needed.

The school board had installed a state-of-the-art computer in the little cottage. It possessed more memory and gadgets than the one Helen had purchased for their condo. Sitting at the desk, Eve quickly accessed the Internet and searched for the university's address. Jumping through the links, she found the faculty directory and quickly scrolled to the math department. As he had said, David's photo, e-mail address, and phone number appeared first, accompanied by the department chair title.

Eve was about to turn off the computer when she saw a link for biographical information under David's phone number. Clicking it, she read the details with great interest. In addition to having a Ph.D. in mathematics, David was a champion sailor, a marksman, and, most importantly, unmarried. According to the creation date on the page, someone had produced the current version of the information the previous week.

Eve frowned and checked her outfit one last time. David had not mentioned any of his extracurricular activities. Perhaps that discussion would come over dinner. He had a doctorate as well as a professorship. His interests were quite different from those of other men she had met, certainly not the same as Brad's. Brad was bold and uninhibited, often taking unnecessary risks. Yet, David appeared to be so down-to-earth, not showy or pushy at all. As a matter of fact, he even spoke of the inhabitants of the more affluent sections of town and transients with disdain in his voice. He was a man of the academic world who, despite his accomplishments, was simply an unassuming guy.

The pendulum clock on the mantel chimed, rousing Eve from her thoughts. Although the day was still bright and sunny, dinnertime had arrived. Eve felt so comfortable in Bermuda and her little cottage that she had not missed being at home. Perhaps after dinner with David, when the gulls no longer swooped overhead, she would miss her condo and the States. However, at the moment, Bermuda offered too many large and small adventures.

A moped sputtered to a halt as the clock struck the last note. Looking out the window, Eve watched as David parked the vehicle outside the gate. He was definitely a punctual man. Eve watched as he swung his long legs over the bike and stood erect, removed the helmet, and ambled through the gate and up the walk. She had not ridden on a moped since her college days but would make the best of it even attired in the flowing skirt.

David appeared relaxed in a white shirt open at the

neck and khaki slacks. He, too, wore sandals. Ordinarily Eve preferred for men to wear shoes that covered their hairy toes, but David strode with such confidence that she could see that the sandals were part of his regular apparel on the island. She wondered if he owned any closed-in shoes other than the tennis shoes he had been wearing when she first met him.

Glancing around the cottage's small but inviting living room, Eve saw that everything appeared to be in its proper place. She had stashed her stuffed bags in the bedroom closet and washed out the coffee mug she had used earlier. Not wanting to keep David waiting, she opened the door on the second knock.

Stepping into the small house, David looked so much taller than he had as they sat on the beach. He ducked his head instinctively as he entered the door as many tall men do although the clearance was sufficient. He adjusted his stride to eliminate the possibility of bumping clumsily into the furniture. He surveyed the room and smiled at the display of flowers against the white walls. Seeing the cottage, David could understand Eve's immediate attraction to the island.

"Nice place," he commented appreciatively. "This is much nicer than the house the university maintains for visitors."

"Really? I guess that's because I'm not a visitor," Eve rebutted.

Chuckling, David replied, "That's right. You're here for a year of teaching experience for your resume."

Feeling the anger starting to build, Eve stated, "Maybe we shouldn't discuss this topic. It seems to put a wedge between us. You obviously have a problem with outsiders coming to the island."

"You're right, I do," David said, stepping aside to

watch Eve lock the door. "Most of them only come here for selfish reasons and leave without having given anything to the country."

"Well, I'm not one of them," Eve said. "Yes, I'm here to teach for a year, and the experience will look good on my resume. However, I'm also here to learn and experience a different culture and people. I want to broaden my horizons and work as part of the community. I don't plan to be an observer. That's not my style."

"Then, why did you lock the door?" David asked, leading her to the moped.

"What?"

"Only city people and outsiders lock their doors. No one lives near you for miles. We have an incredibly low crime rate."

"I guess I did it just out of habit," Eve replied, settling into the passenger portion of the seat.

"The door wasn't locked when you arrived, was it?"

"No, I simply walked in."

With a wry smile, David said, "That should tell you something about your neighborhood. The school system installed a brand-new computer but didn't lock up. Not using your key is one of the first changes you need to make in order to become one of us. We trust each other on this island."

Trying to hold her temper in check, Eve replied, "I'll have to remember that. I wouldn't want anyone to think that I don't have a trusting nature."

When David did not comment, Eve turned her attention to the scenery that sped past the moped. Bermuda's dazzling beauty transcended time and offered many faces and personalities. Although they had not yet entered the town of Hamilton, they had left the miles of unspoiled land behind them. The way David steered as if oblivious of the scenery told her that he knew his island home better than she knew the Maryland suburbs, since she always had to consult a map before venturing beyond her usual haunts.

Holding on tightly, Eve found that she enjoyed the moped ride more than she had initially expected. Somehow, it seemed the perfect vehicle for zipping through the Bermudian streets and seeing the sights up close. The smells of the island's natural elements mingled with those of dinners being prepared behind closed doors to produce an intoxicating aroma.

Having the closeness of David's muscular body was not without its benefits, too. Eve discovered that he wore the faintest of scents, perhaps soap rather than aftershave. His close-cropped hair carried a light brushing of premature gray at the temples that added distinction and character to his appearance. With every turn of the moped, Eve could feel the tightening of his muscles under her arms. His firm back, shoulders, and stomach were those of a man who worked at having an athletic physique. David's closeness was as intoxicating as his island.

Eve wondered if he would become more accepting of her newness to the island over dinner. Soon, she would find out. Even if he was no less hostile, she would have a good meal and see the island with a competent guide. That was worth a few hours of David's critical remarks. If his humor mellowed, she would have the details of a fascinating evening to share with Helen during her call home. Inhaling deeply, Eve hoped that a good meal would soften David's temperament.

Chapter Three

Knowing that Bermuda hosted a myriad of restaurants to cater to the tourist trade, Eve did not know what to expect about the dining experience. The establishment could have exhibited the usual tourist trap tackiness, overly indulged decorating, or been as humble as a fish shack on the beach. She was prepared to be open-minded about any possibility. With his disdain for newcomers, David might have deliberately taken her to the ritzy, upscale, overpriced restaurant complete with local waiters in white jackets and cummerbunds in order to stress his belief that her involvement with the island was temporary and superficial. On the other hand, he could have taken her to a seemingly quaint tumble-down fish shack on the beach that served fabulous food in a seedy décor to show her that visitors do not fit easily into the more traditional life of the islander.

Eve had made up her mind while she was changing clothes that nothing David did would cause her to lose her temper. She had come to Bermuda to teach, gain experience, enjoy a new culture, and, perhaps, find a permanent home. David's dismissal of newcomers would have no visible impact on her since, after that night, she would never have to see him again. Riding behind him on the speeding moped, she hoped that she would see him again.

As they entered the city of Hamilton, Eve felt a sudden rush of irritation, which she suppressed with great difficulty. David was heading toward the high-priced hotels that lined the seaside and the restaurants that catered to their guests. Refusing to acknowledge the obvious, Eve continued to gaze at the scenery and enjoy the tour of the city. Ordinarily she would have complained, but she did not want to give the impression of being a spoiled tourist to David, who seemed to dislike the presence of foreigners in his homeland.

Eve turned her attention to the sights of Hamilton and had to admit that it was a lovely place. She could easily understand its appeal to tourists although she preferred the quiet of the less touristy areas. Shopping in Hamilton would join the list of things that she would seldom do, since her teacher salary would not allow her to frequent the shops reminiscent of Fifth Avenue in New York, Rodeo Drive in Los Angeles, and Georgetown in Washington, D.C. Just like at home, she would have to save shopping in this area for special treats or when family and friends came to visit.

Suddenly, as if tired of the silence, David burst into song that caused his ribs to rise and fall under her hands. Although surprisingly comfortable with the silence that existed between them, Eve found that she enjoyed David's melodious baritone as it floated back to her as much as she did his accented speaking voice. Both displayed the lilting qualities associated with island speech mixed with the perfect English taught in the school system. The music in the people's voices added a magical element to the island experience much like the touch of romance and mystery of the Italian, Scottish, or Irish accent or the hint of elegance in the sound of English spoken properly by a Londoner.

Not wanting to analyze her reaction to David too closely, Eve fleetingly thought about the familiarity that had developed between them so quickly. She usually took her time to become acquainted with people, but with David she felt as if she had known him forever. Perhaps it was the way he had pulled her off guard by attacking the invasion of tourists in summer that lured her from her protective shell and into the open. She could not allow him to speak against people like her without defending herself. Perhaps the warmth of his smile, which he exhibited infrequently, made her step outside herself and want to know him more fully so that she could find the chinks in his armor. Maybe it was being a foreigner in a new place and living without the support of friends that made her assert herself rather than taking a guarded posture. Whatever the reason, Eve was glad that she had spoken out and that their relationship had started with the ice-breaking disagreement.

Stealing a look at the side of his face in the darkness as they left the upscale shopping district, Eve decided that David was an attractive man. He frowned too much and laughed too little, but association with her would soon solve that problem if it developed. Her enthusiasm for the island and desire to try all that it offered would soon lift his serious tone. He appeared dedicated to his teaching profession and his homeland. His dark eyes had sparkled with pride at the mention of teaching at the university. He seemed to be a man who worked hard and enjoyed the rewards of his labors.

Something about the sparkle and directness of David's

eyes when he expressed his love for Bermuda made
Eve determined to know him better. She was aware that
part of her reaction could have been the fact that she
was on her own in an island paradise. She was far from
home and family and already missed being able to share
confidences with her sister. She usually traveled with
Helen at her side and would share her reactions to situ-
ations as they occurred. Now, Eve had to store the
memories to share later or during telephone calls.

However, that touch of homesickness was not the
only contributor to her fascination with David. Despite
his abruptness with newcomers, he exuded a certain
something that caused her to want to know him better.
Maybe it was the quick frowns that darkened his brow
or his grumpy reaction to vacationers that compelled
her to want to see deeper. Perhaps the smile that played
at the corner of his lips had something to do with Eve's
curiosity about him. Whatever the reason, she wanted
to know more.

Eve could not understand why anyone who lived on
this paradisaical island would frown or ever feel unhappy. The sun shone almost constantly, the surf pounded
invitingly on the beach, and the warm breezed caressed
the skin. From fragrant flowers to beautiful people, the
island offered everything that anyone could ever want.
Those facts, too, combined to make David an enigma.
He lived in paradise, yet he did not seem happy.

Pushing thoughts of David's personality aside for a
minute, Eve wondered where they were going. Instead
of setting a true path to anywhere, they appeared to be
taking the scenic route through the island. They had left
Hamilton's glitzy center and had emerged in a quiet
suburb. Although Eve saw numerous restaurants along
the road, David did not appear interested in stopping at
any of them, and she was starving. The aroma of food

from restaurants and homes along the route had made her stomach grumble.

At last, after riding down a dark sparsely paved road, David turned into a brightly lighted parking lot that surrounded a thatched building on the beach. Eve released her hold on his waist as the moped came to a stop. She pulled off the helmet and fingered her hair. Taking her hand, he led her inside the restaurant in which locals laughed at the bar and tables. The fragrance of spiced shrimp, buttery lobster, and assorted delicacies from the sea made her mouth water.

"We're here," David exclaimed as they stepped over the threshold.

"Where?" Eve asked, unable to find the name of the restaurant anywhere.

"The best restaurant on the island. They prepare fresh seafood in such a way that you'll wish you could eat all night," David explained with one of his infrequent smiles.

"But I don't see a menu," Eve said, looking around for anything that might list the island's specialties.

"You don't need one. Just wait. You'll see."

Although a crush of people waited to be seated, the hostess, dressed in a floral jumpsuit, smiled when they entered and beckoned them to follow her to the depth of the dining room. Every table overflowed with the most sumptuously presented food Eve had ever seen. The diners ate as if they relished every bite. Even the floral centerpieces looked good enough to eat.

Surveying the room, Eve saw that the menu and name of the restaurant were not the only things missing from the establishment. She could hear music that sounded like a live band, but she could not see it. Nothing occupied a single space on the floor that might subtract from the total number of diners the establishment could serve or detract from the delight of the dining process. Eve quickly decided that the band must have occupied a space behind the main dining room out of sight and out of the way.

Without mentioning the day's special or suggesting dining possibilities, the hostess lit the candle on the otherwise bare table and clapped her hands. Busboys carrying huge overfilled trays arrived instantly with plates of steaming temptations and the centerpiece. Eve watched in wonder as they transformed the table from barren to heavily laden in a matter of minutes.

"Enjoy your meal," the hostess stated with a kindly smile and left them to tackle the feast.

"Did you order when you made the reservation?" Eve asked as she surveyed the dishes.

"No," David replied with a smile. "This is just the way they do business here. They serve a small portion of everything that would appear on the menu if they had one. Eat what you want and take the rest away in a doggie bag for later. Everything from the kitchen is fabulous. Nothing ever misses the mark. They abandoned a menu years ago after customers started ordering their sampler rather than the entrées. Everyone said that the food was too good for them to decide on just one dish."

"That's incredible! But what if I want more of one dish and not the others?" Eve inquired as she tasted the flavorful, sweet, lump crabmeat cake.

"I guarantee that you won't be able to decide on just one thing," David stated with a quick smile. "You'll think that you only want one thing, but then you'll taste another dish and find a new favorite. I come here all the time and still can't settle on one dish as a favorite. Everything's perfect."

Frowning slightly, Eve tasted a bit of the smoked

salmon. The crab cake had been the best she had ever
tasted, putting Maryland crab to shame, but the salmon
tasted even better. The chef had cooked the rich fish to
perfection and added a sauce that was too light to have
a cream base but too rich to have come from any other
ingredient. Reluctantly leaving her new favorite dish,
Eve tried the shrimp pâté on a thin sliver of toast. The
seasonings burst in her mouth and then melted away,
leaving her wanting more. David had been right; each
bite caused a different culinary experience and left her
uncertain of her former opinion. After sampling four of
the dishes, Eve was sure of only one thing: no restaurants like this one existed at home.

They ate in silence as did everyone else in the restaurant. Eve could think of nothing to say and no words with
which to express her appreciation for the meal and its
splendid preparation. Every time she looked from her
plate to David, she saw that he was sampling something
she had not tried. For once in her life, food was more
compelling than conversation.

The waiter reappeared only after they had eaten every
bite of every dish he had set upon their table. Beckoning
to the busboys, who quickly cleared away the plates, he
smiled, accepted their compliments, and motioned to
the centerpiece. Rather than take their dessert order, he
set two small plates on the table in front of them, pulled
the centerpiece to a prominent spot on the table, and
left them to discover yet another treat.

A flicker of a smile played at the corners of David's
mouth as he waited for Eve to discover the dessert
course. She looked from the centerpiece of carefully
arranged flowers and fruits to the dessert plates and
back to David. When she had first arrived and was trying to silence the loud grumbling of her stomach, the
arrangement had looked good enough to eat. However,

after stuffing herself on that impressive meal, the center-piece looked beautiful but not like a member of a food group.

David motioned toward the colorful arrangement again and pulled off a leaf. Not wanting to be outdone, Eve gingerly reached out and touched a petal. To her surprise, the flowers and fruit were not natural at all but the creation of a talented chef who had crafted the items from marzipan, cake, and other candy. She bit into a rose petal that dissolved instantly in her mouth, leaving the barest kiss of cherry flavor. Next, Eve tried a leaf that contained the crunch of almonds mingled with peppermint. David handed her a wedge of lemon that tasted of rum and summer breezes. Eve was overwhelmed and, again, speechless by the sensory sensations that the treat created. Devouring the centerpiece, they once again ate in silence.

When the table was finally bare and the candle extinguished, Eve tried to find words to express her enjoyment of the dining experience but could not. She opened her mouth numerous times, but words would not come. Thoughts seemed so heavy and earthbound after eating delectable treats that kissed her palate and vanished.

"Let's go for a walk on the beach," David suggested as he led her from the restaurant. Although Eve had learned nothing more about him than she had known when they entered the establishment, she trusted him completely. No man who could possess that level of appreciation for indescribable cuisine could be anything but wonderful.

Whether hypnotized by the exquisite cuisine or the clear warm evening, Eve felt that she was developing a tender feeling toward the stranger who personified the splendor of the island. She was not the type to believe in love at first sight and had never even developed a crush on a classmate at a first meeting. Just the same, she felt a very real attachment to this man who had introduced her to one of the haunts of the natives.

However, Eve knew that the morning sun might modify her thoughts about David. As they walked along the sandy beach, she carefully examined her feelings. Perhaps she would learn something about him that would diminish the glow of candlelight.

"You were right about this restaurant," Eve said. "I've never dined like this anywhere."

"Glad you liked it. The island holds many secrets from foreigners. I'll show you many more," David replied as he guided her along the pink sand that shimmered in the restaurant lights.

Shaking her head, Eve said, "David, I appreciate the offer, but I wouldn't think of monopolizing your time like that. You'll soon have classes to teach, and I'm free until the new school year starts."

Smiling in the darkness, David responded, "You'll never learn the inside scoop on this island without me. Besides, I'd like to show you my homeland. Few foreigners, even the ones who've lived here for years, see the real Bermuda."

"Well, thanks, but I won't hold it against you if paper grading forces you to change your mind," Eve said, returning his smile.

"It won't," David stated firmly. "Seeing your enthusiasm for being here has convinced me that I need to reconnect with my homeland. I've spent too many days plowing through paperwork and too little time enjoying the island. Being your guide will help me to become reacquainted with the islands of Bermuda."

"I suppose that happens when you've lived in a place like this all your life. I take the monuments in D.C. for granted because I grew up visiting them all the time. Whenever a new exhibit opened at the National Gallery, I was always the first in line to see it. The hometown becomes second nature like breathing."

"That's true except I haven't always lived here. I was ten when we moved from the States to Bermuda. My folks were born, raised, and married here but decided to leave after they married. My dad accepted a position at a hospital in Charleston, South Carolina. Mom didn't want to move, but she loved her new husband and didn't want to ruin his chance for success in a big hospital. I was born in the States. Mom had wanted to come home to be near her family when I was born, but I arrived early. Anyway, Dad made quite a reputation for himself. The hospital here needed an administrator, wanted a native son, and lured him back. Mom was reluctant to pull up stakes again. She didn't think that it would be good for me to move too often. The hospital increased its salary offer and the perks. Dad couldn't turn it down, so Mom packed up and followed him. She had never stopped being homesick for the islands and was really glad to come back."

"So you're a foreigner, too?" Eve asked.

"Oh, no. I'm a native. My younger brothers and I spent every summer and all school breaks with my grandparents. They were born here. According to U.S. laws, I held dual citizenship until I could decide for myself at the ripe old age of eighteen. I knew as soon as we moved back that I'd never leave the island again. As soon as I could, I made my intentions known. Anyway, according to Bermuda law, my birthplace didn't matter. I was a Bermudian because my parents had been born here. All of my family was born here and has always lived here. My parents are the only ones who ever left the island."

"Do they still live here?" Eve asked as they strolled in the moonlight.

"They sure do. Dad's retired now, but he'll never leave here again. He confessed as soon as we returned that he appreciated the opportunity of working in the States, but he had always been a little homesick, too. Mom retired as a teacher last year."

"Ah, so that's why you stopped to speak to me this afternoon. You could smell the chalk dust on my clothes," Eve joked as they walked toward the parking lot.

Laughing his rich baritone, David replied, "Something like that. I entered teaching because of her stories and haven't regretted the decision one bit. My brothers are physicians like my dad. Their bank accounts are fatter than mine, but I sometimes get the impression that they aren't as happy. I enjoy being with people despite the paperwork."

"I do, too, although the paper grading weighs me down. I should have gotten my master's in administration rather than English. At least I wouldn't have to read student handwriting." Eve chuckled.

David exclaimed as they fastened on their helmets, "Aha, another similarity . . . Mom was an English teacher, too, until she decided to work in administration. She earned her doctorate in secondary administration and served as principal of the largest high school on the islands until she retired."

"I guess we were simply fated to meet." Eve laughed.

"I guess the pull of the tide in the Triangle was just right," David said.

"The Triangle? Is there any truth to the myth of the Bermuda Triangle?" Eve shouted as they headed back through the upscale Hamilton shopping district.

"It all depends on who you ask," David replied. "Most people think it's a myth fabricated to cover the lack of navigational expertise in the people who disappeared. Some actually believe in the energy created in the area."

"And you?" Eve asked with a little smile of skepticism.

Pulling to a stop at the light, David stated with a broad grin, "For me, it's a great way to say that I'm glad I met you."

"Me too," Eve said with a hearty laugh.

They chatted like old friends for the remainder of the ride to Eve's little cottage. By the time they arrived, Eve and David were the best of friends, knowing much about each other and wanting to learn even more. Eve was definitely happy that she had left Maryland for the pull of Bermuda warmth and people.

Later that night, Eve phoned her sister. She had been so busy that she had almost forgotten to give Helen her desired briefing on the day's activities. Living in Bermuda had already proven to be more exciting than she had anticipated.

"It sure took you long enough!" Helen complained as she answered the phone on the first ring. "I passed up a dinner date with George to wait for your call, and I should have been in bed an hour ago. I have an early day tomorrow."

"George will always be there. Besides, I told you that I'd call after I returned home. I couldn't possibly call from a pay phone or my cell while David was with me, now, could I?" Eve argued.

"Yes! You could have gone to the ladies' room. At least I would have known all the details of Mr. Dream-Come-True," Helen protested.

"That's your term, not mine," Eve retorted.

"Don't tell me that he's turned into a pumpkin already? Most men manage to look real good for at least the first few dates," Helen said with a yawn.

"There you go, making assumptions again. He's still charming, maybe even more now that I've gotten to know him a bit," Eve said, settling into the chair with a view of the starry night sky.

"Well? Tell me everything."

With a contented sigh, Eve said, "David took me to dinner at the most outrageously wonderful restaurant. I've never seen anything like this place. They serve a little of everything in the kitchen without the benefit of a menu, and it's all fabulous. It wouldn't stay in business for two weeks at home . . . go bankrupt in no time. People would chow down and eat them into the poor-house. I don't know how it stays open here. The place was packed. I guess the wages are lower and hauling the fish straight from the pier helps."

"Cutting out the middle man always helps the bottom line."

Eve continued, "Anyway, I thought David had planned to take me to one of those tourist spots since he thinks of me as a foreigner and of little value to his country. Actually, I was sure of it when we rode through downtown Hamilton with its boutiques and dollar signs practically littering the streets. But the place wasn't anything like that. It was practically in the water and very homey. I had the best time."

"Sounds like one of us ate a good dinner. I had tuna on crackers," Helen interrupted with a sniff.

Ignoring her little sister, Eve said, "We talked on the beach after that and while riding on the moped on the way back here. David's a native, a teacher who's still passionate about his job, and a workaholic. He hardly notices the beauty of the island because he's too busy, but he says that knowing me will change all of that."

"He sounds boring. All work and no play makes David a very dull boy," Helen quipped.

Agreeing, Eve said, "He has the potential to be a real stick-in-the-mud, but, with the motivation of having to show me around, I think he'll be just fine."

"You're planning to see him again?"

"If he asks me, I will," Eve said. "David's a nice guy, and I like him. I could see myself falling for him, too. He just needs to schedule time for fun into his day."

"You sound like all of our friends who think they can change a man. Unless their mamas teach them to relax, there's no way that a girlfriend can do anything to change them. You're better off finding another guy while you still can," Helen added sagely with wisdom born of experience.

"I don't want to change him, only add a spark to his life," Eve rebutted. "Besides, David's the only person I know on the island."

"So, you go to the local market, the library, and to church. By the end of a week, you'll know so many people, most of them men, that you'll see very little of that cute cottage of yours until the school year starts."

"You make it sound so easy. Don't forget, little sister, that I'm not as outgoing as you. People don't notice me that quickly; I don't have your pizzazz. David wouldn't have seen me either, if I hadn't been sprawling on the sand with a juice bottle in my hand."

"Don't sell yourself short, Eve. You're the one everyone comes to for advice. You're the silent type. It drives men crazy; they can't figure you out. I tell everything anyone would ever need to know about me when I first meet them, but you keep people guessing," Helen stated.

Chuckling at her sister's honest assessment, Eve said, "Regardless, David's still the only person I know. I will meet other people in my usual quiet way, but the fact remains that, for the time being, he's it. However, I don't intend to fall for a man simply because he's the only game in town. This island has plenty of men. I came here to sample safely, and I will."

"That's the sister I envy for spending a year in a tropical country," Helen said. "You'll return home tanned and fit, and I'll still look like someone who hasn't see the light of day in years. Where's the justice in that? I'm the one who knows how to use all my assets. Think of what I could do with a tanned swimmer's body."

Laughing heartily at the difference between them, Eve replied, "Mostly get into trouble, I'd bet. When I return, I'll be fit from running on the beach, but I won't be tanned . . . bad for the skin."

"That's my big sister." Helen sighed. "I can see you now. You'll run in sweats, long sleeves, and SPF 30 on your nose. You'll be the first person to live and work on an island and return without a bikini line."

"Okay. It's time to end this conversation. I can tell that I'm about to become the butt of your wicked humor," Eve said as she stretched her tired body. Traveling and meeting David had tired her out.

"When will you call again?" Helen asked with sadness in her voice.

"I'll call every Sunday night and e-mail daily. If something exciting happens, I'll phone immediately," Eve reassured her sister.

"I guess that'll have to do. By the way, Brad stopped by tonight. He's really down. I don't think I've ever seen him looking so unhappy."

"He'll get over it. Besides, all he had to do was ask me to stay, but he didn't. He knew that the spark was off our relationship, and we had started taking each other for granted. He knows I've done the right thing."

"I hope both of you know what you're doing. You're pushing each other into the arms of someone new."

Smiling at the stars, Eve said, "I know, and I might have met my new someone. Only time will tell. Let's face reality. Brad and I had a good thing, but it didn't last. We finally faced the facts and broke up. We ended while the memories were still sweet and before the relationship went completely sour. The best part is that we're really still friends. We're starting a new life. I'm excited about living here, and he'll enjoy being single again there. It was time, and I have no regrets."

Rubbing her sleepy eyes, Helen said, "Just keep me posted, that's all I ask. I don't want to receive an invitation to a beach wedding without knowing that it's coming."

"Don't worry. When I'm ready to get married, you'll know. I can't get married without my best friend and maid of honor," Eve stated affectionately.

"Just you remember that when this guy sweeps you off your feet with his wit and charm. The energy of the Bermuda Triangle might make you think and act irrationally," Helen jabbed.

"Hardly. I have no intention of being pulled off course. I'm the one who moves slowly. Remember? I'll call you next weekend," Eve said, rising and stretching.

"Wait a minute. Didn't you say that you'd ridden on a moped?" Helen demanded.

"I was wondering if you'd caught that." Eve laughed. "Everyone rides one or a bike. We shared one for the trip to the restaurant. It's not too bad . . . a little noisy but not bad."

"How's he built? You should have been able to check out his physique."

Eve could hear the wicked wink in her sister's voice.

"You're terrible," Eve chided with a laugh and added, "He's muscular but lean, if you know what I mean. Great six-pack! No love handles. Broad, strong shoulders and wide chest. I think he works out."

"All I can say is that if you don't want him, I'll fly down there and scoop him up." Helen laughed.

"You're bad!"

"Call me next week. Sooner if anything happens with Mr. Muscles. Be good!" Helen advised as she hung up.

Eve looked around the quiet little cottage and thought of home. Her sister was right that Maryland and home were far away. However, she had not seen the undeniable splendor of the island and did not know that Eve had already started thinking of this lush land in the Atlantic as home, too. Perhaps the spell of the Bermuda Triangle was working its magic on her or maybe it was simply the summer breeze that caressed her through the open window. Whatever the reason, Eve was happy that she had made the transition.

Chapter Four

Eve did not wait for David to continue her introduction to the splendor of the island. The next morning as soon as she had finished unpacking her bags, she pushed the bike toward Hamilton and her day's exploration. Seeing the city's luxury shops lighted at night had inspired her to explore further. She wanted to understand the attraction of the city for the tourists who regularly shopped in its stores. Leaving a note on the locked front door, she pedaled toward the big city.

Hamilton offered more than shops; it was the source of upscale hotels and restaurants. To tourists, the city personified Bermudian life. According to locals like David, the real heart of the island resided elsewhere with the people who worked to make Bermuda a vacation paradise.

To the newcomer, it seemed as if everyone in Hamilton owned a bicycle, a scooter, or a moped. Eve loved being able to pedal along the safe streets and sightsee at leisure without the worry of being run over by an impatient cabby or harried delivery person. She definitely was not in the Maryland suburbs anymore. At home, she had to confine her biking to paths in the park.

Spotting a shop with an especially appealing window, Eve parked her bike beside the others that decorated the sidewalk. Fishing into her pocket, she found the lock and quickly connected her bike to the safety of the rack. Noticing that no one else had secured a bike, Eve made a mental note to ask David if anyone locked anything on the island.

Staring through the window, Eve felt like the little girl in the novel who constantly pushed her nose against a shop window. She knew that she could not afford the brightly colored outfits that beckoned from the window, but she wanted to see the treats that encouraged the tourists to pull out their credit cards. Besides, describing the interior and wares of the shop would give her something to discuss with Helen later that night.

Stepping inside, Eve quickly discovered that she had underestimated the price of the items that filled the display cases and hung from padded hangers. Jewelry consisting of dazzling stones sparkled temptingly in the brightly lighted cases. Soft silks and linens fluttered in the breeze of the ceiling fans. The aroma of freshly brewed coffee and potpourri teased the senses.

"May I help you?" a smiling blond saleswoman asked as she quickly approached. Eve wondered how long the woman had lived on the islands and if she still thought of herself as a foreigner. Perhaps working helped to neutralize the feeling of being an outsider. Eve would discover that reality soon enough.

"No, thanks. Just browsing," Eve answered quickly as the woman in silk appraised her spending power.

"Let me know if I can show you anything. Might I offer you a cup of coffee or tea while you're shopping?" the woman asked, not wanting to insult a potential customer.

Waving her off, Eve replied, "Nothing, thank you."

"Call me if you need me. My name's Virginia," the saleswoman stated with a fixed smile as she moved toward the door to greet the newest arrival.

Free to wander independently, Eve browsed the racks and tables. Not even the items on the "sale" table fit into her teacher budget or taste. All of the items were too fussy for her taste; she preferred less frilly fashion. The same did not seem true of the other customers who walked toward the fitting rooms with armfuls of dresses and waited briefly at the counter to purchase items.

Convinced that she could afford none of the shop's trinkets, Eve headed toward the door. She stopped briefly at the accessories counter from which sparkling treats of every description beckoned to her. A beautiful butterfly pin immediately attracted her attention. It would make the perfect addition to Helen's wardrobe.

"Would you like to see something?" the saleswoman asked, seductively sweeping her long fingers over the items on display.

"The butterfly, please," Eve replied softly, afraid to hope that she might be able to afford the item.

"A local artist made it. We've had it on display for several months, but most people just pass it by. It's lovely, isn't it? Most of our customers prefer the genuine stones in the other case rather than the crystals in this one," the woman said gently as her fingers caressed the details.

Cradling the intricately woven silver and gold butterfly in the palm of her hand, Eve knew that her sister would love the way the artist incorporated the crystals into the wing patterns. She could see it sparkling proudly on the lapels of Helen's conservative suits. Even if the pin cost more than she could afford, Eve decided that she would scrimp in another area in order to send the butterfly to her sister.

"Would you be able to ship it for me?" Eve asked as she handed the saleswoman the pin.

"No problem. I'm so glad you bought it. The artist sounds so disappointed every time I have to tell him that it's still here." The woman smiled brightly as she wrote up the sale.

Giving her address in the States and signing the charge slip, Eve thanked the saleswoman and left the shop. Although she would have to pinch pennies for a while, she knew that Helen would love the trinket. She missed her sister and could see her happy face despite the distance that separated them.

Feeling light and happy, Eve continued her bike journey through Hamilton. She passed hotels with doormen waiting to welcome guests. Near the shoe store, a collection of bikers looked her way. From the similarity of their bikes and helmets, Eve decided that they were probably members of a club on a Saturday jaunt. They greeted her as if she had always lived on the island. Everyone was so friendly in this place in which life was slow and easy and people were polite and caring.

Pedaling beyond the city limits, Eve drank in the scenery. Although Hamilton was a lovely city with flowers blooming from every window and door in overflowing pots, she preferred the countryside with its lush vegetation. She pedaled until the rumbling in her stomach reminded her that she had not eaten in hours.

Without realizing it, Eve arrived at the same little food shack by the beach at which she had met David the previous day. She had been so engrossed in the scenery that she had not realized that the road had taken her to a familiar place. Resting her bike against a tree, Eve purchased a collection of fruit and a big bottle of water. Since she was the only customer at that late hour, she had her pick of locations. Settling in the same spot, Eve selected a perfectly ripened mango and began to eat her lunch with the gulls and the surf to keep her company. She felt incredibly happy on the sunny shore.

"I thought I'd find you here when you weren't at home," a familiar deep baritone voice stated.

Eve smiled as the warmth of the sun and the nearness of David spread over her. She was falling in love without a doubt. She just did not know if it was the splendor of the island or the appeal of this undeniably attractive man that made her heart flutter and her mouth go dry.

"It's beautiful here. The road just seemed to bring me here against my will," Eve replied without looking at the form standing beside her.

"It's one of my favorite spots, too. I've been coming here every day since I was a little boy. My family home is just down the ridge," David said as he lowered his tall body onto the sandy spot beside her.

"You didn't mention that yesterday," Eve stated, looking at the handsome man at her side. Today, he was wearing walking shorts that made his long muscular legs look even better, unlike most men whose legs appeared even slimmer in shorts.

"Yesterday, I'd only just met you. I know you better today," David said with a big smile as he munched his fruit. "Yesterday, you were a tourist on vacation in my homeland with the desire to take away memories and leave nothing behind after you left. Today, I know that you've come here to make a contribution."

Eve laughed. "I've already made a contribution to the island's economic prosperity."

"What?"

"I bought a little butterfly pin for my sister. A local artist made it," Eve explained with a smile.

"Do you remember the name?" David asked with genuine interest.

"Only the first name . . . Arty."

"It's probably Arty Shaw. He lives a couple of miles from here and is well known for his butterfly jewelry and other handcrafted decorations. I could take you there, if you'd like," David said, sipping the tea that he preferred to water.

"I'd like that, but I won't be able to purchase anything. I have to watch my budget until school starts again," Eve said.

"No problem. Arty always has items that he gives away to friends," David said as he pulled Eve to her feet.

"But I'm a stranger," Eve sputtered.

"You won't be for long since you're with his best friend," David replied with a big smile.

Standing so close to him, Eve felt strangely dizzy. She was not sure if the cause was the quick rise from the sand or the warmth of David's body, but she liked the sensation. Brad had never made her feel off center and slightly tipsy. David or Bermuda or both definitely made her wobbly, and she liked the feeling.

David's arms were strong, his hands were gentle, and his voice was deep and commanding. He had also been cautious when they first met the previous day but had quickly warmed as he got to know her. Now, he acted more like an old friend than a familiar stranger.

Looking deeply into her upturned face, David felt a bit confused, too. This woman was different from any of the other foreigners he had met while they worked on the island. She was open to living the island life, even if she did lock her cottage door. She wanted to get to know the people whose children she would soon teach. Eve was beautiful, sensitive, and lively. She biked around the island like a local, rather than hiring one of the few cabs and remaining outside the island's usual custom.

In an incredibly short time, David admitted to himself that Eve had gotten under his skin. She had made him forget his usual reserve and drop his defenses. She made him feel as if they had known each other all their lives.

The breeze caressed them as they stood together on the beach. Only the gulls watched the struggle that raged within each of them. The physical attraction was very real and undeniably insistent. However, both of them wanted more than just a passionate romance; they wanted love. During their walk on the beach the previous night, they had shared information about their latest breakups. Although Eve and Brad had ended their relationship as best friends, David and his former significant other harbored considerable animosity toward each other. He did not want to get burned again.

Releasing his hold on her small hands abruptly as if the heat of her skin had burned him, David said, "I think we'd better go before I forget that we're standing on a public stretch of beach. I want to take this slowly. Things have a way of moving too fast on this island. We might find ourselves in a dead-end relationship based on nothing in particular if we're not careful."

"You're right. This island casts incredible spells on people," Eve agreed with a release of breath. She had been only barely breathing as his heat enveloped her.

Gently touching her face with the tips of his fingers, David said, "I've found that I'm too attracted to you. I couldn't get your smile out of my mind. I want more than physical attraction. My ex came here on vacation and stayed for two years after we became inseparable. I fell for her without knowing anything about her except that she was fascinating. Without ever learning more than that, we allowed passion to overpower us. The relationship developed from there. We never really knew each other even at the end of the relationship. We simply enjoyed being together until it went bad. The heat was like the flash of a match that quickly burned out, leaving nothing in its wake. When it was over, she left without saying good-bye. I don't want that for us or for me ever again."

"I understand, and I agree. I didn't come here looking for a relationship. I'm here to teach, to give back, and to renew. I don't want to get swept up in directionless passions," Eve stated as her face burned hot from his touch.

Slowly, Eve grew cold as David pulled his hand away. Although they stood within easy reach, a wall of carefully constructed precaution had developed between them. She knew that David would not touch her with the same intensity until they knew each other better. She would not again have to fight off her desire to throw herself into his arms and burrow deeply into his strong chest. The burning passion within them would have to wait.

They rode side by side on the way to Arty's house. Although she wanted to hear the sound of his voice, Eve had to settle for the sound of the pounding of the surf on the beach. Pedaling in silence, Eve thought about all that she had left behind in the States and all that she still had to discover on this lovely island. She had left a romance that had ended in friendship in her search for herself and something more than the predictable road she had been following.

Coming to the island, Eve had met David with whom she knew she could easily share an enjoyable year. She already knew, though, that she would not be able to leave him behind without further thought. The passion between them was palpable.

However, Eve knew that she did not want a simple romance that would end when her contract terminated; she wanted more or nothing at all. The wall that had appeared between them would protect her until they knew if the relationship would develop into more than a flash of passion.

Yet it would be difficult for her to stay true to her resolve with David near. If she had not met him, Eve knew that she would have passed the year mixing with the people, grading papers, and teaching classes. She would have joined the women in whatever native craft sessions they were engaged in. Now, with David at her side, Eve promised herself that she would still find the time to immerse herself in the island rather than in his life. She needed the time to discover this new life without the cloud of passion obscuring the view of the island and its culture.

Eve could tell from the silence that David shared her thoughts. Unlike many men, he had revealed his reaction to her and his intentions at the beginning of their relationship rather than after the first major argument or as it started to cool off. She liked his up-front manner and honest approach to building a relationship. She knew he had been badly hurt by the breakup of his past relationship. Perhaps the pain had taught him to take small cautious steps rather than plunging into a romance without giving it time to build. Maybe he had learned that passion had its place but so did caution.

Smiling at her, David broke the silence by saying, "Arty's house is at the top of this little hill. He'll probably be in his work shed. It's usually messy, but you'll see great wearable art in the making."

Grinning at the casual friendship that enveloped them, Eve replied, "I can hardly wait to see his work. The shop only had the one item that the saleswoman said hadn't attracted much attention from the tourist crowd."

"I'm not surprised," David said with a shake of his head. "The tourists I've met seem more interested in spending without thought than in searching for the ideal memento. I'd probably act the same way if I only had a week in D.C. or New York, but it's a bit irritating for a local to see people ignore the beauty of the land and the craftsmanship of its people. The visitors who come here via cruise ship are the worst. They charge off the ships, rush through the stores, spend money like water, and flop onto the beach without ever seeing Bermuda. They can brag about their vacation, but they rushed through their limited days here without becoming part of the land. It's their loss, but it makes me sad."

"I promise that I will not do that," Eve said as she followed David up the bumpy driveway. "I'll take my time to make Bermuda my home. Considering my limited bankroll, I think that's the best approach anyway. When I leave here, I want to take only the best memories with me."

"If you leave here, you mean," David retorted with a smile. "This island gets under the skin of people who take the time to know it. My parents have friends who came here on vacation twenty years ago and haven't left yet. I doubt at this stage in their lives that they ever will."

"I don't know if I could live this far from my sister and family permanently. This place has definitely bewitched me, but I'd miss home too much," Eve replied as she pulled her bike next to his against the shabby barn in need of paint.

"You'd start another family here," David suggested.

Eve responded as she stepped around the chickens and scraps of metal that littered the yard, "Maybe, but I don't know if that would be enough. I'd miss home. Helen and I have hardly ever lived apart. I don't know that I want to start now."

"Maybe she'd follow you here," David offered, opening the barn door.

"I doubt it," Eve said as her eyes adjusted to the darkness. "Helen's an investment banker. Her life is the big city. Shouldn't we call Arty rather than just walking in on him? Maybe you should shout his name."

"Still thinking like a city girl? We don't do that here." David chuckled.

"I just don't want to get shot," Eve explained. "That can happen to trespassers, you know."

"Not here." David laughed at her anxiety. "We're too informal for that. People enter each other's homes and shops all the time without calling first or knocking. When you stop thinking like a foreigner, I'll know that the magic of the Bermuda Triangle has you under its spell."

"You sound just like my sister," Eve chided, peering into the bright light ahead. "I don't believe in that stuff. I'm falling in love with this place because it's breathtakingly beautiful and the people are wonderful, not because of an energy force."

"Have it your way," David said. "I just want you to make this little piece of land your home and love it as much as I do. When that happens, you'll stop locking your door and worrying about surprising people. You'll be one of us."

Standing in the glow of the workroom, Eve looked deeply into David's eyes. In them, she saw all the sincerity of his words. She did not know if the passion would bloom into love, but she knew that she would always like this man and his homeland. Maybe one day, she would leave her cottage door unlocked and push through the protective wall between them. Eve knew that she would be completely happy when that happened.

Smiling, she said, "I'll do my best. I won't promise to abandon old habits overnight. It'll take time, but I'll try."

"That's good enough for me." David grinned. "Look, there's Arty. Let's see what he's working on."

Carefully stepping inside the structure, Eve discovered quickly that every wall bore Arty's creations. The items hung from nails suspended from twisted metal clothes hangers. Seemingly running out of space, he had clipped many to Peg-Boards. Eve had never seen so many pairs of earrings, necklaces, and bracelets in every imaginable metal from delicate gold to heavy salvaged automobile steel. In addition, Arty's workroom housed massive sculptures that at home in the States would have fetched a fortune. However, from the appearance of his workshop, barn, and house, Eve got the impression that Arty was just scratching out a living. She wondered if he was really only getting by or if he was an eccentric artist who felt inspired by living in beaten-down conditions.

"Hi!" Arty shouted as they approached. "I thought I heard the dog barking, but I wasn't sure. He's been after a mouse lately and creating quite a racket with his effort."

"Hey, man," David replied. "I brought an admirer to meet you and to see your real work. Eve's from the

States. She's here to teach for a year. She bought one of your pins from a shop in Hamilton."

Extending a filthy hand that he had hastily wiped on his apron, Arty asked, "The butterfly? Good. It's about time someone appreciated it. Those high and mighty tourists don't seem to like my work."

Ignoring the smudges that turned his brown hand black, Eve replied, "They simply don't have the proper respect for a work of art. My sister, however, will love it."

"Is she here with you? I'd like to meet the woman who'll wear my work in the States," Arty said as he turned his attention to the glowing steel on the forge.

"No, she's at home in Maryland. I've asked the shop to ship it to her," Eve responded as she watched him hammer the metal into the shape of a bird's wing.

"Too bad. We could have double-dated tonight. I'm exhibiting at a local gallery. Wanna come?"

"Thanks for spoiling my surprise for the evening," David grumbled.

"What? I'm so lost in this conversation," Eve said.

"After dinner at another of my favorite places, we're going to the art gallery. I thought you might like to meet a few of the local celebrities," David explained with a happy smile.

Chuckling, Arty said, "I wouldn't say that we're celebrities, but we're definitely locals. Every last one of us was born and raised here. You'll see some interesting stuff. Much of it's even larger than my biggest piece over there."

"It sounds like great fun. I'd love to go, and you didn't spoil anything. I can feel the anticipation building until we get there," Eve explained.

"Don't expect too much, and don't rush your dinner. Have dessert and coffee," Arty said, laughing.

"He's just being modest," David said. "The exhibit is a big draw among locals and informed visitors. Every year the shop sells all of the pieces."

"Then your work is on display in the States?" Eve inquired.

Frowning, Arty replied, "No, I haven't been able to penetrate that market yet. They're too snobby to think 'island' art is the real thing. The Japanese have bought a lot of my stuff. Actually, some of it's everywhere except the U.S."

"I'll have to tell my sister that the butterfly is a 'one of.' She'll feel very special," Eve said.

"That's for sure." Arty laughed. "She won't see that pin in the States anywhere. Maybe people will admire it and want to see more of my work. I was about to go inside for a cup of tea. Would you like to join me?"

Before Eve could decline, not wanting to be a nuisance, David had accepted for them and was leading her through the maze of metal and tools that littered the yard between the house and studio. Despite the magnificent sculptures in the yard, the house was in a miserable state of disrepair. A few coats of paint would improve the appearance considerably as would the judicious application of nails in the sagging shutters.

The interior of the house was almost as shabby with bits and pieces of this and that strewn everywhere. Underneath the mess and dust, Eve could see leather upholstery, wicker tables, and a badly stained oriental rug. At some point in his life, Arty had cared enough about the house to decorate it tastefully, but that day had passed.

As if reading her mind, Arty said, "My ex-wife took the place in hand and decorated. It didn't help much since I was always in the barn with my work, and she was always running the streets. She left me after six months of less than marital bliss. She did a nice job on the decorating. The place looks pretty good when it's clean. But I don't have the time to tend to it. I decided years ago that nothing would stand in the way of my work, not a wife and certainly not housekeeping."

Eve cast a glance at David, who smiled indulgently and winked. He had known Arty for so long that his friend's strange habits did not bother him. Watching him step over the mess on the way to the kitchen, Eve saw that David took little notice of the general sloven-liness that matched the overall decay of the house and grounds. She wondered if David lived in similar conditions and she would have to find a tactful way to ask. Eve was not a neat-freak, but she held a great respect for orderliness as a characteristic of personal success. She doubted that David could have earned a Ph.D. in math and risen to the position of department chair if he did not possess an understanding of order also.

Eve was not surprised to find the house overflowing with materials for sculptures, partially finished projects, and sketches of work not yet started. The kitchen held more art supplies than food stuff. He had filled the cabinets with paints, metal parts, and tools. Only the refrigerator held anything edible . . . cans of beer and cantaloupe.

Peering into what should have been the living room, she discovered a collection of haphazardly labeled boxes that held small items that could become lost in the chaos of Arty's creativity. Every chair held something art related except one on which his cat perched territorially. Eve had never seen anything quite like Arty's house.

Seeing her reaction to his mess, Arty laughed. "I need a housekeeper. The only problem is that I'd have to clean up before she could start work. She wouldn't know where to begin."

Smiling, Eve replied, "It is a little lived in."

"That's the diplomatic way of saying that this place is a pigsty," David interjected.

Looking from one to the other, Arty stated with feigned hurt feelings, "This is art in progress. I know where everything is . . . most of the time. The best artists were and still are slobs."

"Well then, old buddy, you must be the next Picasso," David teased, handing a cup of tea to Eve.

Observing her momentary hesitation, Arty commented with a chuckle, "It's clean. I keep a whole set of Styrofoam cups on the top shelf for special company. Since I haven't had any since I bought them, you don't have to worry about catching anything. I don't wash regular dishes so you know I won't wash this stuff. You're the first person to drink from it."

Laughing to hide her embarrassment, Eve said, "Then I'll christen it with relish."

Arty seemed to appreciate her wit and motioned to a chair in the kitchen from which he hastily pushed a stack of boxes. Although it wobbled a bit, Eve accepted the seat graciously and sipped delicately of the tea that actually tasted good. At some time in his life, Arty had taken time away from his art to learn the skill of brewing a truly good cup of tea.

"David, if my memory is correct, Eve is the first young woman other than your sister that you've brought to my humble abode. To what do I owe the honor?" Arty asked as he scanned their faces.

"I wanted Eve to see your work. She needed to appreciate one of the island's foremost artists and the man who created the butterfly that will soon adorn her sister's clothing," David replied with a wink that did not escape Eve's attention.

"I appreciate the compliment and the visit. Not too

many people come to see me. I guess everyone knows the way I live," Arty stated, waving his cup to encompass the messy kitchen.

"That might be part of it, but we know better than to interrupt creative genius. I put our lives in your hands by bringing Eve here," David said. "The main reason is that you exhibit regularly at the gallery in Hamilton. All of your friends attend your opening nights."

"That's true. I do have a very loyal following. That's something you'll like about the island, Eve. We're very friendly here," Arty said proudly.

"I've noticed that already. I'm sure that I'll enjoy my year of teaching here," Eve replied, waving off a refill.

"Maybe you'll find a reason to stay here with us. We could always use an infusion of new blood into our little circle," Arty added.

"Her family's in the States. Permanent relocation would be a little tough on her," David interjected like an old knowledgeable friend.

"We're not that far offshore as the crow flies," Arty said. "Stranger things have happened. Sisters and parents often relocate, too."

"Kip Reynolds's wife is a case in point," David said. "She came here on vacation from Texas, fell in love with the island and Kip, and never returned. Her entire family relocated after the wedding. They built a little cluster of houses not far from here."

"I guess anything's possible," Eve agreed and added, "Falling in love is a good reason for staying. If I fell for a guy, I wouldn't want to leave either."

With a wicked wink, Arty commented, "We'll just have to find the right man for you so that you'll stay."

"That's not an easy task." Eve laughed good-naturedly. "I'm very particular."

"Describe your perfect man, if you don't mind. I'd

like to hear it. I get around a lot and need to be on the lookout for him," Arty said with a smirk.

Playing along, Eve replied, "He's tall and attractive, employed, dedicated to his work but not so involved that he can't have fun in his spare time. He should be fit, but he doesn't have to be a bodybuilder. I like to bicycle and run for exercise. It would be great if he shared the same interests. Other than that, I can't give any specifics. I'll know him when love hits me."

"Fair enough, but I'll keep my eyes open just in case I find him first. I'll steer him in your direction," Arty said, laughing.

Taking Eve by the hand, David stated, "I think she can find her own ideal man. Besides, he might be closer than you think."

Eve looked at the soiled kitchen floor in order to conceal her combined pleasure and embarrassment as Arty gave a tremendous roar of laughter. Her heart pounded so loudly in her ears and chest that she could not hear the cat meowing at her feet. She had not expected David to speak so plainly. Her knees felt so weak that she was not certain that she would be able to stand up.

Eve had never known a man like David. Brad had taken their relationship for granted, hardly ever speaking of love. He certainly had not announced his interest in her in front of others at this early stage of their acquaintance. However, David was different. He had already declared his interest in front of his friend by his words and his presumptive posture. David had certainly dropped the protective wall that had separated them. Like her sister, Helen, always said, a man only needed to know that other men might be interested in his woman, and he would suddenly straighten up and fly right.

They left Arty at the door of his garage-turned-studio and began the ride down the hill. Neither spoke although David often shot glances in Eve's direction as if wanting to say something but not finding the right words for the job. She resolved that she would not help him to verbalize his feelings. In the beginning of her relationship with Brad, Eve had urged him to disclose his thoughts to the extent that she often finished his sentences when he looked reluctant to complete the idea himself. She would not do that again. One terribly shy man where love was concerned was enough to last her a lifetime.

The temptation to start the discussion was almost irresistible as they pedaled in silence through the countryside. The splendor of the Bermuda landscape would have made a lesser man divulge all of his emotions but not David. He had lived so long among the azure water that melted into a slightly darker sky that he was immune to the affect of Bermuda's beauty. Nothing in the sand, sun, and sea could make him give away the feelings at which he had so clearly hinted.

Eve's little cottage loomed in the distance. It would not be long now before their day ended. She slowed her pedaling slightly in order to add a few extra minutes to her time with David as she fought a fierce internal battle. Eve was not certain that she wanted David to proclaim his affection so early in their relationship. She knew that she was not able to separate her feelings for the island from those she felt for him. Yet, she did not want to lose him to her usual tendency to overanalyze a situation.

If David noticed either the change in pace or her confusion, he said nothing or merely thought that fatigue had caught up with her. He was so engrossed in his own thoughts that, for the moment, nothing else mattered. He knew he cared for Eve; however, the feelings might simply have been caused by her newness to the island or the closeness of her velvety skin. He did not know her well enough for more definite emotions. Still, Arty's talk of finding Eve a lover as a reason to remain on the island had unnerved him. David wanted her to stay, and he felt anger at the thought that she might be with another man. He simply was not ready to commit when he was not convinced of his mind.

In silence, Eve pushed her bike to the backyard, leaving David standing by the gate. She took a long time, hoping that David would leave. However, when she returned to the front of the house, he was still standing there with his hands in his pockets and a frown on his handsome forehead.

Thinking quickly, Eve stated, "Thanks for introducing me to Arty. He's a true one-of-a-kind. I'll have to tell Helen about him."

Smiling, David said, "He is unique, but he's also the best friend a guy ever had. I can't imagine not having him in my life. As much as I want his art to make him famous and rich, I'd hate it if Arty ever left me here alone on the island."

"It's nice to have a good friend like that. Helen's that person for me. Although she's my sister, she's also my best friend. I miss her terribly. This is the first time we've been separated by so much distance," Eve confided.

"I know you're homesick, but I hope you'll grow to think of Bermuda as home, too," David stated in a very serious tone.

Twisting the toe of her tennis shoe on the slate walk, Eve replied, "I've seen plenty to make me love it here. Thanks to you, I've toured the island on a bike, eaten in an astounding restaurant, and met an interesting guy like

Arty. When my year is up, it'll be hard for me to leave here."

Placing both hands on her shoulders as if to kiss her, David simply said, "Good."

Quickly, he returned to his waiting bike. Before pedaling off, David asked, "Are you still locking the front door?"

"Of course," Eve replied without hesitation, failing to understand the significance of the question.

Smiling sadly, David said, "Well, there's still plenty of time for you to become one of us. See you later."

Thinking about David's last words, Eve fumbled in her pocket for the key as he rode away. Although he said that the island was perfectly safe, she was not ready to believe that she did not need to lock her cottage. After only two days, Eve still thought like an outsider. She knew that her reaction would change eventually but not this soon.

Eve watched as David pedaled over the horizon. Neither was ready to take the plunge into a new relationship. Perhaps one day the hesitancy would vanish, just like her habit of locking the house. For now, however, Eve was content with the friendship that grew between them.

Chapter Five

The restful summer months passed quickly as Eve toured her new island home with David almost constantly at her side. She sampled water sports that she never would have tried if she had not seen the locals engaged in them. Being surrounded by water and constant sunshine made her want to try everything that the paradise offered, and she did. Eve did not hesitate to enjoy all that Bermuda offered. After all, she would only be new to the island once.

Her sister, Helen, was impressed and amazed with the details of parasailing and scuba diving that Eve shared with her. She knew that Eve liked to have a good time but that she had never been inclined to try the more adventurous activities. Eve was far from being a stick-in-the-mud, but she did not believe in tempting fate either. While dating Brad, Eve had loosened up and become more daring, but not to the point of doing anything dangerous. Now, she was parasailing with the locals, a sport that Brad loved and had never been able to convince Eve to try. The sisters agreed that being away from familiar surroundings and the support of family was proving to be a good change for Eve, who enjoyed the new independence.

Being with Eve was also having a positive impact on David, the normally reserved math department chair. Although he had enjoyed all sports as a child, he had adapted a more conservative approach to life after college and discarded the activities that he considered dangerous or over-the-top. Eve's desire to try everything at least once had worked wonders on him, too. He became reacquainted with forgotten favorites.

Sailing had become one of Eve's favorite sports. She enjoyed working the lines, maneuvering the tiller, and seeing the sails fill with air. Motorboating was also pleasurable, but she preferred the more physical nature of sailing.

If David, Arty, or one of her dozens of new friends was too busy to accompany her, Eve would take the boat that she and David had rescued from Arty's garage and travel around the islands alone. She always stayed close enough to shore that, if something happened that she could not handle, she could get help from the local fishermen. When she had reached her destination, Eve would lower the sails and drop the small brick anchor. She would then extract either a paperback or a sketch pad and spend hours lolling in the ocean as the seabirds argued overhead.

Eve could not remember ever being so happy. The combination of the almost constant sun, brisk breezes, and leisurely days had erased all of the tension that came from spending long hours in the classroom. Papers to grade no longer occupied the kitchen and dining room tables. Report deadlines did not hover over her head. The need to phone parents did not linger at the back of her mind. She slept late, dined on fresh fruits and vegetables, and did exactly as she pleased.

The only way Eve could have been happier would be for her family to relocate to the island, also. She phoned her parents weekly and Helen whenever she had a tidbit to share, which was almost nightly. Between them, their long-distance bills were approaching the budget of a small country.

Waiting for David to arrive on one especially glorious Saturday morning, Eve phoned Helen to pass the time. Helen had recently broken off the relationship with her boyfriend of two years and was starting to see a man in her investment banking field. During their last conversation, she had been neither depressed about the breakup nor excited about the new man. Helen had a way of rolling with the punches that often irritated Eve, who usually had to read her sister's expressions and voice to learn Helen's feelings. This was one of those times that she wished Helen would share her emotions. Being so far from home made it difficult to be supportive of someone who would not acknowledge the trauma of a broken relationship.

"How's it going?" Eve demanded as soon as Helen answered the phone.

"It's okay. It's raining here again and hot and sticky. I just treated myself to a huge bouquet of calla lilies and a pedicure. I don't think I like the polish color . . . too brown. How's it with you?" Helen replied, sounding happy to hear from her sister despite the usual hot, humid, hazy weather of a Maryland summer.

"I'm going sailing with David if he ever arrives, or alone if he doesn't. It's too glorious a day to sit at home. Have you finalized your vacation plans yet? When are you coming for a visit?" Eve asked, settling into a chair from which she could watch the gate and the road.

"Oh, yeah, I wanted to ask you about that," Helen said in her usual relaxed manner. "How's next week?

I'm not too busy right now and thought I'd get away a little earlier than originally planned while things are quiet. The humidity's really bad; I'm ready for a change. I finally bought airline tickets. I arrive on Wednesday at two."

"When were you planning to tell me?" Eve exclaimed. "You didn't say anything last night when you called."

"I know. I kinda forgot about it. I would have remembered on Tuesday night to give you a heads-up." Helen laughed.

"It's a good thing I didn't have any plans," Eve grumbled good-naturedly. "What do you want to do while you're here? How long will you stay?"

"Just chill, sis, and keep it simple," Helen said, laughing again. "I want to meet your new friends, check out your new home, and relax on the beach. I'll stay until your school term starts."

"Great!" Eve replied happily. "I'll gather a few folks for a cookout your first night to introduce you around a bit. By the way, how's it going with Robert, the new guy?"

Helen sighed. "It's not. He's too boring for words. His idea of a good time is checking the stock quotes. I thought I was really into my job, but he's obsessive about it. He can't carry on a conversation about anything other than money. Maybe I'm nuts, but there's more to life than that. Besides, he comes from a loaded family and has never wanted for anything. He'll always be secure. He's just too anal for me. Anyway, I cut him loose. We're not seeing each other any longer. Maybe you could hook me up with someone. I've never tried a super-long-distance relationship."

"No, but I remember the relationship you had with the guy from New York. You two practically burned up the Internet lines and wore a hole in the friendly skies. Whatever happened to him?"

"He sent me a wedding announcement last week. It seems that he's marrying a woman from his firm next month," Helen responded in her characteristic lilting voice.

"If I remember correctly, you found him boring after a while, too," Eve commented as she waved to David, who had just pedaled to her front door.

"I know. Everyone says I'm vivacious and entertaining, but I manage to attract the most boring men on the earth."

Grabbing the lunch basket, Eve responded, "I'll be sure to introduce you only to the most interesting men I know. As a matter of fact, David is the most conservative guy I know. He's making great strides, but he says that before I arrived he was mostly a work-all-day, read-all-night kind of man."

"I hope his friends aren't like that." Helen yawned. "I don't want to be bored stiff while on vacation. I can stay home for that."

"Have no fear. I know some real live ones. David is a fluke, from what I can tell of the other people on this island. He's changing quickly. Speaking of David, I'd better go. He's waiting for me. We're going sailing and then eating a light lunch before yet another of Arty's shows."

"Just make sure that Arty's on my list of people to meet. He sounds like a real live wire."

Rising, Eve replied, "He is. You'll like him. I'd better run. David's starting to look impatient. He's becoming more relaxed, but he's not there yet. He still hears the school bells in his head."

"Okay. See you next week."

Eve could hardly wait until her two favorite people would meet. Hastily locking the front door, she secured the basket onto the bike and pushed it through the gate toward the waiting David. He smiled and kissed her casually on the cheek as they started their journey to their familiar spot of beach.

"My sister's coming next week!" Eve blurted as she sprinted on her bike past David. She always raced him to their spot and usually won.

Shouting, he rushed to catch up saying, "When did she decide this? That doesn't give us much time to throw a party together."

"She'll be okay with something very casual as long as Arty's invited," Eve called over her shoulder.

"What's the big deal about Arty? She's infatuated with a man she hasn't even met," David puffed loudly. Despite being accustomed to the race and the landscape's changing terrain, the ride always left him slightly winded.

"The butterfly pin did it for her," Eve replied as she posed ceremoniously on the imaginary victory line. "Helen says that any man who can create something that beautiful is the one for her. Besides, she's at loose ends right now and looking for something meaningful."

"I just hope she won't be too disappointed when she meets him. Arty's my best friend, but he takes some getting used to. I remember your first reactions." David sighed as he once again more or less graciously accepted second place.

"It wasn't Arty that put me off; it was the mess. Helen won't care about that. She's more understanding of the artistic temperament than I am. Her idea of organizing is placing everything into carefully marked boxes and shoving them under the bed or stacking them on every empty table," Eve stated as she placed the basket into the sailboat and helped cast off from the little pier.

Settling across from her, David watched with pleasure and pride as Eve handled the lines and the rudder. He had been the one to introduce her to the joys of sailing and had been most impressed with the speed at which she not only mastered the tasks but learned to appreciate the craft. Now, when they sailed together, she took control and he relaxed. He helped only if she needed assistance and asked for it. Eve had become so skillful and competent in a short time that she seldom needed more than a brief comment from him.

David watched Eve's trim body bend and sway with the lines. Her skin had taken on a reddish glow from life on the island, and she looked healthier than when she had first arrived. The dark circles had vanished from underneath her eyes. Although she had not abandoned all of her old ways, Eve had assimilated into the island culture well.

Only one thing kept him from speaking of his overwhelming feelings for her. David was still waiting for Eve to stop locking her front door. When she felt sufficiently comfortable to walk away from her home without locking the door, he would know that she had truly become one of them. Until then, he feared that her happiness was simply the effect of the Bermuda sunshine, and that she remained an outsider.

Every time he waited outside her door for Eve to join him on one of their outings, David held his breath that she had finally completed the transition. Unfortunately, she would fumble at the lock before practically dancing down the walk to meet him. Although beaming with pleasure at being with Eve, David would sigh. He had known almost immediately after meeting her that he loved Eve deeply. She possessed all of the qualities he wanted in a woman and so many more. He could tell from the way her cheeks colored when she looked at him that Eve felt the same about him, too.

Watching her handle the sailboat with skill, David smiled and felt warm with the sense of his blessings and love. This wonderful creature had come into his life just when he had stopped looking for love. She had filled his days and his dreams with such happiness that, at times, he was afraid to think of his joy too long for fear that the old loneliness would return. Her smile made his heart sing. The touch of her hand made his throat constrict. The sound of her voice was sweeter than the song of any bird. Eve had made his island home come to life in a way that he had never thought possible. He no longer felt jealous of the vacationers who kissed on his beaches or touched intimately under his moon. One day soon, when the time was right, he would be like them, standing with his love in his arms and looking at the beach without seeing it.

Even without holding her in his arms or touching his lips to hers, David felt Eve's energy and intensity flow through his body. Before she came, he had stopped seeing the island as anything other than home. Its beauty had long ago stopped affecting his heart. Now, he felt the excitement of exploration that had bound him to the island in his youth. Eve had opened his eyes and heart to the world that had once enthralled him but had only recently felt more like a prison than a haven. Even grading summer school papers and working on his latest research project late into the evening felt good again. Eve had given his life meaning and joy. Soon, he would tell her. If only she would stop locking her front door, David would not hesitate any longer. He would know that all was right in Bermuda under the summer breeze.

Eve was aware of David's eyes following her every move as she skillfully piloted the sailboat. She loved watching him, too. No task was too simple. She enjoyed the sight of him carrying dripping ice cream cones to their picnic table. The sight of him trying to lick his cone while holding her dripping one at a safe distance always made her smile. She felt secure as he pedaled his bike beside her and knew that David could beat her in their races if he really put his heart to it. She knew he always let her win.

Under his watchful gaze, Eve sighed happily. Although they never spoke of it and David never did more than kiss her cheek, she felt secure and happy in the glow of his affection. Sometimes, she wondered why he hesitated to tell her of his emotions. Surely he realized that she felt the same way even though they had not known each other very long. Eve knew her feelings glowed on her face at the sight of him at her front door. She laughed more frequently when she was with him. She looked for every opportunity to touch him. Her fingers flew to his arm in praise of anything witty he might say and lingered longer than necessary. She listened contentedly when he shared stories of his students. She cared little for the topic but loved the sound of his rich, sexy baritone.

Turning her attention to the shoreline, Eve breathed deeply of the sweet sea air. She had fallen in love with the island when she first set foot on it the day of her interview. She had fallen in love with David when she first met him. He filled her life with happiness just by walking beside her. The weeks that had passed since her arrival in Bermuda had convinced Eve that her feelings were not caused by the sea air or the island's mystic energy pull. She knew love when it enfolded her, and she was in love.

With the sails safely folded and the anchor dragging behind them, Eve and David nibbled at their simple lunch. She always packed his favorites and savored the way he relished every bite. They did not talk. Instead, they listened to the water lapping at the side of the boat and the birds gliding on the hot air currents overhead. They never even brought a radio on their trips, preferring the sound of life on the water to the intrusion of a deejay.

Only telling David of her love could make the day more perfect. Although she wanted to say the words, Eve could not bring herself to be the first to speak of love. It was an old-fashioned idea, but she could not shake that habit any more than she could stop locking the cottage's front door. Sometimes Eve wondered if the locked door kept David from speaking of his feelings for her. He was as bound by tradition as she was. He occasionally mentioned the lock with a genuine sadness although he usually pretended that he no longer noticed that she continued to lock it. Eve knew that the lock meant to him that she did not feel completely at home on the safe island. However, locking the world out was one habit that she was not ready to abandon. She had lived too long in a metropolis, making a secure lock a necessity.

They had floated on the placid water and enjoyed their time together for a few hours when David suddenly noticed an ominous darkening of the sky. All of the seabirds had vanished, leaving the bay silent. The sea had turned black and angry, and the wind had begun to increase.

"We'd better get back quick. A storm has blown up," David shouted over the wind that increased in intensity rapidly.

"Should we head for that little island?" Eve demanded as she steadied the rudder while David worked the sails that had broken lose from their bindings and flapped dangerously over the boat.

"Good idea," David replied. "Steer west, northwest. Tack her across the wind."

"The wind's too hard. I can't hold her," Eve shouted. Her voice was amazingly calm and free from fear.

"Hold her a few more minutes. I've almost finished here," David called as he tied the last of the line and started toward Eve.

Suddenly, a strong wave crashed against the side of the boat, nearly capsizing the small craft. Eve held tightly to the rudder and seat, but David was caught off guard. When the boat righted herself, he was not on board.

"David!" Eve called into the wind. "David!"

Although they always wore life vests, Eve knew that David was in terrible danger of drowning. Her calm exterior cracked, and she shouted his name repeatedly through the tears that blinded her vision.

Straining to see through the salty water that further stung her eyes and drenched her clothing, Eve searched the angry sea for any sign of the bright orange vest. Tearing the life preserver from its harness, she threw it overboard and watched it float on the choppy waves. If David surfaced anywhere near the buoy, he would be able to grab it and allow the boat to pull him to safety.

For the first time in her life, Eve was so scared that she could not think. She set the coast guard radio signal to SOS and prayed. Relying on instinct, she encouraged the little boat toward the island. The craft shuddered and sighed as it pressed forward.

Tacking carefully, Eve crouched low to brace against the thundering sea. Periodically she would look out to see if she had managed to close the distance. Scanning the darkness, she saw the empty life preserver riding high on the waves but nothing else. She was alone.

Wiping water from her streaming face, Eve held so tightly to the rudder that her palms started to bleed, but she hardly noticed, so great was the pain in her chest. David was gone! She would never see him again. Never smile at the sound of his voice or have the chance to kiss his lips. He would never again allow her to beat him in their race. He would never again lick the melted ice cream from his fingers like a little boy. He was gone.

The sailboat tacked hard across the tossing sea until it finally reached the island. Although Eve and David had not sailed far from the main shoreline, the boat seemed to take an eternity to cross the distance to one of the smallest islands in the chain. As often as she dared, Eve rechecked the life preserver and scanned the churning sea behind her. Each time, she saw no sign of David on the pounding waves.

By the time the boat reached the relative quiet of the island, Eve was exhausted. She managed to drag the battered boat to dry land before collapsing on the wet sand. She did not notice that the waves washed across her legs. She was too tired and far too miserable to care.

When Eve awakened, the sun was beating down on her and burning her skin. The sleep had helped to restore her strength, but it had done nothing to lessen the pain in her heart. She covered her eyes with her hands and tried not to remember the storm and David's disappearance. She wanted to remember his smile and his voice. She had to will him to be alive on the teaming sea. The tears mixed with the dried salt water on her face and ran into her sand-matted hair.

Barely able to stand, Eve dragged herself to the boat. Although its paint carried the scars of the battle with the sea, the trusty vessel sat on the beach where she had left it. She would not wait for the coast guard to find her. The sea looked calm enough for her to try the journey home. Eve was thirsty, but the island was so small that hardly any vegetation covered its sandy surface. Scanning the island from where she stood, she saw that she was completely alone on a landmass that was only slightly larger than a swimming platform.

Before Eve pushed the boat into the water, she tried the radio only to find it had gone dead. If another storm blew up, she would be completely without communication. The cloudless sky and the return of the squawking seagulls gave her the courage to try.

Working the wet sails skillfully, Eve soon had the boat on a true course for the shore. Although the rudder was balky, she managed to steer well enough as she scanned the water for David and the life preserver that the angry waves had ripped from its rope. She saw neither as she left the deserted channel and headed toward open water again.

Now that the storm had ended, boats once again dotted the sea. Some of them were fishing crafts, but most were pleasure vessels. Their passengers waved to her gaily as she passed, without knowing of her loss. No one could read the pain on her face.

Unseen, a coast guard cutter slowly approached Eve's sailboat. She hardly noticed when it pulled as close as it could come without capsizing her craft. Her heart was so heavy and her mind so clouded that Eve saw and heard nothing. If the wave action on the mostly calm sea had not increased, Eve would not have pulled herself from the stupor that enveloped her to take notice of it. The voice of instinct inside her head guided her reactions, and then returned to her tortured thoughts.

"We received a call for help from this craft during the storm. Are you okay?" the skipper asked through the amplifier in his ship.

"I'm fine, but I've lost my friend. He washed overboard and didn't resurface," Eve replied as the tears tumbled down her cheeks again.

"I'll send a crew member over to pilot your craft," the skipper stated briskly.

Eve did not reply. She simply waited as two young men sailed a small craft the distance between them. One of them asked for permission to board and accepted her silence for agreement. He gently removed the rudder from her bleeding hands. His sympathetic and well-trained eyes surveyed her face and body for signs of injury. Not seeing any, he waved away his vessel and turned his attention to the task of sailing toward shore.

Staring dazed at the water, Eve saw practically nothing. Occasionally, a seabird would fly low, make a dive for the water, and fly up with dinner in its beak. Jumping fish and shouting children sometimes shook her from the thoughts that dulled her mind and caused tears to run down her face. For most of the trip, however, as the shore drew closer, Eve saw nothing.

Eve's thoughts and prayers were of David as the young crewman helped her ashore. She had known that she loved him and had been hesitant to tell him. Now the opportunity had slipped into the stormy sea. She had lost him and happiness just when she had thought that her life would be happy forever.

As she followed the crewman toward the coast guard station, the loud voices of a gathering of people on the beach jarred Eve from her thoughts. At first, she thought someone had caught an especially large fish after the storm. People liked to display their catch for the praise of others. She had turned away and returned to her thoughts when she heard someone shouting her name. She stood frozen on the deck and wondered if, for the rest of her life, she would hear the voice of the man she had loved and lost to the sea.

Slowly, through the depths of her emotions, Eve listened to the sound of excited voices and calling birds. Again, she heard the voice, familiar but muffled by the crowd. Shaking herself, Eve moved forward.

The crewman looked from her drawn face toward the parting crowd, but Eve continued to press on. Her mind needed the order of her having to appear in the coast guard office. She needed something to do so that she would not feel.

Again, the voice called her name. This time it was closer, louder. Eve stumbled as if she had stubbed her toe in the darkness.

"Eve! Eve! Wait! Eve!" the voice called.

Eve stopped and covered her face with her trembling hands. Her shoulders shook as the sobs wracked her body. Her knees bent, and she slumped toward the deck.

Strong hands caught her and pulled her to her feet. Strong arms enfolded her and made her feel safe. A strong baritone voice broke through the turmoil of her mind as the crowd gathered around them.

"Eve, darling, I'm here. I'm safe. Fishermen found me. I was so worried about you. When the coast guard lost your signal, I just knew I'd lost you forever. Oh, Eve, I love you so," David said soothingly as his lips caressed her cheeks and wet eyes.

"David! I love you! I thought I'd lost you. David, hold me," Eve cried tears of joy as she buried her face in his warm chest. Her arms clung to him so tightly that they ached.

The crowd at first stood silently and then erupted into songs and shouts of joy. They had watched David pace the beach, check every boat that anchored after the storm, and demand information from the coast guard. They had seen him cling to fading hope. Now, they watched him cradle the woman he loved tenderly in his arms. The sea had separated friends and reunited lovers.

Chapter Six

The room at the back of the coast guard station was quiet, dimly lit, and smelled of the sea. Unlike the main room that bustled with activity, the room had the feeling of a relaxing den. A small television occupied one corner and a seating arrangement consumed the opposite wall. The aroma of fresh coffee filled the air, mingling with that of hastily reheated lunches.

Eve and David sat close together on the sofa as they waited for her clothes to dry. David had carefully wrapped her tired body in a big scratchy blanket after she had changed into oversized sweats donated by one of the officers. Now he held the bundle close as Eve sipped tea and munched cookies.

"I still don't understand," Eve muttered. "Explain it to me again."

Looking pained by the memory, David stated, "When I washed overboard, I thought I'd never see you again. I tried not to become disoriented, but the wave action was too great and the sand was churning too much. The current was so strong that I couldn't fight my way to

the top. I've never stayed under so long. I dived for
coral and played with the fish when I was a kid, but I've
always surfaced sooner than that. Anyway, when I finally surfaced, I didn't know where I was. I bobbed
around for a while, calling your name just in case you
were in the water, too, until a fishing party rescued me.
Most of them were mighty green in the face, but at
least their boat survived with only a little damage. We
patrolled the area looking for you but saw nothing. We
finally gave up. By then, we'd raised the coast guard,
but they had already picked up your SOS and lost it."

"Oh, David, it must have been so awful for you!"
Eve cried, snuggling closer.

David continued, "The worse part was not knowing
if I'd ever see you again. I just knew that you'd drowned.
The boat took so much water when I washed overboard."

Smiling bravely, Eve said, "It did, but it's a mighty
sturdy little sailboat. I had to bail a little, but she kept
afloat. I watched for you for the longest time, and then
sailed in circles hoping you'd surface."

"I was nowhere near where we'd been at anchor
when I surfaced," David continued. "The water's a
tricky thing. I had to tell myself constantly which way
was up. The whirling sea is very deceptive. I thought I
was directly under the sailboat the entire time until the
fishermen straightened me out. I'm just glad we were
both wearing life jackets."

"Me too," Eve agreed. "I towed a life preserver behind the boat for a while, hoping that you'd grab hold
of it. Silly, huh?"

"No, wonderful," David stated, kissing her lightly on
the lips. "You know that something good has come
from almost drowning."

"What's that?" Eve asked without moving from his shoulder.

Smiling, David said, "We've finally stopped hiding our feelings for each other. I've loved you from the first day I met you at our spot. I was completely bowled over that night at dinner. The way you warmed to Arty finished me off. I knew that you were the woman for me."

"I've loved you from the first, too," Eve confessed. "We were silly not to have said something sooner."

"We have now, and that's all that matters," David said, pulling her closer.

"I don't ever want to feel that frightened again," Eve stated.

"Neither do I. Your clothes should be ready by now. If you're feeling up to it, we should grab some tea and then go to see Arty. He was very concerned about both of us. Besides, we haven't told him about your sister's visit."

"And here I was thinking that I'd never have to move from this spot again." Eve yawned delicately and stretched.

David laughed. "We can't occupy their break room forever. I'm surprised that no one has come in. I'll stand guard while you change."

"I'll get my clothes and meet you outside," Eve agreed reluctantly.

Kissing her, David hurried from the room. The coast guard captain looked up as he heard the movement in the connecting hall. Seeing David lingering outside the door, he decided that Eve must have been feeling better and getting ready to leave. Closing the gap between his desk and the break room door, he joined David on sentry duty.

"You folks thinking of going home?" the captain asked.

"Eve's feeling much better now. It was just the shock. She's getting dressed," David replied.

"It was quite an ordeal for someone so new to the island. I hope she won't think that the Triangle had anything to do with it. It was simply one of those storms that blows up now and again," the captain commented.

"She hasn't said anything, but I doubt that she believes in that old myth. Besides, she loves it here. Nothing could change her mind," David replied proudly.

"That's good. Take good care of her," the captain said as he returned to his desk. He was so busy that he barely noticed when Eve and David left the station a few minutes later.

Eve and David pedaled leisurely to their favorite spot for afternoon tea. Although they had eaten at the coast guard station, they felt a compelling need to return to their customary routine after their ordeal in the ocean. Unlike their usual travels, they did not race. Instead, they rode abreast and chatted almost constantly. The afternoon storm had blown a new wind in their direction.

Chuckling, Eve said, "I can't believe that I'm saying this, but for the first time in my teaching career, I'm actually looking forward to school starting. I enjoy our leisurely time together, but I want to become more involved with the people. I don't want to feel like an outsider anymore. Everyone has been so nice to me. It's time I repaid the kindness."

"I'm glad to hear it. I know you like it here, but I want you to become one of us, too," David replied with a broad smile.

"I don't know if I ever told you this, but I hope the

year passes slowly. I really don't want to leave here and I'll have to once the school year closes," Eve added as they spread out the tablecloth and set up for tea.

Waiting in line with the others who had stopped by the roadside booth for afternoon refreshment, David said, "You don't have to leave, you know. I'm sure the government would grant you the proper visa, and the school system needs teachers."

"I know that, but my family's in the States. I've missed Helen and my parents so much these last months. I don't want to live away from them, but I don't want to leave you and this island either," Eve said gently.

"Maybe Arty will give Helen a reason to relocate here. They might fall in love. Helen could relocate. Who knows, they might be kindred souls," David said as he watched Eve skillfully pour their tea.

Since their first tea time together, Eve had learned the proper way to bring the cup to the pot, the offering of the little cookies, cakes, and sandwiches, and, in general, the formality of tea. Tea time was a formal affair, even while enjoying the feel of the ocean breeze and the sand.

"We'll have to give love a little push," Eve replied as she handed David a cup.

"I don't know about that," David said, shaking his head. "I'm not one for meddling in other people's affairs. The last time I played matchmaker, the relationship soured and I almost lost two friends."

"You won't have to do anything," Eve retorted as she nibbled a little cream cheese and cucumber sandwich. "I'll do all the work. As a matter of fact, knowing Helen, she'll do everything if she likes Arty. I think she will. I sent her a photo of him last week."

"You did what?" David demanded.

"I sent her a photo. He's a good-looking man, and she likes his art. I'm only helping. What's good for Helen is good for me," Eve explained.

"Does he know?"

"I doubt it. I sent her the latest catalog of his work. His photo just happened to be on the back. There's no harm in encouraging my sister to purchase more of Arty's work."

"I guess not," David conceded reluctantly. "But just because she buys his work doesn't mean that she'll like him, or that he'll like her for that matter. Don't forget that it takes two."

"There's nothing not to like about my sister," Eve said with a jerk of her chin. "Helen's beautiful and incredibly sweet. She's a lovely person."

"Maybe I've fallen in love with the wrong girl. I should have held my tongue until after Helen's visit," David teased.

"Very funny! You'd better be careful or the Fates will capsize your boat again," Eve retorted with a chuckle.

"So true! Anyway, it's not possible for Helen or any other woman to surpass you in beauty or charm. My fate was sealed the first time I saw you," David stated, resting his hand on hers.

"Oh, David, I'm so happy." Eve sighed. "That's what I want for Helen. I want her to fall in love with the island, its people, and, if she's lucky, one special person. I don't know if the Fates arranged our meeting or if the Triangle exerted its power or if we just happened to be in the right place at the right time. All I know is that I'm happier now than I've ever been. Even if we hadn't finally gotten around to telling each other how we felt, I still would have felt happier being here with you on this island than at any other time in my life. Having you as a friend made me feel secure."

Moving closer on their little square of sand, David slipped his arm around Eve's shoulders. Any other time, he would have remained on his little square of the tablecloth, but loving Eve and almost losing her had made a huge change in him. He would not hesitate to show his affection regardless of the number of people sitting on the beach with them.

"I've never been happier either," David stated as he kissed Eve gently on the lips. "You've made me see my island again. I had grown too comfortable with the beauty and had stopped enjoying it. I allowed work and research to consume too much of my life. Since I met you, I've put life in perspective. Love is what's important. Research will get done; it always does. You've taught me that I need to live on this beautiful island, not simply exist. For that, I'll be forever grateful."

Eve smiled through tears as she rested her head on David's strong shoulder. They hardly saw the people who sat on the beach enjoying the view and the last of their tea. The island in the Atlantic Ocean was theirs. The only thing that could have made Eve happier was to know that she would never leave. Maybe Helen's visit would make that dream a reality.

As the afternoon shadows lengthened into early evening, Eve and David left their spot of beach and biked toward Arty's. They still had not told him about Helen's visit. So much was riding on his ability to make a good impression that they felt a need to give him a heads-up.

True to his habits, Arty was hard at work in his studio when they arrived. The barking dog and the piles of scrap metal provided their only greeting. Even Arty's cat was nowhere to be seen.

"Hey, Arty!" David shouted as they entered the studio.

"Hey, bro! Glad to see you. You guys really gave me

a scare. That's one way to stop me from working. I thought I'd lost my best friend and his girl. I love you, man." Arty greeted them with big hugs and tear-filled eyes.

"Back at you. You should have been on my side of the action. I've never been so scared in my life. We had some pretty close calls on the water as kids, but never anything like this," David said, accepting the offered bottle of beer and taking big gulps to hide his emotions.

"Thought you'd drown?" Arty asked as he studied his best friend's face.

"Yes, and, when I finally fought my way to the surface, I thought I'd never find Eve. I just knew she'd gone down with the boat. I love this woman and don't want to lose her," David said.

"You okay, Eve?" Arty asked, turning his attention to the subject of David's admiration. The expression on David's face clearly stated his emotions. Arty could see that David was in love in a big way.

"He can't get rid of me that easily," Eve joked with lightheartedness that she really did not feel. "When I fall for a guy, I hook him and reel him in good. I use every trick in the book, even calling on Poseidon for a little shipwreck. Besides, my sister's coming for a vacation, and I have to show her around the island."

"Helen's coming?" Arty asked with raised brows. "She just e-mailed me with the purchase of another brooch. She's turning into my guardian angel. She's sent me a lot of referral business and has arranged an exhibition of my work in D.C. She's gotten me notice that I've never been able to obtain on my own. I'd like very much to meet the woman behind all that. I owe her a lot."

"She wants to meet you, too," Eve said, smiling. "I'm sure you'll become great friends."

David did not say anything as he watched the play of emotions across Arty's face. He could see that his buddy suspected something. However, Eve had anticipated his suspicion and was ready with a response.

"Helen supports many causes, but her favorite is the arts," Eve explained with a smile. "She has helped several photographers by arranging shows for them. She's great at doing that kind of thing. For the most part, she stays in the background and doesn't even meet the artist until the day of the show. She has great connections but is shy about her role in the process. You'll probably be the first artist she's met prior to the big day."

Looking from one to the other, Arty replied, "Great! I like being the first. I'd like to meet her, too. She's done a lot to help my dream of a show and wider distribution come true. If she's anything like you, I'll like her immediately. Besides, she has a great voice. If she's half as intoxicating, all she'll have to do is reel me in just like you did with David. That's what you have in mind, isn't it?"

"I take the Fifth on that one. Besides, Helen's much more interesting than I am. Her interests are so diverse. She'll love the island. There's so much to do and see here. She loves water sports as well as golf and tennis. She's just a great person."

"She certainly has a fan club in you," David said as he stole a glance at Arty's latest project. He managed to see the corner of a very elaborate beaded project before his friend tossed a towel over it. Arty did not like for anyone, not even his best friend, to see his work before he completed it.

"You'll join it, too, after you meet her," Eve stated.

"That's right. You haven't met the sister of the woman who has won your heart. They say that it's the mother the guy should meet," Arty teased.

"I'll start with Helen. I don't think we've reached the mother stage yet. We've only just today confessed that we're more than friends," David replied, avoiding the suggestion that they might be ready for the big step.

"Yeah, start small and build up. That's what I always say. That way, the foundation will be nice and strong," Arty commented without looking from his work. A collection of sparkling colorful beads covered the table in surprisingly neat piles.

"If that's your approach to life, why is it that you're not married?" Eve asked. "Your patience would make you an ideal husband."

"That's what I think, too, but my ex-wife would disagree," Arty said. "She claimed that I put so much time into my work, building it from the foundation up, that I didn't have room in my life for anything else. I guess she was right 'cause I haven't remarried and there's no line of women waiting for me to finish a project. It's not easy building a business. It takes a slow, easy touch, too. I think I'm a confirmed bachelor."

"That's what I thought until I met Eve," David said. "She certainly turned me around."

"Is that a bad thing? I can turn you loose just as quickly if it is," Eve said with a mischievous grin.

"Oh, no, you don't. You've made an irreversible change in my life, and you're stuck with me," David replied as he kissed Eve possessively on the lips.

"Any time you feel confined, let me know. I've been in a dead-end relationship and don't want another," Eve stated, returning the kiss but remaining wary.

"Meeting you is the best thing that's ever happened

to me. With Arty as my witness, I promise that I'll never let you go," David responded seriously.

Chuckling, Eve said, "That's some witness. The man's so busy with his work that he didn't hear you and hardly notices that we're here."

Arty laughed. "Not true. I hear everything even if I don't comment. I stand witness to hearing both of you speak of love. You're stuck now."

The three friends enjoyed a hearty laugh that put an end to the worry and anxiety that the day's ordeal in the water had started. For the rest of the afternoon and evening, they would simply enjoy life and being together. They had been frighteningly close to losing both.

After helping Arty tidy his studio for the evening, the trio decided to go out for dinner. Since meeting David, Eve had enjoyed almost every restaurant recognized by the locals as offering good food. Tonight, it seemed fitting that they would return to the first one to which David had ever taken her. They were marking the beginning of a new phase in their relationship, and no other restaurant would do.

The three friends pedaled off into the sweetness of the evening. Along the way, Arty pointed out the houses of the island's rich and famous residents. Although David had already given her the tour, Eve enjoyed Arty's often gossipy commentary about each of them. She wondered if his reputation as one of the island's eccentric artists had given him a chance to meet any of them, but he certainly told a good story.

The restaurant was just as noisy and crowded as on their first visit. Strangely, however, the hostess quickly seated them as if the capacity were endless. Eve did not ask, but she wondered if the owner kept a few tables unfilled in case the line of hungry patrons grew too long. She was hungry and did not care as long as they could eat.

As the waiter delivered their meal, Eve said, "The first time we came here, I thought the idea of serving a little of everything on the menu was bizarre and a waste of money. Now I think I can see where the practice would speed things up. There's no wasted time looking over the menu or waiting for the entrée to cook. Everything's ready."

"That's probably what the owner had in mind," Arty said as he dove into the Manhattan clam chowder.

"Helen will love this place," Eve interjected. "This is a gourmand's paradise."

"Yeah, that's why I like it so much," David added. "Where else can a single person have a filling, satisfying meal without going home to Mom?"

The trio ate in relative silence for the rest of the meal. The food was too good to ruin it with idle chatter. While they waited for dessert, Eve excused herself and headed to the ladies' room.

"Speaking of moms, has yours met Eve yet?" Arty asked as soon as Eve rounded the corner.

"Not yet, but soon," David replied quickly. "The timing didn't seem right until today. Now I definitely want them to meet her. I don't want to scare her off. Maybe I should wait until Helen's in town. My folks would hold one of those infamous island cookouts."

"Good idea," Arty agreed. "It won't look as if you're introducing your girlfriend to your folks if her sister's with you. Can I come, too? You know I'm always up for a free meal."

"Sure. We'll invite a few good friends to keep the evening informal," David offered.

Rejoining them, Eve asked, "You guys look so serious. Did I miss something?"

"No, not a thing. Just two old friends talking," David replied, kissing Eve on the cheek.

"Good," Eve said and added, "The last time I left men alone together, I returned to find that they had volunteered me to serve on a committee. Because of them, I had to give up my Saturdays for four months. I was not happy, but it taught me a lesson."

Arty laughed. "Don't worry, we have not assigned you any disagreeable tasks."

"No, we were talking about holding a cookout to introduce Helen to the island," David offered.

"Oh, really? You didn't do anything like that for me," Eve said with a touch of sarcasm mixed with jealousy.

Fidgeting a bit, David said, "No, and maybe I should have. I didn't think of it, because I wanted to keep you all to myself. Besides, I know that you'll meet everyone during the school year anyway."

"That's a good save," Arty stated with praise in this voice.

Laughing and passing on the chocolate mousse, David said, "I'm not saving anything. It's true. I knew from the first time I met Eve that our relationship would be special. I didn't want to waste valuable time by sharing her with others. You're the only one of our group to meet her."

"I know and the others have complained loudly," Arty said.

Eve asked, laughing, "Do you have so little to do here that you have time to monitor each other's social life?"

"No, we're just very close-knit," Arty offered, finishing the mousse and starting on the apple pie. "Besides, David has never brought a woman to the group for approval. You're the first one."

With a serious face, David replied, "The first, last, and only. Until you, I didn't have anyone in my life that I wanted to introduce to my friends. In front of my best friend and the world, I love you deeply and completely."

David's tone was so serious that Eve initially did not know how to react. Something in his behavior and facial expression said that the declaration in front of his friend in their favorite restaurant meant more than the one in the coast guard's break room or Arty's studio. The expression on Arty's face confirmed her suspicions that David was, indeed, displaying his emotions in a way that was new and unique.

Eve's eyes welled at the realization that David's heart was so clearly on his sleeve. She swallowed hard and waited for composure to come. She had never been so completely moved or felt so overwhelmed by love.

In the flickering candlelight, Eve matched her mood to David's and stated, "I love you, David, with all my heart."

With Arty watching, David cupped Eve's chin and gently kissed her in the restaurant. Their first truly public display of affection was a confirmation of their love. Relocating to Bermuda had given Eve not only a new perspective on life but a true love.

Chapter Seven

Helen arrived on the late afternoon flight from BWI. As always, she traveled with only one bag of favorite items, believing that she could purchase anything that she really needed and had forgotten to bring. She grinned happily when she saw Eve holding red, white, and blue balloons to welcome her to the islands. Her face broke into a huge smile when she saw David at Eve's side. He looked every bit as handsome in person as in the photograph that Eve had sent. Helen was thrilled that her sister looked so happy with the man of her dreams beside her.

"Helen, you're finally here!" Eve gushed as she hugged her sister close.

"I've missed you so much!" Helen gasped. "We've been separated forever."

"Welcome to my new home, this wonderful island. Helen, this handsome guy is David. I told you about him," Eve said, motioning toward David, who had taken a few steps back to allow the sisters to enjoy their reunion.

"I'd have known you anywhere," Helen replied, holding her arms open for a hug from David.

David, usually shy on first meetings, found that he could resist Helen no better than he had stood his ground against Eve. Both women were so openly warm and gregarious that he found his reserve melting away. Before he knew it, David was locked in a tight embrace.

"Let's get you home. You must be tired," Eve stated as they joined the flow of travelers. "You'll love my little house. It's so cute and so appropriate for a place like this. It's not at all stuffy or pretentious like the cottages at home that really want to be colonials."

"I'm hungrier than I am tired. You know they don't feed people on the flights anymore. I had a sandwich before I left home, but I haven't eaten since," Helen replied as she matched her stride with theirs. Eve and David were so clearly a couple that they modified their pace to accommodate each other without even thinking.

Eve and David exchanged glances. Helen was playing right into their plans. They had anticipated her need to eat and had arranged to meet Arty at their favorite restaurant at seven after dropping her bag at the house. If only they would fall in love, everything would be perfect.

"The house is on the way to our favorite restaurant. We'll drop off your stuff and then go to dinner," Eve said with a happy smile.

"What's wrong with you?" Helen demanded. "You're grinning like the Cheshire Cat."

"Nothing," Eve bubbled. "I'm just so happy to see you."

"Maybe, but the last time you acted like this, you had filled my backpack with melted chocolate candy bars.

That gross mess covered all my books and gym clothes," Helen stated with a wary smile.

"They hadn't melted when I put them in there," Eve said, defending herself, looking at David, who only smiled. "How was I to know that you'd leave your stuff sitting in the sunshine? I only wanted to share my candy with you. I helped clean it up."

"That's true, but I haven't trusted that smile since," Helen replied with a chuckle.

They did not say much on the walk to the car. Eve was afraid that she would arouse Helen's suspicions if she sounded too happy. She would wait until the drive home when her enthusiasm for the island would give her actions the needed cover.

David drove the most direct route to Eve's little cottage but still managed to show Helen some of the homes of the rich and famous expatriates who called the islands their home. Eve enthusiastically pointed out the home of a movie star and, later, a spectacular view of the beach not far from another celebrity's home. She talked nonstop about all the water sports and shopping that the island offered. By the time they pulled to a stop in front of the cottage, Helen felt as if she knew the island well.

"This is cute!" she exclaimed as they walked through the gate and up the path that led to the house.

"I couldn't have asked for more," Eve replied as she fumbled in her purse for the door keys.

"How do you get around?" Helen asked. "I don't see a car."

"I bike. We bike almost everywhere or use a moped. If I need a car, David drives me. I'm spoiled. I don't know how I'll ever survive in the big city again," Eve said, unlocking the door.

"That's so unlike you. You're the windows-up, air-conditioning champion," Helen exclaimed.

"The weather's too perfect for that. In D.C., the only way not to have a permanent bad hair day is to use the a/c. We don't need that here," Eve said.

"The speed limit's so slow on the island that it's not really worthwhile to own a car. Most of us only use it for driving to the airport or the grocery store," David added as he followed the women into the house.

"I suppose we'll bike to the restaurant. I haven't been on one in a long time. I hope I'll remember how to do it," Helen said as she looked around the living room.

"You will. I did. We'll pedal slowly, won't we, David?" Eve said.

"Don't worry. We won't lose you," David stated from his perch on the chair by the window. He knew that the sisters needed time to reconnect, and he would only be in the way if he ventured further.

"The school system really gave you a nice place. This is charming, and the view is breathtaking," Helen proclaimed as she meandered from one room to the other, peering out the windows as she walked.

"Let's go upstairs. You'll really like the view from your room," Eve said.

"Coming, David?" Helen asked mischievously.

"I'll wait for you here," David replied with a wink.

The sisters vanished up the stairs, leaving David in the living room. From above, he could hear Helen's exclamations of praise for the little cottage as she followed Eve through the two bedrooms and one bathroom that made up the second floor of the cottage. When he heard low murmuring, David smiled, knowing that he was the topic of discussion.

"Have you two . . .?" Helen asked in a low voice.

"No! We hadn't even talked of love or affection until the day of the storm. We're taking it slow," Eve replied in an even softer whisper.

"You take it any slower, and you'll be in stop mode. I know old couples who move faster than you," Helen teased.

"I want to go slowly this time. I've been through whirlwind relationships as you know. I want to enjoy the 'getting to know you' stuff this time. David's really good with that stuff. Handholding, light kisses, flowers. I couldn't be happier," Eve replied as she helped Helen unpack her belongings.

"Speaking of relationships, I saw Brad the other day. He is doing well and sends his regards," Helen said, watching her sister for her response to the mention of her former love.

"That's good. We e-mailed a little when I first arrived, but I stopped after a while. I'm really busy getting to know the island and David. To be honest, I haven't thought much about Brad," Eve said without pause.

"Did he mention his new girlfriend?" Helen asked, her focus completely on her sister.

"No, he didn't. Who's he dating?" Eve inquired, pausing momentarily to remove the wrinkles from Helen's linen blouse.

"Her name's Gina," Helen said. "I think he said that she's a tapestry artist."

"Really? I didn't know he liked the artistic type. He seemed so traditional to me," Eve said with a disquieting tone in her voice.

"I guess he's changed his tastes. Anyway, Brad sends his regards. I showed him the brooches that Arty made, and he was impressed by the skill level. I even told him that I've helped Arty arrange a show."

"I certainly hope he appreciated Arty's work; it's

very delicate and complicated. What did what's-her-name, Gina, think about it?" Eve asked, waiting for her sister at the door.

"She loved it! She weaves handmade beaded items and really thought the brooches top quality. She's anxious for the show so that she can buy a few items," Helen explained.

"Good. I'm sure Arty will welcome that," Eve replied through slightly tight lips.

Eve did not like the extra little hop her heart gave at the mention of Brad's new love. She had thought that she was over him. Later, when she was alone, she would assess her reaction. For the time being, she decided that she simply did not like the idea of the man who had promised to remember her forever finding someone else. She did not want a relationship with him, but she had not anticipated that Brad would bond with someone else so quickly.

"When will I meet him?" Helen asked, interrupting Eve's thoughts.

"Tonight," Eve replied absently. The discussion of Brad and his new love had soured her reunion with her sister and spread a pall on the evening's planned festivities.

"Oh, no! Not tonight! I look terrible. Travel always makes my face look tired. My eyes look as if I've been up all night," Helen complained, scanning her beautiful face in the mirror and looking for imaginary wrinkles and dark circles.

"It's too late to make changes now," Eve said irritably. "Arty doesn't keep a phone in the studio, so I can't phone him. He's probably on his way to the restaurant anyway. Besides, you look terrific. Slip into a pair of slacks to show off your figure and let's go. We've been up here so long that David has probably fallen asleep downstairs."

"Fine," Helen replied snappishly. "Will these do? Is this place fancy?"

"Not at all. That's perfect. This little rainbow-colored sweater would look great with those slacks, too. I'll wait for you downstairs." Eve tossed the freshly unpacked item to her sister.

Changing quickly, Helen pulled on the outfit and checked her appearance. Even after washing her face, she still thought she looked tired. A touch of lipstick helped a bit but not as much as she would have liked. This evening was not going the way she had envisioned her first meeting with Arty. Although she had done him a favor by using her contacts to set up his show, Helen wanted to impress him with more than her brain on their first meeting. If pressed, she would have admitted that she had a little crush on the artist who had created the lovely brooches. She had not told Eve, because she did not want her sister to make a big deal of it. Still, Helen wanted to knock Arty's socks off when she first met him and felt that her travel-weary face would not do it.

David had been trying to hear their whispered conversation and rose at the sound of the sister descending the stairs. Although Helen looked stunning in her simple outfit, to his mind, Eve in white linen slacks and blouse was the more beautiful of the two. She was almost two inches taller, tanned from the Bermuda sun, and the woman he loved. He sighed contentedly, knowing that he was a lucky man to have a woman like Eve in love with him.

Joining the women at the front door, David pulled Eve into his arms and lightly kissed her. He smiled into her eyes and felt the warmth of love spread over him as the love Eve felt for him replaced her surprise at his impulsive behavior. He had come a long way from the conservative university professor.

"Should I wait for you lovebirds outside?" Helen asked with a chuckle.

"No, we're right behind you. I'll bring your bikes around." David laughed as he reluctantly removed his arms from Eve's slim body.

As he vanished down the path that led to the backyard, Eve locked the door and walked with Helen to the garden gate. The sisters chatted happily although Eve's mind was not completely on the little tidbits she shared about the island. The nagging thought of Brad with another woman nipped at her mind. She no longer loved him and had not for a long time. However, she did not like to think that the man who had so recently loved her could now love another.

Although their relationship had ended long before they agreed to call it quits, Eve still thought of Brad as hers when she thought of him at all. He had been so sad when she left for Bermuda and had promised, in his way, to be there when she returned. Eve had not wanted him to make that kind of commitment, knowing that she could not reciprocate. She had wanted him to fall in love with someone else. After all, she had. Still, she felt betrayed as she had any time her former boyfriends had fallen for someone else. In time, Eve knew that she would get over the shock, or at least she hoped she would.

David's love was more important to her than anything else in her life. He was a more perfect lover than Brad had ever been. However, Eve could not stop the sour taste that filled her mouth when she thought of Brad with Gina. When she had left the States that day,

Brad looked so sad. During their short e-mails, Eve
had imagined that he still wore that hang-dog expression. Now, she had to change the image of Brad that
she carried in her mind and, perhaps, her heart.

Thanks to Helen's refusal to give a description of Gina,
Eve could imagine a small toadlike woman in Brad's
arms. Perhaps Gina was cross-eyed or bucktoothed. She
might have a large hairy mole on her neck and spindly
legs. Her IQ was probably barely trainable. Eve consoled herself with the thought that Gina would certainly be lacking in not only beauty but brains.

By the time David returned with the two bikes, Eve
had managed to conjure up a very ego-satisfying image
of Brad and his new woman. With little effort and a
sense of triumph, she pushed the thought of Brad from
her mind. She refused to allow thoughts of him to ruin
the evening that she and David had planned so carefully as Helen's introduction to the island and to Arty.
If all went well, this matchmaking might prove to be
one of her most successful undertakings.

"I'm doing it! I'm doing it!" Helen cried as she pedaled slowly down the road behind Eve and David.

"You'll look like an islander by the time we reach
the restaurant," David shouted.

"Great job, Helen!" Eve said.

"This isn't half bad. This is a great way to enjoy the
scenery," Helen commented loudly as she grew more
confident with her ability to propel herself and the bike
forward. She even dared to glance at the stunning vis-
tas as she wobbled down the road.

By the time the trio reached the restaurant, David's
prediction had come true. Helen no longer lagged behind but pedaled confidently beside them. To her surprise, she had enjoyed the ride as she had as a child when
she used to tear through the neighborhood at speeds

that made her mother shudder. Not that she planned to
do wheelies, but Helen was pleased with her ability to
negotiate the turns in the road.

Once inside the restaurant, Eve and Helen quickly
vanished into the ladies' room as David went in search
of Arty. Finding him waiting somewhat impatiently at
the bar with an untouched glass of wine in his hand,
David approached him with a smile. Arty's slightly crooked smile showed that he was nervous about the evening.

"Hey, man! I hope you haven't been waiting long,"
David said as he clapped Arty on the back.

"No, I really just got here. I've been walking on the
beach. I was afraid I'd be late so I . . . Man, am I nervous! Couldn't I have met Helen at the shop? At least
there she would have seen me on my own messy turf,"
Arty complained, wiping the sweat from his palms onto
his trouser leg.

"Don't worry. She's an okay person, real normal, if
you know what I mean," David explained.

"She's probably the real cool type, good under pressure, even under the stress of a blind date. I hate this,"
Arty continued to complain as he allowed David to guide
him into the dining room.

"Smile or at least look pleasant. You don't want Eve
and Helen to think that you're not happy about being
here," David advised as they approached the table.

"I'm not," Arty whispered through tight lips drawn
into a fake smile.

"Look who I found in the bar." David announced as
they sank into the extra chairs.

Eve greeted him cheerfully. "Hi, Arty. This is my
sister, Helen, the one who purchased your art."

Taking a deep breath, Arty said, "Greetings, Helen.
It's really nice to meet you finally. Thanks for the sup-

port and the contacts and the show. I really appreciate everything you've done for me."

Smiling with a calmness that she did not feel while her stomach did back flips, Helen replied, "I'm the one who owes you the thanks. It's not every day that someone with your talent comes along. I'm really looking forward to the show and to seeing your workshop. Eve tells me that it's messy but a trove of unexpected treasure."

Beginning to relax, Arty said, "Eve's right about the mess, but I'm not sure about the treasures. You'll have to judge for yourself."

"Believe me, the workshop's worth the visit. You just have to be careful where you step. Art, or elements of it, is everywhere," Eve teased.

Slapping his buddy on the back, David said, "If you can believe it, Arty was a neat guy until he discovered his true calling. When he was in college, he always had the perfect room. It wasn't until grad school and the discovery of an artistic soul that he changed."

"It seems to me that most of the people we know have changed," Arty replied with a smile. "You were a daredevil once, able to hang ten with the best of them. Your brother almost killed himself paragliding. My cousin did the same thing with skydiving. We've all mellowed a bit with age."

As the waiter set the platters in front of them, David said, "We had to grow up sometime."

"Yeah, but we've become not just grown but staid. You're a professor, my cousin's a lawyer, and your brother is a dentist. Sounds dull as heck to me," Arty commented as he offered Helen a spoonful of an aromatic shrimp dish.

Surveying the table, Helen asked, "Who ordered all

this food for four people? Are you expecting someone else?"

The three regulars laughed at the familiar reaction to the restaurant's style. Eve felt smug at being able to witness her sister's reaction from the superior seat of a person accustomed to the restaurant's uniqueness. She placed her hand on David's and smiled; Eve was home.

Leaning closer, Arty explained, "Believe me, we'll finish most of it. Whatever we don't eat, we'll take the rest home. That's the way this place operates. It offers some of everything to its patrons. Great idea, don't you think?"

"It sure is. I wonder if this would work at home," Helen said, accepting the food and serving herself small samples from the other platters.

Joining the conversation, David said, "We've wondered about that, too, but decided that people in the big cities would probably turn their noses up at the idea. I think it would work in the resorts like Vegas. It's a fast way to get 'em in and out."

Studying Helen's face, Arty asked, "Do you know someone who'd give this approach a try?"

"As a matter of fact, I do," Helen replied. "Before I left home, a client asked me to be on the lookout for a unique opportunity. He might like this concept."

"If he likes good food with an interesting presentation, he'll love it," Eve added, munching happily on pineapple shrimp.

The couples ate in silence for a while. Each was occupied in thoughts that required as much attention as the meal. Helen was working out a presentation to her client to whom she intended to pitch the restaurant's concept. Arty was designing a new brooch that he would fashion for Helen as a special thank-you gift for her help. David was thinking that Eve had never looked more beautiful with that smear of barbecue sauce on her chin. He had never been happier.

Eve, however, was being tossed between her love for David and her former attraction to Brad. Breaking up with Brad had been a no-brainer activity since the relationship had changed into friendship with no physical contact before it officially ended. She had no regrets. However, she still felt unsettled at the idea that he had a new woman in his life. When she last saw him, Brad was sad about her leaving and still appeared to be in love with her. Now, only a few months later, he was involved with someone else. Eve found herself contemplating the fickle nature of people. She did not want to deny Brad the chance for happiness and love, but he should have moped and missed her a bit longer.

By the time they reached dessert, the nervous first-date tension between Arty and Helen had vanished. In its place, a budding friendship grew with indication of more to come. Eve smiled broadly and congratulated herself on a job well done. Even David, who initially objected to Eve's interference, had changed his mind and now believed that the introduction had been a good idea. He had not seen Arty looking so happy in a long time.

Deciding that they were too full from the enormous meal to pedal to Arty's home, the couples took a walk on the beach. Slipping off their shoes, they linked arms and walked four abreast in the wet sand as the dark sea tickled their toes. The night air smelled sweet and the stars sparkled in the darkness.

Night on the beach was one of Eve's favorite times. She knew the frightful power of the surf but still loved hearing it pound the sand. Its strength seemed muted by the darkness. Somehow, the ocean was not as scary when the sun did not highlight its depth.

"This is the most beautiful place I've ever seen."

Helen sighed. "I can understand why you wouldn't want to leave here."

"I hope the year passes slowly," Eve replied with a tinge of sadness in her voice.

"I'll just have to find a way to keep you here forever," David said, breaking the chain and hugging her close.

"That sounds like a discussion of commitment," Helen teased.

Before David could answer, Arty chimed in, saying, "Women always hear commitment. Maybe he meant a business venture."

"Funny business, if you ask me," Helen replied. "Just look at those two."

In the darkness broken only by the distant stars and the few restaurant lights, Eve and David stood in a tight embrace. Their arms encircled each other as if to block out the future and cling only to the present. The surf splashed around their ankles like icing on a cake.

"Should we break that up?" Helen asked Arty playfully.

"No, I don't think so. People who've almost lost each other deserve a break," Arty replied seriously.

"Then, what should we do? We can't simply stand here until they remember us. From the way they're clinging to each other, we might have to wait a long time."

"I have an idea." Arty pulled Helen into his arms. "We've only just met, but I've had a crush on you for months."

"Really? I'm glad to know I'm not the only one," Helen confessed as she allowed herself to melt against him.

Kissing her lightly on the forehead, Arty said, "I asked Eve to show me your picture after you bought the second brooch. I wanted to see the woman who liked my art. I liked what I saw. Not long after that, I heard your voice for the first time when you phoned with information about the show. I was hooked."

"I think that's when I stopped denying my feelings for you. Your voice was so mellow, matching the photo that Eve sent me perfectly," Helen stated softly.

"I didn't give her a picture of me. I don't have any," Arty said, studying Helen's face.

"She snapped it one day when the three of you were out sailing. I had asked for a heads-up before I lowered my guard. I didn't want to fall for a troll." Helen laughed.

"That little sneak! I had no idea she was doing that. Well, if it worked to get us together, I won't complain." Arty gave Helen a big hug.

"What are you two talking about over there?" David demanded as he and Eve approached.

Arty chuckled. "Oh, just some fancy photograph."

"You told him?" Eve asked accusingly.

"He might as well know that your talent as a shutterbug is what helped to bring us together," Helen confessed.

"Well, I guess there's no harm after all," Eve conceded as the four of them walked toward their bikes.

The evening had turned out better than she had expected, and Eve felt contented and smug about her accomplishments. Unlike her other botched attempts at matchmaking, this one seemed to be on solid footing. Helen and Arty certainly gave the impression of being two people who were falling in love.

The ride home took longer than usual, but none of them seemed to notice. Along the way, they stopped at a brightly illuminated beach behind one of the famous and expensive hotels. Surprisingly, they had the beach all to themselves on a glorious evening. Eve was so in love with the island that she could not understand anyone's desire to sit inside a casino or club when the beach beckoned.

When they finally reached Eve's little cottage, they were incredibly tired but very happy. They stifled yawns and stretched bodies stiff from leaning over the handlebars. The women lingered at the front door while the men stowed the bikes around back. A strange shyness overwhelmed all four of them as they said good night on the steps. The women disappeared into the little cottage as the men began their journey home.

"He's wonderful!" Helen breathed as soon as they had locked the door behind them.

"Yes, David is a great guy and very different from Brad," Eve agreed with a smile that reached from one ear to the other.

"David? I'm not talking about him. I mean Arty," Helen snapped, looking at Eve as if she failed to comprehend an earth-shattering event.

"Oh, yeah, he's terrific. I knew you'd like him," Eve said, staring at her glassy-eyed sister.

"I knew from looking at his art that he had a warm, compassionate soul." Helen sighed as she climbed the steps with Eve behind her.

"He's sensitive but messy," Eve commented, adding a touch of reality.

"There's nothing you can say that'll change my mind. I don't care if he lives like a pig. I can handle anything," Helen replied, giving her chin a jerk of obstinacy.

"I just thought I should warn you. You like order and everything in its place. Arty's not like that. He doesn't clean up often," Eve said with a small smile.

"Are you trying to convince me not to fall in love with him? I got the impression that you were playing matchmaker," Helen stated, looking at her sister as if Eve were a specimen under the microscope.

"Not at all," Eve replied. "I like Arty, and I think he'd be perfect for you. But I know you. Can you handle a relationship with a man whose idea of organization is stuff strewn everywhere?"

"Of course I can. I'm not a shallow person."

"Good. When we go over there tomorrow, you won't be shocked."

"That's right. I can overlook anything for the man I love."

Smiling, Eve asked, "Can you forget the distance that'll separate you two as soon as your vacation ends?"

A shadow fell over Helen's beautiful face as she replied, "I know that'll be rough, but, if this turns out to be more than an infatuation, we'll work it out. What about you and David? I thought you were in love with him. How do you plan to handle distance?"

"I don't know yet. We haven't dealt with that. We're just enjoying the days as they come," Eve replied sadly.

"Well then, big sister, I'd say that we both have something to work out," Helen said.

The sisters stood in subdued silence for a few moments and then parted for bed. Neither of them had a solution to the larger question of distance. For the moment, they would ignore the inevitable and enjoy the time they had on the island with the men they loved.

Chapter Eight

The sun was hot and high in the sky when David arrived the next day. As usual, he waited beside the gate as Helen waited for Eve to lock the door. The sisters were wearing similar shades of red and white and looked stunning. David always felt a little dowdy beside Eve in his cutoff jeans and scuffed scandals. Since she did not appear to notice his lived-in appearance, he did not break with his routine.

Arty had been hard at work for hours by the time David freed himself from his pile of papers and joined Eve and Helen for the trip to the studio. He had spent half the night cleaning up until he decided that his efforts were only making a path in the mess. After that, he turned out the light and went to bed. Although he usually slept fitfully as designs swirled through his dreams, he fell asleep as soon as his head hit the pillow and slept until his alarm sounded five hours later.

David, however, had not spent a peaceful night. He loved Eve and was often tortured by the thought that their time together was limited. He knew the reality was that, as soon as the new school year ended, she would leave him and the island behind to return to her old life and school. School years passed so quickly, and grading papers consumed so much time that there was little left for building a relationship. David often wondered how his married colleagues managed to keep their spouses happy with so little free time. Perhaps they graded papers and prepared lessons together.

David did not want that kind of life with Eve if he could convince her to stay on the island permanently. With luck, they would be able to find time to be together rather than spending every waking minute tending to school business. His books were doing well as were his patents and, perhaps, that income would be enough to free both of them from the chore of punching a clock. He enjoyed the simple, uncomplicated life and needed few frills; he hoped that she felt the same way.

He had not as yet shared any of these thoughts with Eve. Although their relationship had turned the corner after the boating accident, David had not wanted to scare her by coming on too strong or putting forth his ideas of permanence prematurely. With Helen spending her vacation on the island, intimacy and conversation would have to wait.

"You're awfully quiet, Helen," David commented as they biked toward Arty's studio. "Is anything wrong?"

"No, nothing. I was simply enjoying the scenery. I'm even more impressed by the beauty of the island now than yesterday. It'll be difficult to leave here," Helen replied, adjusting her hair and blouse for the tenth time.

"You could always set up shop here," David suggested. "We need investment bankers, too."

"No, I'll go home when my vacation's up. Maybe one day I'll make enough money to be able to move here. I just hope I won't have reached retirement age

when that happens," Helen stated, giving her belt another tug.

"David has a good idea, Helen," Eve said. "If you
were to move here, I would ask the school board to hire
me permanently. With the two of us here, we might be
able to convince Mom and Dad to join us in this paradise."

Smiling, Helen responded, "Don't count on me for
that. I need to be where the big money is. That means
D.C., San Francisco, or New York. As much as I like it
here, Bermuda will have to be a vacation spot for me.
You can stay here if you want."

"You could always scale back your lifestyle. The
beauty and freedom of living here would quickly replace the stuff you'd leave behind," Eve suggested.

Shaking her head, Helen said, "I'm not ready to do
that yet. I want it all, but who knows? I'll do a little in-
vestigating after I return home. I might be able to have
my cake and eat it, too."

"I don't want to live that far away from you and Mom
and Dad. I guess I'll have to cherish every minute of
this year and take the memories home with me," Eve
replied sadly.

The trio felt a heaviness fall over them as they continued their ride. Each one silently promised not to discuss departures again. The reality of not being able to
stay in Bermuda added a somber note to their visit.

By the time they arrived at Arty's studio, they were
feeling like having a conversation again, and Arty's
home provided plenty of material. Entering the yard,
Eve was once again impressed by the level of messiness
with which he lived. Scrap piles of this and that littered
the front and backyards, making it impossible to sit
outside to enjoy the view of the ocean.

"Wow! You said he was messy," Helen commented as she picked her way past one of the lesser piles of scrap.

"Creative," Eve replied, echoing Helen's initial defense of Arty's lifestyle.

"Messy," Helen stated in a matter-of-fact tone.

David said nothing. He could think of no words to reduce the impact of seeing Arty's homestead. Instead, he walked silently behind the women, listening to their muttered conversation but adding nothing.

Chickens from the neighbor's coop scratched and pecked at the ground at their feet. A big red cat sat on an overturned wheelbarrow watching them. Occasionally the beast would flick its tail or bat at a fly. A huge dog with one floppy ear lounged under a tall palm. When motivated, he would lift an ear and survey his territory.

Leaving their bikes, the three approached the converted garage that functioned as a studio. They stepped carefully along the path to avoid the overflowing piles of scrap metal that threatened to tumble in front of them. Although Eve and David cast quick glances at Helen to judge her reaction to the clutter, they could not read her expression. She maintained a calm, composed, almost poker-face expression that had not changed since her initial comment.

Inside, the studio's messiness melded with Arty's creativity to produce an intriguing combination of artistic energy. Helen immediately recognized the change and became animated by the complete creations that hung from the ceiling, filled baskets, sat on easels, and leaned against the walls. Watching her, Eve could not tell if her sister was in love with the man or his work. Whichever it was, Helen was definitely affected by the colors and textures that filled Arty's studio.

"Stunning!" Helen exclaimed as she gingerly fingered a beaded tapestry that was still connected to its loom.

"Arty's been busy since the last time I was here," Eve commented to David.

"He's been staying up nights, trying to get ready for the show," David replied, amazed at the quantity and quality of his buddy's work. "I've known Arty's creative spurts since grad school, but he's never produced this much at one time. He has captured every color of the sea and sand in his work. It's remarkable."

"I've never seen anything so vibrant," Eve said as she studied a metal sculpture that reminded her of the waterfall in her favorite swimming hole.

"I don't think all of these are new. Even Arty on caffeine can't have created this quantity in so short a time," David remarked.

Finding discreet tags hidden in the framework of the designs, Eve interjected, "He made this one last year. He must have had it in storage for the day that he'd have a show."

"That must have been what he had in that locked back room. I sure hope he has insurance on everything," David said as he stood in the middle of the huge room in disbelief.

"Do you really think that Arty has insurance?" Eve joked. "That's too conventional for him."

"He doesn't have insurance on these?" Helen asked in horror. "Do you realize that we're standing within a treasure trove of creative genius? These are worth hundreds of thousands. I have a client in mind who would pay top price for these, and I'm not talking about the sales from the upcoming show. A fire would destroy invaluable art treasures."

"I could make more," Arty stated as he joined them.

He was wearing a shirt that David had not seen before. He had also managed to remove the flecks of paint that had seemed to stick to his hands permanently. David could not believe the transformation that had occurred in his friend. Love had certainly had its impact of Arty. David wondered if he was as transparent.

"You couldn't possibly replicate these items. They'd be lost forever," Helen commented.

"I take photos of everything I make. I might miss a twist here and there in a recreation, but not by much. Would you like to see my album?" Arty offered, setting the tray of tea-filled glasses on a workbench.

"I'd love to, but first, which of these will we ship to the States for the show?" Helen asked, accepting the offered glass. "The gallery's huge and could handle all of them unless there're some that you don't want to show."

"You know the clientele. As far as I'm concerned, they're all for sale," Arty replied.

"Then, we'll ship all of them. This show will be an incredible success. I have clients who've been asking me to find new artists for them to support. They'll love you," Helen enthused.

"From them I want purchases. From you I want love. Has the appearance of my studio turned you off?" Arty replied, studying Helen's face.

"Not at all. This is your creative domain. It should have an appearance that feeds your art," Helen responded with affection in her voice.

"We better not show her the main house," David interjected.

"What does he mean by that, Arty?" Helen asked.

Sighing, Arty replied, "My house is messy, too. I'm not the homebody type. I really need to hire a housekeeper."

"Don't worry about a thing," Helen stated firmly. "While I'm here, I'll take care of that for you so that you can concentrate all of your energies on your art. I want this show to wow everyone in the D.C. area. The gallery has a sister shop in New York and will exhibit a few of your pieces there at the same time. You don't have time for the mundane."

David and Eve exchanged glances. Helen, who hated to clean her bedroom in the condo, was biting off more than she could imagine. David was glad that someone would tackle the mess in the main house, but Eve knew that her sister would regret offering to do the work without seeing the condition of the house first.

"In that case, let's go inside. I'll give you a tour of the house and show you my album," Arty replied, so blissfully happy that he ignored the fact that Helen's decision to help him came prior to seeing the way he lived. They had fallen in love with each other without seeing more than photographs. Now the affection was deepening with every word of praise and understanding that Helen uttered. He could think of nothing in his house that could affect their love.

Arty led the way as the others carefully stepped around and over the obstacles in their path. From the outside, the house needed only a coat of paint and judicious straightening up. The inside, however, was another matter.

The sun streamed through the large windows in the living room highlighting every misplaced, dropped, or abandoned article on the floor and tabletops. Helen, despite her adoration of Arty, gasped at the sight of the messy room. Peeking in the kitchen and dining room, she quickly learned that each room was just as messy.

"Well, I have a lot to do. Where's the broom?" Helen asked with a tone of acceptance that surprised Eve.

"You're planning to start now?" Eve asked incredulously.

"There's certainly no better time," Helen replied, further shocking her sister.

"I had planned to take you on a tour of the island. I hadn't thought that you'd spend your vacation cleaning house," Eve stated.

"It needs to be done, and I'm happy to do it. I'll see you back at the house later," Helen said as she bent to pick up the unopened newspapers on the floor.

As Helen applied herself to making a path through the mess, Arty happily returned to his studio. As David and Eve escaped before Helen could hand them a dust cloth, they could hear his happy singing through the open windows. Rushing to their bikes, they quickly pedaled up the path toward David's family home.

While Helen toiled, Eve would spend her time under Mr. and Mrs. Scott's scrutiny. David had arranged for the meeting to take place while Helen vacationed on the island so that Eve would not have to go through the ordeal alone. Although David was well past the age of feeling that he needed to introduce his girlfriend to his parents, Eve was one woman whom David wanted them to meet. Just the same, he knew his mother would put her through a mild form of the third degree.

The Scott home sat on prime hilltop land overlooking a lush tropical valley. They had built it away from everyone for privacy and economy. At the time of its construction, all of their friends thought they were making a big mistake. Now that the island's population had increased, they all wished they had the same views.

As soon as Eve and David leaned their bikes against the big frangipani tree in the front yard, Eve sensed that she had arrived in a special place. Unlike her small, comfortable cottage, the house was massive and sprawling

yet intimate in color scheme and very welcoming. She
could feel it encouraging her to enter through the deep
red door encircled by fragrant flowering vines. From the
outside, it was the kind of house that any child would
look forward to returning to after school.

Without knocking, David ushered Eve through the
unlocked front door into the stunning living space decorated in cool color and vases of flowers. Paintings and
tapestries hung from the walls, depicting scenes from
various parts of the island. Eve could see breathtaking
views of the island from every window. A wall of rocks
housed a fireplace that the family probably only used
on special occasions.

While Eve stood at the window admiring the view,
Mrs. Scott entered silently on the gleaming hardwood
floors. She was a sturdy woman who looked as if she
could have raised an army of sons without flinching.
Although she emitted an air of being a no-nonsense
person, she had a kindly smile and an inviting twinkle
in her eye.

"It's beautiful, isn't it?" Mrs. Scott stated, quietly
joining David and Eve at the window.

"I've never seen anything like it," Eve replied softly.

David almost burst with pride and happiness at Eve's
reaction to his family home. His mother was a very fair
woman who tried not to judge people too quickly, but
first impressions were often lasting ones with her. He
could tell from the way his mother hugged Eve in greeting that the woman he loved had made a good one.

"Welcome to our home, Eve. Feel free to visit any-
time, even without David. That view will call you back
often," Mrs. Scott said warmly.

"Thank you. I appreciate that and will definitely accept your hospitality. I'm a very amateurish plein air
painter, but I'd love to set up my easel here one day. I'm

sorry that my sister couldn't be with us. She would have loved the view, too, but she's helping Arty tidy his working environment," Eve said, barely able to turn her eyes from the view of the birds playing happily in the flowers.

"She'll never finish that task. You'll have to rescue her, I'm afraid." Mrs. Scott chuckled and turned to her son, leaving no room for argument. She intended to be alone with Eve for a little girl talk. "David, your father's in the sunroom. After we chat for a while, Eve and I will join you there."

Looking briefly at Eve, who smiled and seemed comfortable being left alone with his mother, David left the room as instructed. He knew that Eve would survive his mother's gentle probing, yet he wished he could be in attendance to help her withstand the inquisition. In due time, he would ask Eve for her reactions. Eventually, his mother would offer hers.

"It's about time my son brought you to see me," Mrs. Scott stated as soon as she heard the door close behind him. "David wanted to wait until the cookout that we're hosting to welcome you and your sister, but I insisted on meeting you today. I've waited long enough to meet the woman who has turned around my usually reserved son and made him more outgoing."

"I really haven't done anything, Mrs. Scott." Eve chuckled. "David's simply seeing the island through the eyes of an outsider. That makes all the difference. He's no longer taking his homeland for granted."

"Well, whatever the reason for the change, thank you. I haven't seen my son this happy in a long time. Being outdoors again and not cooped up all day in a classroom or an office has made him look healthier, too," Mrs. Scott added.

"I've enjoyed his company and definitely seen parts of the island that outsiders usually don't," Eve stated.

Studying Eve closely, Mrs. Scott commented, "You and David had a close call a short time back. The storm could have killed both of you."

"It was frightening, but surviving it was instructional. We were always careful, but we're even more so now. I hope that we'll never get caught that way again," Eve said, reflecting on the harrowing experience.

Mrs. Scott nodded and agreed, saying, "Well, I guess the ordeal wasn't too dreadful as long as you learned from the experience. Let's hope that son of mine did. He spends too much time in the analysis of a situation and not enough immersed in the emotions of the moment. He needs to blend the two functions. He was better about being in touch with his feelings when he was a little boy. Somewhere along the line, he became so reserved and analytical. I'm happy to see him living again."

"I love it here, so I guess we're good for each other," Eve said, waiting for the deeper questions to begin.

On signal, Mrs. Scott cut through the casual conversation and asked, "You've opened the world to my son. What do you plan to do with him when your time ends here? The school year will speed by. What are your plans?"

"I haven't thought that far yet. David's a big boy now and can take care of himself. Both of us have a lot at stake if our relationship can't survive the separation after I leave. If it doesn't, I guess that means that we were only meant to be friends," Eve stated gently but firmly.

"Are you two in love?" Mrs. Scott asked bluntly.

"We're just beginning to explore the possibility. It's too early to speculate as to the depth of our emotions for each other. We'll have to see if it's infatuation or a deeper affection that will survive the test of time," Eve replied with equal honesty.

"I hope you'll decide that you two will have a future. It would be wonderful if you'd stay here after your contract ends. I'd hate the thought of your taking the sun from his life again. You've given him so much," Mrs. Scott said as she placed her hand over Eve's.

"We'll see. David adds immeasurably to mine also. I'd feel a great loss if we ever separated," Eve said and added, "Let's not think about June of next year. I prefer to concentrate on the hours and days we have together in the future."

At that moment, before his mother could delve more deeply, David returned. Gazing from one to the other, he judged that the conversation had been satisfactory. Neither looked upset or angry. As a matter of fact, both were smiling.

Hugging Eve around the shoulders, David said, "Dad's becoming impatient to meet you. Sorry, Mom, but I have to steal her away from you."

"We'll find time for many more long chats. Tell your father that lunch will be ready in fifteen minutes," Mrs. Scott replied as she kissed Eve on the cheek and headed toward the kitchen.

"She likes you," David said as he led Eve to the family room.

"The feeling's mutual," Eve replied, linking her arm through his.

As soon as Eve saw David's father, she knew the source of his height and handsome features. Even at sixty-five, Mr. Scott still stood tall and straight. The loose-knit shirt barely disguised his broad shoulders, muscular arms, and wide chest. His face showed smile rather than frown lines as if he had always lived a happy life surrounded by the people and the land he loved. His broad hands bore calluses, and the sun had tanned his skin a deep red brown. Squint lines populated the skin around his eyes as if he had spent hours gazing across the water. David had told Eve that his father was an avid fisherman who had spent every free minute on the water while he was the president of a large consulting firm and had increased his time on the water considerably upon retirement.

"Ah, so this is the woman who has restored my son's sense of fun," Mr. Scott said, hugging Eve close. "I'm so happy to meet the person who could get David out of the classroom and into a boat again."

Accepting the hug and compliment, Eve replied, "I'm a teacher, too, and understand the need to grade those papers. David has done me a great favor in serving as my tour guide to these wonderful islands. I'd never have learned Bermuda this completely if he hadn't given up his time to show me around."

"You would have learned our ways just fine. Teaching has a way of putting people at the grassroots level," Mr. Scott said as he motioned to the sofa.

Eve and David settled opposite Mr. Scott, who immediately indicated the view from the large picture window. "Have you ever seen anything like this? I can't imagine living in a place that doesn't have this view," he said.

"It is lovely," Eve agreed. "The entire island is fabulous. I've seen so much of paradise that I didn't even know existed until I came here. I love the ease with which people interact here, too. No one seems in a hurry or obsessed with making an impression. It's wonderful."

"I'm sure that some people here display type-A personalities," Mr. Scott stated. "I can't image how they survive on an island where there's really nowhere to go so there's no need to rush. They must drive themselves crazy, rushing to and fro for no reason. That son of mine had that tendency. You've worked wonders in turning him around."

"Dad, I'm not like that at all," David objected with a chuckle. "It's just that I can't stand a desk full of papers waiting to be graded. The students like speedy turn-around, and I understand that need completely. If I had my way, I wouldn't require so many intermediate tests. I'd simply administer a midterm and a final. However, the powers won't approve that idea, claiming that the use of only two assessment tools would put too much stress on the students, although it would certainly relieve mine."

"Your ideas are ahead of their time. One day, they'll agree with you. Educational consultants have been telling school systems the same thing for years. It's time for a change, but no one's willing to make it," Mr. Scott said, defending his son.

"I hope so," Eve agreed. "Whatever trends the universities embrace eventually trickle down to the high school level. I'd love to save my eyes a bit."

Entering the room, Mrs. Scott declared, "I can't believe that you folks are talking shop with that view out the window. Summer's too short. Before you know it, you'll be back in the routine. I can clearly see that it's my duty to save you from yourselves. Lunch is ready."

Smiling, Mr. Scott rose and embraced his wife. "Let's go, children. When Mother calls, you know that there's something good on the table."

Mrs. Scott beamed at her husband's compliment. She was, indeed, a good cook, having won ribbons for her pies and cakes; however, she always loved flattery when it came from her husband. He had been the love of her life since she was six years old, and she took great pleasure in pleasing him.

Mr. Scott had been correct in anticipating a feast fit for a king. Mrs. Scott had decorated the table with fresh flowers, all of which were edible, and fruits from her garden. She had, as usual, used her bone china luncheon service in the belief that every meal deserved special treatment. The crystal stemware and sterling flatware glistened in the sunny dining room, inviting the family and its guest to dine on the steamed and buttered shrimp, crispy lettuce salad garnished with tomatoes, radishes, and nasturtiums, asparagus with a drizzle of clarified butter, and freshly baked rolls.

"I hope you didn't go to all this trouble for me," Eve said as she admired the table. "The table is stunning!"

Smiling at his mother, David replied, "Mother feeds us like this all the time. She serves every meal like this."

"I've stayed married to this woman all these years not only because I love her but because I live in a five-star hotel and eat gourmet meals every day. She's a wonder," Mr. Scott commented proudly.

Mrs. Scott's deep red-brown complexion deepened with embarrassment. "It's what I do for my family. It's not a big deal. I love to cook. As for the presentation, I can't take this stuff with me; I might as well use it. George, will you bless the table?"

All heads bowed as Mr. Scott offered thanks for the food, the hands that prepared it, and those who were about to enjoy it. Eve felt warm and comfortable in the home of David's parents as if she had known them all of her life. Everything from the sunlight streaming through the window to the view of the lavish gardens to the aromas coming from the sumptuous meal invited her to make herself at home among them.

The meal was as flavorful as it was aromatic. No one spoke for the first few minutes as they feasted on culinary delights that would make any famed chef jealous. Mrs. Scott's work definitely bested any that Eve had tasted in D.C.

"This is so good!" Eve exclaimed when at last she could tear herself away from the meal. "Good isn't a strong enough word. It's heavenly."

Mr. Scott beamed with pride and said, "I told you my wife was a talented chef. People have tried unsuccessfully to convince her to open a restaurant."

"I'll never do it," Mrs. Scott stated flatly. "I cook for the ones I love, not for a bunch of paying patrons. I create these meals as my way of telling my family that each and every one of them means more to me than life itself. God gave me this talent to share with them; I won't commercialize it."

"You can see that my wife's a woman of strong convictions," Mr. Scott declared proudly.

Mrs. Scott only smiled at her loving and indulgent husband. Eve and David exchanged glances, too. In the midst of all that love, Eve saw the kind of husband David would make and liked what she saw. He had grown up in a family in which the members felt safe to share emotions and opinions and genuinely cared for and about each other.

After such a fabulous lunch, Eve could not think of eating another bite. Helping Mrs. Scott in the kitchen gave her another opportunity to get to know the woman who had prepared the sumptuous meal. While cleaning up, they chatted amiably.

"How does your sister like our islands?" Mrs. Scott inquired.

"She loves it here. It'll be hard for her to leave although she has Arty's art show to look forward to when she returns home," Eve replied, stacking the clean dishes on the table.

"He told us about that. It's very nice of her to take an interest in our popular local artist," Mrs. Scott said, placing another dish in the drain board. The kitchen contained every amenity, but she preferred to hand-wash her delicate china and crystal.

"Helen's a good kid. Besides, she loves his work," Eve replied.

"And Arty?" Mrs. Scott asked with the tiniest of smiles playing at the corners of her mouth.

Chuckling, Eve said, "I think something might be developing between them."

"Just as it's developing between you and my son. I saw the way you looked at each other. Falling in love's a wonderful time. The only thing that's better is looking across the room and seeing the face of the man you've loved all your life," Mrs. Scott said casually as she inspected a sparkling wineglass.

"I love David," Eve stated. "We really haven't known each other very long, but I think we're compatible in a quiet kind of way. He's fun to be with, has a great sense of humor, and doesn't mind showing me around the island."

"That's good to know because David's 'fond' of you, too. You're the first woman he's brought home since his college days," Mrs. Scott said, allowing the importance of her statement to speak for itself.

"We're proceeding cautiously. I don't want to be swept away by the Bermuda Triangle's powers, you know."

"Oh, that old myth! The only power that matters between two people is the power of love."

The women continued their work with only the clicking of china and crystal to break the silence. Both were consumed by their thoughts and felt sufficiently comfortable not to need conversation. Eve was astounded by the fact that she had not been in the least nervous in David's mother's presence. Not only was Mrs. Scott a phenomenal cook, but she also had the knack for making a visitor feel at home.

After they had put away the last dish, Eve joined the men on the veranda. She felt content to the point of needing a nap on the inviting hammock; however, she resisted and listened to the conversation instead. Since the men were discussing fly-fishing, a topic that interested her not at all, Eve spent the time studying David's face and wondering how he had looked as a little boy and how he would look as an old man. One she would only know from photographs, and the other she would meet if they grew old together.

When Mrs. Scott rejoined them, she carried a colorful fruit salad onto the veranda. At first, Eve thought that she would not be able to eat a bite of it. However, the fruit looked so appetizing that she soon began to feast on yet another treat. Mrs. Scott had purchased the fruit from the local produce stand to augment what she did not grow in her garden. Although incredibly fresh, the flavors mingled perfectly.

While the men resumed their conversation, Mrs. Scott showed Eve the gardens that thrived under her expert care. The color of the flowers was so vivid and the greenery so lush that Eve felt as if she were strolling through the controlled environment of the National Arboretum in D.C. She had never seen a private garden of such a magnitude.

Mrs. Scott explained that she had lavished as much care on the plants as she did her children and husband. That, in addition to careful weeding and feeding, produced a garden that all would envy.

As the women rounded the corner that led to the front of the house, they spotted David and Mr. Scott waiting for them beside the bikes. The men waved happily at the sight of their favorite women. Advancing on them, the women returned the greeting, pleased that they could elicit such a welcome from men they had only just left on the veranda.

"It's time to rescue your sister from Arty's messy house," David announced as he righted the bikes and prepared to leave.

"Poor Helen! I'd forgotten about her. She's probably exhausted by now," Eve lamented.

"No, she's fine. I just called her. She and Arty even went out to lunch," David replied after kissing his parents good-bye.

"It seems that he's so taken by your sister that he took a few hours from his work and helped your sister in her effort to clean up his place," Mr. Scott added as he kissed Eve on the cheek.

Hugging Eve, Mrs. Scott said, "It seems that both of you girls have the magic touch. I'll see you later this week. The door's always open. Don't wait for David to ride over with you."

Waving good-bye, Eve said, "I won't and thank you for an absolutely wonderful afternoon."

Eve and David pedaled swiftly down the road. Although neither had missed Helen and Arty, they were curious as to the extent of the makeover that Helen had produced in the house. She would have to be a miracle worker to turn that pigsty into a livable space.

As they biked in silence, Eve could feel a change settling over them. After the success of the afternoon, they seemed closer and more relaxed. They had passed into a new phase, one that led to deeper comfort and insight. They were now very definitely a couple.

David, too, sensed the transition. Having his parents approval of the woman in his life had been very important to him, not that he needed it since he was grown and self-sufficient. Still, their family was close and the woman he loved and eventually married would have to fit into his family harmoniously. The island was too small for petty family quarrels due to mismatched personalities. Eve, to David's delight, had immediately warmed to his parents and fit right into the flow of his family. If Helen and Arty had succeeded in working in harmony as they cleaned the chaotic house, all aspects of the afternoon would have been a success.

Chapter Nine

The afternoon had left Arty's front yard as they pedaled up. As usual, bits of this and that littered the unkempt yard. Helen's helping hand had not yet extended to the front of the house, although Eve was confident that it would eventually.

"Let's talk for a minute before we enter the shop. There's something I'd like to discuss with you, and we haven't had any time alone," David suggested.

Eve agreed reluctantly. "Okay, but can't it wait? I really want to see the changes to the inside of the house. I'm skeptical about Helen's ability to help Arty. She's not exactly the neatest person I know."

Smiling, David said, "What I have to say won't take long. With Helen here, we don't have much time alone, although, if I'm right, she won't stay with you much longer."

"What do you mean?" Eve demanded.

Taking Eve's hand and leading her to the garden bench, David said, "I saw the way Helen and Arty looked at each other. The chemistry and electricity between them is incredibly strong. I don't expect her to stay with you now that she's made a path in the mess."

"I saw it, too, but I didn't want to think of Helen leaving me so soon. She's only just arrived, and I haven't seen her since I left home. I want more time with her." Eve sighed, easing a sleeping cat off the seat so that she could sit down.

"If I'm right, you'll see her plenty, but Arty will be with her every time," David said, sinking onto the bench beside her.

"That's okay. I don't mind sharing if that's the only way to have time with her," Eve stated.

"I'd like for us to spend more time together, too," David began.

"More time?" Eve questioned. "We're together all day and into the evening now. You'll never get your papers graded or the book finished if we spend more time together."

"I have a solution for that."

"Really? What?"

"Let's live together. We love each other and are wasting time commuting between residences. I have a huge condo with a fabulous view of the ocean. You have that cute cottage on the beach. We could live in either one or split the time and live in both. We'd see each other every day and night," David suggested.

Touching his hand lightly Eve replied with a sweet smile, "David, as much as I love being with you and can't wait to see you every day, I really want to live alone for a while. I've lived in my parents' house, a dorm room with two roommates, and now a condo with my sister. I need time alone or else I'll never learn to be self-sufficient. I'm lonely when we're not together, but I need to find myself so that I can be a better person when we're together. Let's compromise and spend nights together. There's no reason for you to kiss me good night at the door."

Shaking his head, David said, "I'm disappointed, but I can live with that. If you don't mind riding a man's bike, you could use my extra one when you sleep over."

"I don't mind a shiny blue bike, but how do you feel about fuchsia?" Eve asked, chuckling.

"It's not my favorite color. Maybe I could ride the red one," David offered.

"Fine with me. See, already we've compromised twice. We're a wonderful couple." Eve grinned.

"However, on this point, I won't negotiate or compromise," David stated, pulling Eve into his arms.

"Neither will I," Eve replied as she melted against his chest.

Their lips touched in an incredible tenderness that made Eve's toes curl and the nerves at the back of her neck tingle. David's hands alternated between caressing and possessing her back. Her body responded by becoming one with his. Neither of them noticed the steady parade of chickens at their feet or the threatening clouds in the sky above them. Their world consisted of only themselves.

Separating slightly, David whispered, "I love you, Eve. For the first time in my life, I've found someone who makes me completely and totally happy."

"So have I. I never thought that love could be like this," Eve said as his lips closed on hers again.

Long after Eve and David loosened their embrace they sat on the bench and watched the chickens pecking for food amongst the piles of scrap metal. Occasionally, a seagull would fly over their heads, adding its voice to that of the other seabirds as they dove for their meals. The late afternoon sun cast a reddish glow on the windows of Arty's house. Swathed in the glow of love, their world looked unspeakably beautiful.

"I guess we should go inside," David said reluctantly.

"I suppose you're right," Eve agreed without moving.

"Your sister might need rescuing," David continued as he gently stroked Eve's arm.

"That's true; she might." Eve nestled deeper into his shoulder.

"We left my parents' house to liberate Helen. I guess we should do it."

"Helen is a big girl. I think she can take care of herself," Eve said as she traced hearts on David's tanned thigh.

"She might need reinforcements. Arty can be overwhelming sometimes."

"Helen grew up in the big city. She's up to the task," Eve said, nibbling on David's earlobe.

Suddenly, a crash and the sound of breaking glass shattered the silence. Looking at each other, Eve and David rose, clasped hands, and walked toward Arty's house and studio. Perhaps they had underestimated Helen's need for rescue. At any rate, their moment alone had ended.

To their surprise, it was not Helen who was in need of help but Arty, who hung by his hands from the garage rafters. He looked quite helpless as he tried unsuccessfully to throw his feet over the beam while the ladder lay on the ground below him in a pool of shattered glass. Helen, unfortunately, was not in the garage.

"Boy, am I glad to see you! Help me get down, would you?" Arty asked as he dangled above them.

"What happened?" David demanded as he steadied the ladder.

"I should have waited until Helen returned, but I do

this all the time. I climbed up for another sheet of glass, and the ladder tipped over. I'm glad you guys returned when you did. I wouldn't have been able to hold on until Helen got back," Arty said, rubbing his arms and flexing his hands.

"Where's Helen?" Eve asked, sweeping the broken glass into a neat pile and looking for the dustpan.

"She left over an hour ago for groceries. Now that she has cleaned my kitchen, she thinks I should have a little food in the refrigerator," Arty explained. He took the broom from Eve and finished the sweeping.

At that moment, Helen appeared. She had entered the house by the front door and missed the commotion. Now, surveying the last of the cleanup, she was confused about seeing the trio looking so intense.

"Is something wrong?" Helen demanded.

"The ladder fell over. I'd still be hanging from the rafters if Eve and David hadn't rescued me. This just shows that I need a wife to save me from myself," Arty explained as he pulled Helen into his arms and kissed her soundly.

"I don't doubt that, but who will save me from you?" Helen asked, returning his embrace.

"I guess that job falls to Eve and David," Arty stated and continued, "They'll get married too, and live next door to us. When you can't undo one of my messes, you'll call on them."

Joking, Helen asked, "What makes you think they want to get married any more than I do?"

"Look at them. They have the marrying look written all over their faces."

Helen studied Eve and David as directed and replied with a chuckle, "I guess they do, but I don't have that goofy expression on my face."

Joining the comfortable exchange, David asked,

"Have you looked in the mirror lately? The longer you stay here, the more obvious it becomes."

Laughing, Eve added, "Soon you'll have Arty's name tattooed over your heart."

Looking at both of them suspiciously, Helen replied, "Not on this skin, I won't. I work too hard to keep it smooth. He'll have to settle for a button pinned to my blouse."

They all broke into gales of laughter at the picture they must have made. Little wonder that Arty's dog had crawled under the table and refused to come out. Glass breaking, ladders falling, and humans acting like playful children were all too much for the old companion.

Wiping tears, Arty said, "That about does it for me. I'll clean up, and we can go to dinner."

"Not tonight. I bought steaks, all the trimmings, and a hibachi. We'll cook here," Helen said.

"Oh, yeah. Domesticity is setting in big time," Arty proclaimed, slipping his arm around Helen and leading her into the house.

The foursome stopped abruptly at the kitchen door. Rather than the usual clutter, the kitchen was sparkling clean. Helen had not only put away the groceries, she had completely reorganized the cabinets so that all of the items that usually sat on the counter fit securely behind the closed doors. The table, once hopelessly messy and scarred, shone under a carefully applied coat of polish.

"Is it safe to open the door? All the mess that was in here isn't stashed in the hall, is it?" Arty asked as he approached the door to the hall.

"You'll be pleasantly surprised," Helen promised while David and Eve looked on.

Stepping into the hall, Arty discovered that the haphazard path from the kitchen at the back of the house and the stairs at the front no longer existed. In its place, he could now see the sparkling hardwood floors. He had not seen the floors since his ex-wife left him.

Walking past the living room and dining room doors as the others followed him, Arty exclaimed, "Wow! This looks great!"

Peeking around him, Eve and David gasped in surprise. The living room furniture no longer held clean and dirty clothes, magazines and newspapers, animals of all description, and supplies for the shop. The dining room table actually had a deep, luxurious finish and was clear of incoming mail and packages ready for shipping. Instead, the rooms glistened and smelled clean. Helen had placed cut flowers in all the vases.

"Your house is wonderful," Eve exclaimed. "Now that I can see it, it has a lot of charm and a friendly appeal."

"It had been a long time between thorough cleanings," Arty joked.

"Years," David interjected.

"It takes years to make that kind of mess," Arty said, defending himself.

"Yes, but we won't do that again, will we?" Helen asked rhetorically.

"No, General, I won't let it happen again," Arty agreed as he climbed the steps.

The friends joined in to prepare the first meal that anyone had made in Arty's house in years. Helen had, indeed, purchased all the fixings for a steak and potato dinner. David and Arty grilled the steaks while Eve and Helen made the salad and dessert. Everyone was touched by the domestic scene.

Dinner in the glistening dining room was a big success. Although simple in preparation, the meal contained a robustness of flavor that satisfied their hunger and their emotions. They were together, two couples, friends, and family. It was the best meal that any of them had ever eaten.

After dinner, the conversation turned to the immediate future and the show. They wondered if Helen would be able to handle making all of the final arrangements for shipping Arty's work to the States for the show. Arty, however, was more concerned with the days immediately after the show. He wondered if Helen would return to the island with him.

"I've taken care of everything," Helen said. "The shippers will arrive in two days. Once they finish packing to our satisfaction, the mover will transport everything to the airport. Their company has coordinated for another mover to accept the items and convey them to the gallery. I sent the final itemization to my friend today from the fax at the grocery store. Everything's done. All that's left is to enjoy the show and accept the accolades."

"I told you she was organized," Eve said proudly.

"And after the show?" Arty asked.

"The same thing happens in reverse. You don't have to lift a finger," Helen explained.

"Will you return, too?" David asked, knowing that his best friend was trying in his awkward way to ask the question.

Looking from one to the other, Helen replied, "I don't know yet. If I do, it'll only be for a few days. I have to work."

"You could set up shop here," Arty suggested gently.

"I made contacts as soon as I knew that Eve had been offered the contract. Unfortunately, the opportunities in my field are just not here," Helen explained, touching Arty's cheek softly.

"Then end that career and start another one," Arty replied. "You can do something else. I make enough to support us in style here. At least, the house looks stylish now that you've cleaned it up. You could be my manager."

"You could open a little boutique that specializes in Arty's work," David said.

"Those are great ideas!" Eve agreed. "What do you think, Helen?"

"I'll have to think about it. I like my job. Besides, you'll leave at the end of the school year. I don't want to live here without you. You said that it's too lonely without family," Helen replied.

"Maybe we can talk Eve into staying here. She could teach here permanently, then you could relocate," David offered.

All eyes turned to Eve, who shrugged her shoulders and responded, "I think we'll have to table this discussion for the moment. First, I don't know if the school system will want to hire me on a permanent basis, or if I'll like teaching here. Second, our parents might not want to live here. Three, I . . . Three is personal and will have to wait until later."

Chuckling dryly, Arty joked, "From the sound of that, I guess it's on your shoulders, David. This is definitely not the time for performance anxiety."

With the tension of the discussion broken, Eve and David prepared to leave. As David predicted, Helen decided to remain at Arty's for the night. Now that the house was clean, Helen had her choice of bedrooms, although no one thought she would sleep in either of the ones set aside for guests.

"I'll stop by to get my stuff tomorrow," Helen said quickly.

Eve and David exchanged glances. Eve was glad that she had not entered a wager on David's prediction. She certainly would have lost that money.

Eve and David left the couple on the porch as they

pedaled toward home. Helen had looked happier than Eve had seen her in ages. In fact, Helen had not looked that content since she decided to move in with her big sister while they were still in college.

On the trip home, Eve and David chatted like an old established couple about the expression of fear and surprise on Arty's face as he had dangled from the rafters and Helen's cool demeanor during the discussion of the future. They remarked that everything about the show and Helen and Arty's relationship pointed to success. Eve thought that Helen was on the brink of changing her mind about living in the States and, instead, moving to the islands. The only real obstacle was their parents, and they might be more flexible than anyone had anticipated. They would love the island's leisurely pace of life, the almost constant sunshine, and the temperate weather. Eve felt in her heart that all other concerns would resolve during her year of teaching in Bermuda.

"If all the pieces fall into place, maybe you'll decide to make this your home, too," David commented as they walked their bikes to the back of the house.

"Let's just wait and see. There are still too many variables to suit me. We've only just begun to discuss love and commitment. I haven't even met the kids yet. Helen doesn't know Arty's little oddities. Let's talk about this later. For now, I just want to enjoy what we have," Eve replied, unlocking the front door.

The delightful little cottage welcomed them home. The flower-filled vases added a lived-in look. The only thing missing was a dog or cat waiting at the door. With David lounging on the sofa, the picture was complete.

Eve settled beside David as they sipped their soda and watched the nightly news. The atmosphere was so domesticated that Eve could easily picture the scene as a preview of her long happy future with him. At least she could until she remembered what Helen had told her about Brad.

Eve was sure that she no longer loved him, but the thought of Brad with another woman grated on her emotions. She wanted him to be happy, but she was not sure that she liked the idea that he had replaced her with someone else so quickly. He had been tearful when she left, but now he was happy again. Something in the scenario did not set right. She wanted to see him for herself. In his last e-mail, Brad had written that he planned to visit the island over the winter holiday break. Solving that piece of the puzzle would have to wait until then.

Snuggling deeper into David's shoulder, Eve decided that December would come soon enough and so would June. She would have her answers then. In the meantime, she was with the man she loved. Nothing and no one else mattered.

As the telecast ended, Eve and David looked at each other and smiled. If they had been in their separate homes, they would have gone to bed without giving it a second thought. Now that they were together, they lingered long past their bedtimes. Neither could think of a way to get past the awkwardness of sharing sleeping arrangements for the first time. Arty's mention of performance anxiety hung between them, making both of them think about the sexual nature of their relationship that they planned to consummate that night. It was a big step, but after knowing each other so well, they were ready.

As if on cue, when they could find nothing on television to watch, they rose and turned off the lights. Standing at the foot of the stairs, David pulled Eve into his arms. His kiss was slow and tender, but his hands were suggestive of his need to make her his.

"I love you, Eve, but I can go home if you're not ready to take this next step," David said, holding her close.

"I love you, too, and can think of no better time than the present to move our relationship to the next level," Eve replied.

Taking his hand, Eve led the way up the stairs to her bedroom. She was uniquely aware of every detail of the house as if seeing it through new eyes, which, in some ways, she was. She hoped that David would like the cottage as much as she did.

Looking into the bedrooms as they passed, David commented, "This is a great house. These rooms are as well decorated as the ones downstairs. I've heard horror stories about corporate rentals that look good but are really cardboard and empty."

"That's right. This is your first time in the inner sanctum. I can't complain about the accommodations. I can't think of a better place to live. All the furnishings fit my taste perfectly," Eve said as she led him through the last door to the oversized master suite.

"No wonder Helen didn't complain about Arty's mess. Her bedroom could do with some cleaning up compared to yours," David said as he surveyed Eve's bedroom.

"It's not so bad. Besides, I'm a neat freak." Eve chuckled as she turned down the handmade quilt.

"I wouldn't say that. You like order and tranquillity. I'm the same way," David rebutted, grabbing a corner and pulling gently.

"Good. I won't have to step over your dirty clothes on the way to the bathroom."

"Or get hit in the face by wet panty hose."

"I doubt that anything like that would happen down here. It's too hot for panty hose." Eve laughed and then asked, "Which side of the bed do you prefer?"

"I usually sleep in the center of the bed, so I'm flexible," David answered with a touch of nervousness in his voice.

Now that they had finished discussing the more casual nature of sleeping together, David felt a little apprehensive about taking the next step. Actually, it was not the step that made him nervous; he knew that sharing themselves physically would be as natural as breathing. However, the fact that he had wanted a permanent living arrangement that would lead to marriage still existed between them. Eve's need for self-discovery made him question her commitment, a thought that he pushed from his mind. For the time being, David would be content with spending nights in both homes.

David's concerns stemmed from a past relationship that suffered because of distance. The woman had accepted a job in the States and left Bermuda for the excitement of a bigger world. When she left for New York, they promised to keep in touch and visit often, but they never did. Strangely, he had not missed her. Both of them knew that the foundation for a lasting relationship of true depth did not exist between them. Although their lovemaking had been fueled by incredible passion, the relationship had not contained that soul mate quality that David desired. He had decided that he was searching for an impossible quality until he met Eve. Meeting Eve had shown him that it was possible to find the one person whose being fit his completely.

"Me too," Eve exclaimed a little too cheerfully. "I love the center. I can stretch out in all directions and still have a mattress under me. Well, should we flip a coin to see which one of us gets the right side closest to the door and the bathroom?"

"Here's the coin. Best two out of three," David said, producing one from his trouser pocket.

Eve called heads as David flipped the coin. Inwardly, she wished they had agreed on the best eight out of ten in order to prolong the first miserable minutes of uncertainty during which all of her insecurities about her figure blossomed. Her sexual experiences had actually been few compared to other women she knew. This would be the first time that she had known the man for less than six months before going to bed with him. Somehow, however, Eve did not need to know David longer to realize that he was the love of her life.

Eve had fancied herself in love while in college, but the relationship ended at graduation. He had been in most of her first-semester required courses and lived on her floor. She saw him every day coming and going from the bathroom. It did not take much imagination to figure out what was under his Jockey shorts or her oversized T-shirt. Her college love affair had consisted of cramped sleeping conditions on a twin-sized bed and cold lumpy accommodations in a sleeping bag. The relationship had lasted all of their senior year at a time that both were ready to move into the future and put the past behind them.

After a period during which she was too busy for interpersonal relationships while getting used to writing lesson plans, grading papers, and phoning parents, Eve had dated a few guys before settling into a comfortable pattern with Brad. Somehow, those did not amount to much either. She had not even slept with two of the three and quickly ended the relationship with the third as soon as they received their master's degrees.

The romantic element of Eve's relationship with Brad had been only slightly more sensual. Since they had known each other as friends and then as lovers, most of the nervousness had not existed. They had boated, surfed, and skinny-dipped as buddies. Seeing each other partially clothed or nude dulled the first-night jitters. As lovers, they had been compatible but uninspired.

The lack of passion in the relationship with Brad had been the reason that Eve ended it and put distance between them. She wanted sparks and fireworks. She wanted a man who excited her. Now that she had one, Eve was so nervous that she feared she would do something to spoil their first night together.

She need not have worried. As soon as she won the toss, David pulled her into his arms and kissed her deeply. His kiss made her go weak at the knees and her heart pound. He had impressed her as a good kisser from their first embrace, but Eve had no idea of the extent of this quiet man's talent. Usually, David's hands held her possessively, but this time his fingers burned with an unfamiliar passion as they explored her body and unbuttoned her blouse. Eve was so swept up by the passion that David aroused in her that she hardly felt her blouse fall away to be followed by her bra. She sighed softly as his lips touched her breasts.

Sweeping her into the air, David deposited Eve gently on the bed and, in one motion, removed her slacks and panties. Releasing her only long enough to remove his own shirt and trousers, David covered her body in kisses and words of admiration for the softness of her skin. No longer did either of them feel nervous as their passions blazed.

The bed, usually too large for one person, now seemed small as their limbs tangled and their hot bodies warmed the cool sheets. The pillows were the first casualties and were quickly tossed on the floor in an effort to achieve the perfect union. Stopping only long enough to don a condom, David continued to explore Eve's body with his hands and lips. She tasted sweeter than any woman he had ever kissed. The light sheen of perspiration added a delicious saltiness to her skin that tasted of all the ripe fruits on the island.

Clinging to David and matching his enthusiasm with her own, Eve delighted in feeling the strength of his shoulders as David hovered above her. She matched her rhythm to his as he pressed into her. She wrapped her legs around his waist and allowed herself to ride the thrilling waves that swept over her. They called each other's name and held tightly as their passion peaked. Spent, they cradled each other and breathed deeply of the sweaty sweetness.

Lying in David's embrace, Eve only fleetingly thought of her sister and hoped that Helen was as happy as she at that moment. Memories of Brad's touch vanished as her skin continued to tingle from the caress of David's hungry fingers. Sighing, Eve relished the thought that she was at home with the man she loved. She never wanted anything to change their passion and their love.

David, too, longed for the moment to continue. Loving Eve had been everything he had imagined and more. Her body had melded to his as if made for him. Her lips had sought his with a passion that had matched his own. He had loved Eve without touching her since the first day they had met on the beach. Now he loved her with every nerve in his body.

Neither felt the need to speak or move. The sound of each other's breathing was comforting, and the gentle movement of their chests matched perfectly. Never had either of them felt so completely loved and secure. Sleep soon overcame them as Eve and David formed an inseparable mingling of arms and legs. With the sound of the ocean outside the window, they fell asleep, safely locked in each other's body.

Chapter Ten

The days passed quickly with the foursome being practically inseparable. They spent long days on the beach, walking, swimming, and talking. Occasionally, they sailed to one of Eve and David's favorite grottos, taking a picnic lunch of sandwiches, salad, and wine.

When they were not together, David graded the never-ending pile of papers that plagued members of his profession while Eve lounged on the sofa with one of the books she had neglected during the school year. She would lure him away from his work as often as possible but usually settled for gazing at him across the room. Often when David realized that she was watching him, he would put aside his work and join her on the sofa. The conversation would be about nothing in particular but so meaningful that Eve would think about it whenever they were apart. Their love grew daily and quickly became visible to everyone who met them.

Arty, under Helen's watchful, loving gaze, finished all of the projects that he had previously started and abandoned, producing an incredible quantity and quality of work. She was definitely his muse, who empowered him with insights and creative energy. Their long walks on the beach provided the inspiration with Helen as the catalyst for stunning sculptures, jewelry, and tapestries.

Unfortunately, the time soon came for Helen and Arty's work to depart for the States. The couples spent the last evening together, knowing that Helen and Arty would not return until after the show. They felt a charge of energy and excitement just knowing that his dream had finally become reality.

Over dinner in their favorite restaurant, Eve said, laying her hand on David's, "I can't believe that your vacation and summer are over. School starts for me next week. These months have passed too quickly. I've fallen in love with this wonderful island and its delightful people."

Pausing in the middle of spreading soft butter on a piece of French bread, Arty commented, "I have a hard time believing that I have a show in a few days. That's what I can't believe. All those years of contacting people and receiving rejections and hoping that someone would appreciate my work have finally paid off and with an unexpected bonus. Not only has my dream of selling my work in the States come to reality but so has my dream of finding the perfect woman to love. I'm truly blessed."

"What about me?" Helen chimed. "Let's not forget that I've kissed a fair number of toads before meeting you. I had begun to think that I'd never find a man whose personality so perfectly matched mine. I'm happier than I've been since I was a kid running downstairs to see what Santa had left for me."

Joining the conversation nervously, David stated, "Since it looks like we're into true confession, let me add that I didn't remember that my island home was so beautiful until Eve moved here. I had forgotten about all the secret places, the waterfalls, the fun of sailing, until she opened my eyes. Touring the island with her at my side has provided me with incredible joy that I hope will never end."

"What about me again?" Helen joked. "You didn't say anything about me."

"Knowing you has been good," David added with a chuckle.

"I'll remember that," Helen jabbed.

They laughed so uproariously that people at nearby tables looked at them and smiled. They smiled and wondered about the reason for the joyous dinner among such obviously well-matched friends. Not being able to learn the cause, the others shrugged and returned to their meals.

"What time's your flight tomorrow?" Eve asked as she dabbed the happy tears from her eyes.

"One-thirty but we have to report to the airport early to supervise the loading of Arty's work," Helen replied.

Arty added, "I don't call that supervising. With all the security at the airport these days, we'll be so far away from the crates and boxes that we'll be lucky to see if they leave one on the runway."

Waving her hand impatiently at him, Helen retorted, "I'm not as worried about the runway as about the possibility that security will destroy one of the boxes thinking that the art inside constitutes bomb parts. Some of your stuff is kinda strange looking."

With his insecurities showing, Arty demanded, "I thought you liked my art."

"I do," Helen said with a sigh of exasperation at dealing with Arty's artistic temperament. "I wouldn't have gone to all this trouble if I didn't think that it and you are wonderful. I'm just saying that to the untrained eye, the components of some of your larger pieces look like items from a pipe bomb shopping list."

Feigning injury, Arty stated, "I certainly hope the art critics take more pity on my humble work than you. You're tough."

Turning her side to Arty, Helen said, "I think he should stay here with you. The pressure of the show might prove too much for him."

"I heard that!" Arty snapped with a chuckle. "I'm just a little nervous, that's all. You'd feel the same way if you'd waited all your life for something wonderful like this to happen."

"He's an old hen clucking over her babies," David said, laughing.

"We'll see who's laughing when I make my fortune and return to this island only long enough to see my house and move to the States," Arty declared.

"You'd never leave this island any more than I would," David said. "It's the source of your inspiration and your artistic muse."

"I have a new muse now," Arty replied, placing his hand on Helen's. "I don't need this island any longer."

"How can you say that?" Eve demanded. "How can you say that you no longer need this paradise? The colors, the textures, the feel get under your skin."

"Like a mosquito bite that I can't wait to scratch," Arty retorted.

"He's just mouthing off," Helen said. "Arty's more in love with this place than anyone I've ever met. He's just afraid that his work will be so popular that he won't be able to leave the States."

" 'If wishes were horses, we'd all take a ride,' " David teased. "You might return with as many crates as you took to the States. Maybe no one will like your stuff."

"Don't tease Arty like that!" Helen objected. "You know he'll be a big success. After all, the gallery owner would not have spent so much money to host the show if she didn't think that he'd be an instant sellout."

"Don't pay any attention to him," Arty explained. "He's just jealous that he can't come along."

"That's not it at all," David said. "I just want you to know that we love you and will stand behind you regardless of the outcome. Your inflated ego won't prevent us from caring about you."

"I feel humbled," Arty replied with a grin. He needed David's playful support to ease the tension he felt. The show was a big deal to all of them, and his success meant as much to them as it did to him.

After dinner, the foursome returned to Arty's to do last-minute packing. All but the smallest, most delicate items had already been transported to the airport. Knowing that everything was in good hands did not stop them from worrying.

After they carefully placed the last items into Arty's rented truck, they took a long walk on the beach. This would be the last time that they would be together until Arty and Helen returned from the States. They would phone with the highlights, but it would not be the same thing as watching their expressions as the events of the special evening unfolded.

"We'll miss you," Eve stated as they reached the halfway point in their walk.

"This place won't be the same without you," David said and added, "This is the first time you've left the island since you returned after college graduation."

"Yeah. It feels strange," Arty said. "I have everything I could possibly want right here. I have no reason to leave home, but now I am. I don't like it. My energy feels out of whack because of it."

"Oh, Arty, you'll survive," Helen insisted with a touch of irritation. "He's been singing the same song for the last few days. Despite his comments over dinner, he really doesn't want to leave. This island is his muse, not me."

"I can't help it if I'm homesick even before I leave," Arty said in his defense and added, "But you're wrong. Without you my island muse lacked direction. I need both of you."

Smiling at him, Helen said, "Don't worry. We'll both be with you always."

"I know exactly how he feels," Eve explained. "I was terribly afraid of leaving home until I met David. If it hadn't been for him, I would have felt miserable being here alone. Meeting him was the best thing that has ever happened to me."

"Yes, but I'll be with Arty. He's overreacting," Helen groused.

They walked in silence for a while until Arty stopped and asked, "Will you really return to the island with me? You're not going to change your mind at the last minute and stay in the States?"

"With my sister and David as witnesses, let me tell you one last time that, as of this moment, I plan to return to the island after the show but only for a few days."

Arty sulked. "See? She equivocates. She 'plans' to come back with me. Where's the commitment?"

Helen explained for the one hundredth time, "Look, there's always the possibility that someone will know that I'm an investment banker and offer me a huge sum to work for his company. Stranger things have happened to other people."

"Helen, I love you and want you with me," Arty asserted without embarrassment. "I won't ask you to promise that you'll return. Just remember that you are the source of my happiness."

"That's so sweet!" Eve exclaimed and then turned to David and asked, "Why don't you ever say anything like that?"

"Thanks, Arty," David complained. "I don't say it because I show you every day. But if you need to hear it, here goes. I love you, Eve, and want you in my life forever. Will you marry me?"

"What? You're just trying to one-up Arty. This is not a time for jokes with Helen and Arty leaving us and his big day looming over our heads," Eve scolded.

"I'm not joking," David insisted seriously. "I hadn't planned to ask you here or tonight. I had planned to take you to dinner and dancing while Arty and Helen were away, but now's as good a time as any. Will you marry me?"

"Eve, say something. Don't just stand there," Helen urged gently when her sister continued to stare rather than speak.

Eve's eyes filled with tears. Softly, she replied, "Oh, David, you know I love you. I can't think of anyone with whom I'd want to spend the rest of my life, but I have issues to resolve before I can get married."

"I can think of a quick way to put them out of your mind. I won't take no for an answer. There are no issues that we can't work out," David stated.

"But, David, I need time to think," Eve said, looking into his incredibly handsome face.

"I'll help you," David replied, kissing first Eve's eyelids, then nose, and finally lips.

Pulling her into his arms, David kissed Eve soundly, forgetting the presence of Helen and Arty. No one existed in the world except the two of them. They had found each other in the Bermuda Triangle.

"Not to interrupt at a moment like this, but I'll make the rings if it's okay with you," Arty said.

"I'll plan the wedding. We'll have it here, not in the States," Helen said joyfully.

"Did you hear what we said?" Arty asked when neither Eve nor David responded. "We'll make all the plans for you. Just tell us the month. We'll take care of everything."

When Eve and David did not break from their embrace, Helen said, "I think our presence is unnecessary at the moment. Let's go back to the house and check things over one more time."

"Helen, one more thing," Arty began hesitantly. "We could make it a double wedding, you know."

"Oh, Arty!" Helen exclaimed, kissing him tenderly. "That's so sweet, but I can't think of anything other than the show at the moment. Ask me again once that's over."

"Fair enough," Arty said, beaming. "I'll ask again as soon as the show ends. You might want to start working on your acceptance reply."

Laughing softly, Helen replied, "You're a nut! Let's check everything one more time. I'd like to tuck you into bed early tonight. We have to get up before dawn, you know."

"You can put me to bed any time you'd like," Arty agreed as they linked arms and walked toward his house.

Alone on the beach, Eve and David slowly parted. Looking into each other's eyes, they smiled and wordlessly began to stroll the empty beach. Not once did they think about Helen and Arty. For that magic evening, they thought only of each other.

Finding a secluded spot sheltered by a boulder, Eve and David slowly undressed under the starry sky. David spread his shirt on the sand to make a bed for them to lie upon. The warmth of the sand soon embraced them as they lay close together. Slowly with fingers, lips, and bodies that had memorized every curve, they brought each other to new heights of passion and love. The warm breeze dried the perspiration that glistened on their bodies in the moonlight.

By the time Eve and David finally pedaled home, Helen and Arty had been asleep in each other's arms for hours. Exhausted from the intensity of their love-making and the anxiety about the show, they slept with visions of their futures playing in their minds . . . futures that would begin when the show ended.

The next morning as Eve and David headed to their classrooms to prepare for the first days of the new school year, Helen and Arty supervised the loading of his life's work into the bowels of a 727 bound for the States. Although they stood in the window of the observation tower, they frantically motioned to unseeing eyes every time a new crate appeared. By the time they boarded the plane's first-class section, Arty was a nervous wreck, and Helen was in the throes of an anxiety attack.

While Eve and David slaved over gathering supplies, arranging desks, and preparing lessons, Helen and Arty opened crates, scrounged additional wall space, and supervised the hanging of the wall art, lighting of the sculptures, and displaying of the wearable art. Although both couples were busy, they thought of each other often, each creating visions of the other lying on the beach or dining in a famous restaurant. Neither phoned, knowing that they were too busy to talk.

When Eve and David returned home, they slumped exhausted into the wicker chairs on the cottage's front porch. Neither thought about preparing dinner after the long, demanding day. They were content to share anecdotes about new and old colleagues and tales of the horrors of preparing for the new school year.

Gazing at the flowers blooming in mad profusion, Eve mused, "I wonder when Helen and Arty will call. Do you think they're busy?"

"They're probably putting the finishing touches on the show arrangements. Let's wait until later. They'll need to shower and change before the show," David replied, waving aside a persistent bee.

"I hope it's a success. Helen will bounce back if it's a flop. I'm not worried about her, but Arty has worked too hard and dreamed so long of this event," Eve said, tossing her shoes onto the welcome mat at the door.

"It'll be fine. Arty's a realist. He's done his best and knows that the rest is beyond his control," David said.

"I hope you're right," Eve said, searching in her purse for the door key.

David watched in silence as she finally retrieved the unnecessary item from the depths of her bag. He was still waiting for the day that she would not feel the need to lock the little cottage's door. Eve had assimilated well but had not as yet embraced the habit of leaving the door unlocked.

"I guess we should start dinner," Eve stated, reluctant to move from the porch.

"Let's take the boat out for a bit. Sailing will help us to relax, and we'll catch fish for dinner," David suggested.

"Good idea! It won't take me but a minute to change," Eve exclaimed, rising as quickly as her tired body could accomplish the task.

"Let me help you," David said as he swooped her into his arms and carried her into the house. Along the way, he gently kissed her cheeks and forehead.

Nuzzling his ear, Eve murmured, "I don't know if this is a good idea. We might miss dinner completely."

Pulling her into his arms, David replied, "Sounds like a good idea to me."

Instead of fishing for dinner, Eve and David climbed the stairs to the bedroom level. Putting all thoughts of Helen and Arty from their minds, they concentrated on relaxing their tired muscles and restoring their fatigued minds through one of the oldest revitalizing techniques known to happy couples. By the time they lay spent on the expanse of sheet, they had nothing on their minds except each other.

However, Helen and Arty had plenty on their minds as they rushed through a hasty shower that barely restored their spirits and grabbed several of the tiny canapés that sat like lead in their nervous stomachs. The lighting had still not been adjusted on several items, and Arty's bio sheet had not returned from the printer.

Helen was so uncharacteristically nervous that she donned mismatched shoes and had to return to the hotel to change. She got a run in her stocking as soon as she closed the hotel room door and had to spend valuable time buying another pair at the pricey lobby shop.

Although everything Arty wore matched, he felt incredibly uncomfortable in the suit and tie that Helen had insisted he wear. He was a shirt, shorts, and, sometimes, sandals kind of guy. Anything else was too much. Now, he was buttoned and belted so tightly that he could hardly swallow. The wool of the summer-weight suit scratched his unaccustomed legs.

Both wondered if they would survive the evening.

Helen pasted a smile on her lips and set about doing little unnecessary things that would help her conquer her nerves. Arty, however, sulked and fretted.

The gallery door opened promptly at eight. For the first half hour, no one arrived except the art critics for the local newspapers. They hungrily munched sandwiches and gulped cups of hot coffee while staring at Arty's life's work and scribbling in tattered notepads. They left without speaking to anyone other than the gallery's owner.

Helen and Arty stood in a corner licking their imaginary wounds and nursing their bruised egos until the nine o'clock hour arrived. Neither had ever felt so violated, ignored, or unimportant. They were so crushed that they could take little comfort in the presence of each other.

"This was a mistake," Arty whined.

"No, it wasn't," Helen said, trying to console him. "The critics didn't run screaming from the gallery or anything. They must have found something praiseworthy in the collection."

"They didn't even speak to us. Not one of them picked up a copy of my bio," Arty stated without feeling any better.

"The bio arrived late. Maybe they didn't see it," Helen offered.

"They saw all right. I watched them read the copy and leave it. This was a bad idea," Arty repeated.

"You're just nervous. You'll think differently as soon as the patrons arrive," Helen said.

"No, I won't. This suit is itchy and the tie's trying to choke me. My feet are hot and they hurt from the damn shoes that you made me wear. I wanna go home," Arty concluded, refusing to be consoled.

"You're not going anywhere until this evening is

over. It's your big night. Every artist needs a touch of reality sometimes. The press was yours. You'll bask in your own reflected glory soon enough," Helen snapped, holding his arm tightly.

"Yeah, I needed a bunch of pompous jerks to tell me that I should stick to making tourist trinkets and trash and leave the real art to other people," Arty stated sarcastically.

"You're being particularly petulant tonight," Helen said through clenched teeth. "I don't especially like this side of you."

"I don't like this side of me either. That's why I'm returning to my little island. I don't need this frustration," Arty replied as he laced his arms across his chest in a huff.

Not wanting to get into a fight with him in public, Helen left Arty standing in a darkened corner nursing his ego and hurt pride. He was the personification of the temperamental artist. She preferred the man she had met on the island a few days ago—the gentle, witty, sweet man with the highly defined but often raunchy sense of humor. This one was a stranger.

Suddenly, a swarm of well-dressed and obviously well-heeled patrons alighted from a limousine and descended upon the gallery. Ignoring the sandwiches, they daintily nibbled the caviar and sipped the champagne that the gallery's owner had selected for their enjoyment. Circulating in groups and pairs, they whispered critiques of Arty's work, nodded discreetly at favored items, and smiled knowingly at the gallery's owner.

To Helen's amazement, small red dots started to appear on the description cards that accompanied the items although she had not seen anyone make a purchase. She later learned that the gallery owner simply added the items to the client's regular bill. The transactions happened so quickly and silently that Arty, standing alone in his darkened corner, missed them.

Gliding to his corner, Helen said, "You're a success! People are buying like crazy."

"You don't have to say that to make me feel better. I'm disappointed, but I'm a big boy. I'll get over it," Arty replied.

"You're such a baby," Helen said angrily. "See those red dots? They mean that the item has sold."

Steeling himself for disappointment, Arty stepped from his corner for a better view of the gallery. To his surprise, he felt as if he had entered a world in which measles proliferated. He could find few items that did not bear the dot.

"Wait until I tell David about this. He won't believe it," he said softy.

"How does it feel to be the new artistic toast of the town?" Helen asked, smiling.

"I can't believe it," Arty gushed and hugged Helen tightly.

Helen did not stick around long enough to see his reactions as the final dots appeared and the gallery owner locked the doors. Now that everyone had left, she wanted to learn the grand total. When she finally returned to the hotel, she wanted to be able to share as much with Eve as possible. Besides, she was feeling put out by Arty's childish behavior. Helen had expended so much effort in persuading the gallery's owner to take the chance on an unknown and helping Arty to arrange his pieces for display that she did not feel the need to comfort his ego at his moment of success.

The next day, Eve and David left school early to pick up Helen and Arty at the airport. The newspaper

reviews they had read on the Internet said that the show
had been a huge success. Helen had been so excited on
the phone that she was hardly able to describe the
evening's events. They managed to learn that Arty had
become so successful overnight that he returned to
Bermuda with advanced commissions that would take
him a year to complete. He had also developed an
artist's temperamental streak.

Standing in the crush of people at the airport, Eve and
David struggled to see Helen's and Arty's familiar faces.
Unlike their departure, they were returning with only
their suitcases; the crates of art had found homes in the
Washington, D.C., area. The successful travelers were
returning with empty hands and a bulging bank account.

"Have we missed them?" Eve asked, standing on
tiptoe.

"Not unless they took another flight and didn't tell
us," David replied, slipping his arm around Eve's shoulders to calm her fears.

Smiling at this open display of affection from an
originally conservative David, Eve said, "No, Helen
confirmed the flight last night. She would have phoned
if they had changed their plans unexpectedly."

"I see Arty now. Helen must be behind him in the
crowd," David announced, peeking over the heads of
the shorter people in the crowd.

A very drawn Arty joined them. His face looked as
if he had not slept in weeks. His clothing was disheveled.
He did not look the part of a newly acclaimed rising
star in the art hemisphere.

"Where's Helen?" Eve asked, looking around him
for her sister.

"She stayed in the States," Arty stated dryly.

"What? Why? What happened? When did she change
her mind?" Eve demanded in rapid succession.

"This morning," Arty said as they walked toward the parking lot. "We had an argument of major proportions. We stayed up all night trying to figure out where everything had gone wrong, but we couldn't patch it up. She even went to the airport and flew as far as Charleston. She's not coming back. She left the plane there and is on her way home now. She gave me this note for you."

Quickly tearing open the envelope, Eve read in Helen's scrawl, "I'll explain when I phone tonight. What a mess! I'd say that the Bermuda Triangle sank me."

Looking from Arty's tortured face to David's inquisitive one, Eve could only shrug her shoulders. Something big had shattered their romance, or maybe a collection of little things became more than Helen could bear. She would have to wait until Helen phoned later that evening. In the meantime, they drove Arty home in silence. His face said that some things were too painful to discuss. Eve hoped that her sister would seek out their parents for comfort. She hated the idea that Helen was going through the heartbreak of a breakup alone.

Eve and David waited anxiously by the phone that night for Helen to call. Since Arty had refused to say anything about the argument on the ride home, Helen would serve as their only source of information. Arty's silence frightened both of them. Instead of being euphoric over his triumphant entry into the Washington art scene, he was morose and taciturn. He barely spoke to them on the drive to his house.

Helen, however, gushed out her version to Eve of the breakup as David listened on the bedroom extension. Sniffing loudly, she exclaimed, "I don't think I'm asking too much to expect a man not to whine, pout, or otherwise act like a child. Arty sulked and hid in a corner when the sales weren't as brisk as he had hoped. I know artists can have their temperamental streak, but

Arty acted like a child. It was embarrassing. He wouldn't mingle with anyone. I can understand being shy or nervous, but he was rude."

"Why didn't you come back? You still have a few days of vacation left," Eve said, holding the phone slightly away from her ear so that David could listen.

"David, I'm sorry, I know the man's your friend, but I couldn't stand the thought of being on that island with him. It isn't worth the frustration. I'll spend my last few days here where I don't have to deal with a prima dona. It's a good thing I didn't leave anything at his place. It's a clean break," Helen explained and added, "Did Arty say anything?"

"Nothing," David replied. "We could barely get him to tell us about the show. He was silent most of the trip."

"I'm not surprised. It probably shocked him when I refused to continue the trip," Helen stated somberly. "We had talked all night. He tried to explain his behavior, but he couldn't say anything that could justify his childishness. He insulted me and the gallery owner. I had hoped that the show would be the start of great exposure for Arty, but he ruined it. I doubt that my friend will even touch Arty's work again. She's used to artistic temperament but not to rudeness. He snubbed all those high-powered paying clients."

"He seems genuinely affected by your absence," David interjected.

"Good! Maybe he'll realize that he acted like a jerk," Helen replied angrily.

"I think he feels dreadful about messing up the relationship that you had. He didn't say it, but he looks awful," Eve commented.

"Whatever," Helen quipped.

Suppressing a chuckle, Eve said, "It's getting late, and we could all use some rest. Sleep well, Helen."

"You too. Good-bye, David. I wish it could have worked out with Arty, but he's too needy for me." Helen sighed.

"Good night, Helen," David and Eve said in unison.

Turning to David, Eve asked, "Do you think we should try to patch things up between them?"

"I don't know," David replied. "Let's sleep on it. My gut reaction is to leave it alone. If they're meant to be together, Arty will do something to make amends."

As Eve and David settled into their bed for a good night's rest, Arty paced the floor of his studio. He was furious with himself and exhausted from the show and the all-night discussion with Helen. She was right in saying that he had behaved badly. He could not explain what had caused him to turn into the kind of artist he despised. One thing for certain, Arty would never be that person again. He had lost too much to make that mistake again.

Arty knew that he had failed to earn Helen's forgiveness even before she left him at the Charleston airport. She had barely spoken to him on the flight from D.C. to Charleston. Her decision not to return to Bermuda had not surprised him. She had worked hard to make the connections for him, and he had acted like a spoiled brat.

Arty needed sleep but could not settle down. He did not want to enter the bedroom that only recently Helen had transformed into a paradise for him. He had not been able to bring himself to go into the house that she had so carefully organized for him. Her touch was present in the studio, too. He missed the sound of Helen's voice and her loving smile. Arty had made a colossal mistake and would have to live with it for the rest of his life if he could not think of a way to win her back.

Turning to the only thing that would bring him comfort, Arty began working on a project that had been teasing him since he first met Helen. He was not a sculptor, but he wanted to make something that would represent Helen and the love she had given him and awakened in him. Turning to the clay that he had recently purchased, Arty consoled himself by letting his hands do this thinking. For now, art was all he had.

Chapter Eleven

The weeks and months passed with a steady stream of papers to grade, parents to call, and lessons to prepare. Whenever they could, Eve and David took the boat out and sailed to their favorite cove. On weekends, they would pack a lunch and picnic or sometimes fish for dinner. They loved being together and cherished the time although they still lived separately. Eve was not ready to move in with David permanently and enjoyed living among the people whose children she taught. He understood and was content with alternating between her cute little cottage and his luxurious condo.

Helen phoned regularly with details about friends and family. She missed Eve and their quiet times together during which they unwound from their demanding days. However, she never asked about Arty. She seemed to have purged that part of her life from her memory.

Arty worked nonstop to satisfy the orders that resulted from his show in D.C. He seldom left the studio although he was happy to see friends when they visited. His studio overflowed with supplies and completed orders waiting to be shipped. Surprisingly, he managed to keep the place looking as it had when Helen left. It was impeccably clean and orderly as if he were waiting for her to return. Eve often caught him looking at the door with his head cocked to the side as if listening for Helen's footfalls. He would smile and turn away sadly.

One night when Helen called, she chatted with more energy than usual. Lounging in her favorite chair in the living room that she and Eve had so painstakingly decorated, Helen dangled a shoe off her big toe as she talked. She had snared another big client and felt especially pleased with herself.

"You'll never guess who I saw this morning," Helen said as she admired her manicure and without pausing in her story. "I had just finished signing a new client and was in the mood to celebrate. You know me, I'm a big spender, so I went next door to the coffee shop for one of their special creations. While standing in line, I felt someone tap me on the shoulder. You'll never guess who was standing behind me. Brad. Seems he was on a coffee run from the hospital. Anyway, he looks great and is planning to take a week off at Christmastime. He's going to Bermuda."

Accustomed to her sister's rambling approach to storytelling, Eve hardly noticed that Helen had stopped talking and had reached the end. Suddenly the silence caught Eve's attention, and she realized that Helen was waiting for her to say something.

"Really? Christmas? That's in a few weeks," Eve said.

"Yeah, he says that he's bringing his girlfriend with him," Helen stated. "You remember that I told you about her. Anyway, I get the impression that the trip is their Christmas gift to each other."

"Did he say where they'll stay?" Eve asked as her interest increased at the mention of Brad's girlfriend.

Helen responded, "No, but you can count on it that he's made reservations at one of those big swanky hotels. I don't think he's the beach bungalow type. From what I saw of her, I doubt that she would relish the idea of catching fish from the kitchen window. Hey, you're not still interested in him, are you? You shouldn't be, with a guy like David to love."

"Not at all," Eve protested. "I was simply curious. I remember that Brad used to like to spend big bucks whenever he traveled. I was just wondering if he had changed his ways. This island will definitely help lighten his wallet if that's what he wants."

"If I see him again, I'll find out," Helen offered. "You're right about his free spending. I remember that, too. Did I describe his girlfriend to you? She's really pretty in a pampered, spoiled kind of way. I didn't like her at first sight."

"I'm sure she must have qualities that you didn't see in that short meeting. She must have something or Brad wouldn't be interested in her," Eve commented as lightly as possible.

Helen laughed. "She has long, shapely legs and a healthy chest. What more would a man want?"

Eve said nothing. She did not find the description comical. Brad had often lain in her arms and complimented her on the shapely legs that encircled him and the perky breasts that he loved to fondle. Now it seemed as if he had found replacements that satisfied him just fine.

"Maybe a brain to match? Or maybe wit and a sense of humor or style? A fun-loving personality?" Eve suggested.

"Are you describing yourself? I thought you were

over him," Helen said, suddenly losing interest in her crimson nails and the dangling shoe.

"I *am* over him," Eve stated firmly. "I'm just suggesting that there's more to a relationship and a woman than legs and boobs. I'm sure that Brad considered the entire package before building a relationship with her."

"Let me tell you this, sister dear, if I hadn't seen David for myself, I wouldn't believe you. You were just that unconvincing. Anyway, you'll have a chance to meet her over the break. I gave him your address and phone number. Brad said that he'd definitely call you."

"You what?" Eve shouted into the phone.

"I didn't think you'd mind," Helen protested. "You are over him, remember? Besides, the island's small. You would have run into him anyway. This way there's structure in your reunion."

"I think I'd rather just run into him," Eve said. "This looks too planned. Besides, I live out here in the countryside, and he'll stay in town. We might never have seen each other. I doubt that he'll rent a boat to sail to the secret cave that I like so much."

"Well, maybe he won't contact you. He might even lose the paper on which he wrote your number," Helen offered, feeling her sister's irritation through the phone lines.

"When have you ever known Brad to forget or lose anything?" Eve asked rhetorically. "He'll contact me. Have no fear."

Helen commented, trying to make Eve feel better, "You don't have to do more than be polite for a few minutes. After that, he'll do his own thing without you."

"I hope you're right," Eve stated and then added slowly, "It would be nice to see him again. It might be fun for us to double-date. David and I could show him the island. I have nothing to worry about. It'll work out just fine."

"Good. I'm glad you've come to that realization. You were certainly overreacting for a while."

"I know. Silly, wasn't it? Besides, he's with someone else now. I still can't believe that a man who was dying from the breakup is now with someone else. The curative processes in the human male are amazing."

"He might not really be over you," Helen offered. "The girlfriend business might just be a cover-up, not that it matters. You broke off with him. You left the city and the country. You didn't give him the chance to convince you that the relationship was worth saving. You tossed in the towel and left. You can't blame the guy for finding someone else. No one wants to be alone."

"No one? What about you?" Eve exclaimed. "You haven't mentioned finding anyone since you broke up with Arty. Aren't you lonely? I worry about that sometimes. You don't even seem to be looking for anyone."

"After Arty, I don't want anyone. To tell the truth, I still love him. It's hard to find someone else when he's very much in my thoughts," Helen confessed.

"Why, Helen, this is the first time you've admitted that in all these months," Eve exclaimed. "I wondered if you were really over him."

"It doesn't matter anymore. I won't ever see him again. We're just too different to make a life of it."

"Maybe not as much as you think. Arty's really changed since you left him. The house, grounds, and shop are cleaner than I've ever seen them except when you were cleaning for him. He's organized and even keeps a calendar. You really had a profound impact on him."

"That's nice, but it doesn't matter. I want a man like David, and until I find him, there's nothing for me in Bermuda or anywhere else."

"David's not without his flaws, you know. He's not much on trying something new. I have to push him into it. He is an awfully sweet guy. I'm very lucky to have found him," Eve said, the smile sounding in her voice.

"So's Arty. He's just . . . confused. He wouldn't be David's friend if he wasn't a good guy. I just wish . . ." Helen sighed.

"I know. Maybe you should visit at Christmastime, too," Eve suggested.

"No, thanks. The time's not right for that. Maybe for your spring break if I can tear myself away from here. Being my own boss has a few drawbacks. If I'm not here, I don't make a living. I'm not complaining; I love being self-employed and should have gone this route years ago."

"I'll remind you. I really miss our talks. Your phone bill's going to be terrible this month."

"I don't care. I needed to talk to you. I miss you, too. We have to promise to live close for the rest of our lives," Helen said.

"Will you move here when I marry David?" Eve asked. "He really wants to live here, you know."

"I don't know. Maybe. David's right; I really can do this kind of work almost anywhere. Besides, I'm sure that David must have other interesting friends. There must be someone else for me on the island."

"Does he ever! However, none is as unique as Arty," Eve said fondly.

"I'd better go before we start talking about him again," Helen said. "You might convince me to overlook his shortcomings and return to the island at Christmas. I'm not ready for that yet. Besides, I don't want to add any confusion to Brad's visit."

"I'm sure nothing will happen. Talk to you later. Happy Thanksgiving," Eve stated as she hung up.

Eve sounded far more confident while talking to Helen than she felt. She dreaded the idea of seeing Brad. Just hearing that he planned to visit the island made her heart flutter. The thought of him being with another woman made it pound. Eve knew that she loved David, but there was still at least a small warm spot in her heart for Brad. Perhaps it would always be there, harmlessly occupying its little niche, or maybe it would blaze into a flame when Eve saw him again. She had to know. She could not marry David as long as she felt the slightest doubt.

David entered the living room at that moment with a pan of freshly cleaned fish. They had sailed the little boat to their cove despite the chill in the air and would have fresh catch for dinner. Eve had completely forgotten that it was Thanksgiving until one of her teacher friends had wished her a happy holiday. She had become so completely immersed in the island that she had put away her old traditions. Eve did not know how long she would stay in this paradise, but Bermuda was definitely her home now.

"Ready for dinner? Since it's your holiday, I'll cook," David announced, walking toward the kitchen.

"I've never heard of anyone eating fish for Thanksgiving." Eve laughed. "Where's the turkey, stuffing, gravy, and pumpkin pie?"

"You'll have to use your imagination for those," David replied. "How's Helen?"

"She's doing fine professionally, but she misses us . . . and Arty," Eve responded, setting her table. "If she could abandon her hurt feelings and disappointments, she'd see that he has made an effort to change. He's so contrite that it breaks my heart to see him. They belong together, and they're miserable apart."

"He's certainly unhappy," David said. "I saw him

yesterday. He's becoming a hermit. He needs her badly. Have you seen the volume of work he's finished since she left? Arty's never worked so feverishly. She was a good influence on him."

"He was good for her, too," Eve said, tossing the salad. "She laughed a lot when they were together. He made her forget that hectic, high-pressure life she lives. She really needs him now that she's self-employed."

"I don't usually play matchmaker, but maybe we'll have to do something to help them," David mused. "We could get them together for a special occasion like a wedding."

Laughing, Eve replied, "Good try, buster, but I'm not ready to walk down the aisle even for my dear little sister. I still have some issues to resolve."

"Issues? Like what?"

"I'm not completely sold on living here. My family's in the States. I'm a U.S. citizen. The United States is my home. I don't know if I can leave it permanently," Eve said, disclosing the least complicated issue that tossed in her mind.

Serving their plates, David replied, "We're close to the coast. You'd be able to hop over any time you wanted."

"It's not the same," Eve explained. "I'd soon become a visitor in my own country. I have to make up my mind where my heart lives . . . here with you or in the States with my sister and parents. Until I do, I have issues."

"I certainly hope this fish dinner isn't one of them." David chuckled, realizing that further discussion of marriage was fruitless.

"Actually, it is," Eve stated. "This is Thanksgiving, and I'm eating fish. This is my first Thanksgiving without turkey. I'm not fond of turkey without lots of cranberry sauce, but it's part of being an American."

Pulling Eve into his arms, David said, "If you'd said turkey with all the trimmings was so important to you, I would have found one and learned to cook it. Lots of U.S. citizens live here. Even some of the grocery stores on the island stock the dry, tasteless bird for Thanksgiving and Christmas."

Sighing, Eve said, "I didn't know it was important to me until you brought in the fish. Let's have turkey for Christmas at least."

Grinning into her upturned face, David relied, "We'll have turkey and goose. I have my traditions, too."

Settling at the table, Eve said, "We'll never eat all that fowl."

"Then, we'll eat Christmas dinner at my parents' for the goose and Christmas Eve here for the turkey," David suggested, serving their plates.

"Good idea!" Eve agreed quickly.

"See what I mean? With a little effort, you can still have all of your U.S. customs while enjoying ours as well."

"That still doesn't solve the problem of being a little homesick for familiar sights and faces," Eve said, enjoying the meal.

"This might be wishful thinking, but the longer you know me and the more we love each other, the less that will matter," David stated with a big smile.

"You are growing on me." Eve chuckled. "I think it's your modesty that I love the most."

"I'm definitely not modest where we're concerned. I'll do everything in my power to win your heart and make it impossible for you not to stay here when your contract's up," David replied.

"This is a pretty good start. Besides, you already have my heart. You know, this fish isn't bad. It's not turkey, but it tastes great," Eve remarked.

"Made with my special recipe," David quipped with a slight bow.

Eve sighed. "I can't think of anything more perfect than having a handsome man wait on me."

"Unless it's turkey for Thanksgiving dinner?" David joked as he pulled Eve to her feet and kissed her. The rest of the fish would have to wait for a few moments.

Eve and David spent the rest of the meal and evening in casual conversation. Anyone observing them would have seen that they were a perfect match despite Eve's reservations about marriage. Their devotion was complete.

A growing sense of anticipation filled the weeks between Thanksgiving and Christmas. Eve's students were extremely excited about the upcoming holidays and, for the first time, difficult to inspire. With the local shops sporting holiday decorations and water-skiing Santa's constantly on the television, Eve could understand their reactions. She was feeling the preholiday tension, too. She would be away from home for her first major holiday. Although Helen would spend the time with their parents, Eve would not be there to experience the joy of being together and of opening their gifts. Christmas was the one holiday that she looked forward to with great expectation.

This year instead of happily awaiting her mother's award-winning pumpkin pie, Eve anticipated her reaction to seeing Brad again. Since Helen's call at Thanksgiving, Eve had thought of him every day and could hardly wait until he arrived. Her love for him had turned into warm friendship long before she left the States for Bermuda; however, the idea of seeing her former boyfriend with another woman bruised her ego and tweaked her curiosity. She needed to see him so that she could get over the past once and for all.

Like most of her neighbors, Eve decorated her little cottage for the holiday. Although Boxing Day celebrations would mean little to her, the Christmas holiday promised to be entertaining among people who enjoyed a good time and threw great parties. She had received numerous invitations from her students' parents inviting her to their homes for holiday parties. She had decided to drop in on each of them for a few minutes and then move to the next. Fortunately, David's parents had planned one for the same evening, making long stays impossible.

David was excited about the holidays, too. Although they often visited his parents on Sunday and stayed for dinner, their party would be the first official introduction of Eve to his family's friends and associates. Even though everyone knew that he and Eve were a serious item, their public appearances had been few and mostly limited to friends in their age group. However, after his parents' party, the rumor mill would quickly contain every detail of their relationship, Eve's appearance, and her attire. David was happy to see that she handled the scrutiny so well and did not appear nervous about attending a party that would mark her debut to the island's society.

David did not know that the reason for Eve's seemingly composed demeanor was due to her growing anxiety over seeing Brad. Helen had phoned again with the details of Brad's trip, including when and where he proposed that he and Eve might meet for a cup of coffee. Although he would be vacationing with his current girlfriend, he had told Helen that he very much wanted to see Eve to be sure that island life agreed with her.

Helen had not seen any reason to tell him that Eve was involved with someone else since the relationship with Brad had ended prior to the relocation to Bermuda. Eve had not mentioned David in her early e-mails to Brad. Instead, she had simply chatted about the island. The communication had stopped when Eve discovered that she was in love with David.

Knowing the size of the island and the likelihood of seeing Brad, Eve had decided to tell David about Brad's vacation trip. And with David's desire to show off Bermuda's tradition, she knew that he would insist that she invite Brad and his girlfriend to her cottage for tea. The four of them would pass a delightful afternoon and then go their separate ways. At least, in Eve's imagination, the events would transpire in that way. She hoped that the reality would match.

Adding finishing touches to the collection of hand-painted glass ornaments that sparkled in bowls around the little cottage, Eve turned her attention to the garden. Despite it being the end of December, roses, carnations, verbena, and other assorted flowers still bloomed. The Bermuda climate produced a never-ending supply of cut flowers for her table. Carefully snipping a variety of stems, Eve collected enough to fill the four vases scattered around her house.

After hurriedly finishing her decorating, Eve locked the front door, jumped on her bike, and pedaled to the home of her nearest neighbor. The children of the family were her students and had invited her to join them for caroling. To her surprise, Eve was beginning to feel the Christmas season's excitement descend upon her despite the warm weather.

Eve was surprised to see David's bike leaning against a tree as she parked hers in the front yard. Although she

had asked him to meet her at the house, he had feared
that his late class would cause a conflict. Smiling, Eve
knew that he had ridden at suicidal speeds in order to
arrive early. She delighted in the warmth and security
of being loved as completely as David loved her. Pushing
from her mind the thought of the ocean that might one
day separate them, Eve thought that David's love was
the best thing that had ever happened to her. If only the
nagging thought of Brad would go away, she would be
able to enjoy their time together completely before she
would have to face the real hurdle . . . staying in Bermuda
or returning to the States.

Passing the vibrant flowers that bloomed along the
Petersons' walkway, Eve thought about home. Helen
had said that the D.C. area lay under its first heavy Christmas snowfall after years of dustings. While Eve strolled
along flower-strewn paths, Helen trudged in foot-deep
drifts. Shaking her head at her own silliness, Eve wondered why she would even think about returning to the
world of four seasons—two of them either hot and
humid or cold and snowy. If her family would only relocate to Bermuda, she would embrace the thought of
living here forever.

David touched Eve lightly on the elbow as she entered the elegant home. He had been standing at the door
when she arrived, but she had not seen him in the crush
of people. She joined him in the living room where
they sipped a heady rum punch and sang along with
the others. A silent wait staff mingled, offering sandwiches, cakes, and other finger foods to the revelers.

Eve, leaning against David's chest, felt happier than
she had in years. The decisions she needed to make
were far from her mind as they enjoyed the camaraderie
of the other guests. She had missed Thanksgiving, but,

thanks to the warmth of the Bermudians, she would not miss Christmas. Warm temperatures could not dull the Christmas spirit of the island people.

"I'm glad we came tonight. Thanks for meeting me here. I know you had to jump through hoops to arrange your schedule," Eve whispered, looking into David's sweet face as he towered over her in a very reassuring way.

"You said that it was important for you to attend," David replied, kissing her lightly on the forehead. "I wouldn't have missed it. I haven't been to a party like this since I was kid."

"I love carols. I love Christmas. I love being with you at Christmas," Eve said as the caroling continued around them.

"That goes for me, too, kid," David replied, beaming. "This will be an especially blessed Christmas because I have you in my life."

Feeling the tears well in her eyes, Eve smiled and kissed him lightly. She did not care if her students witnessed her happiness; David had surprised her at school by visiting her classroom on more than one occasion anyway. Her students already talked about her handsome boyfriend in a very convivial way. Besides, Eve was so in love that she did not care who saw the exchange of affection or kisses.

By the time they left the Peterson house, Eve was feeling not only relaxed from the punch but passionately in love with her adopted homeland. She looked forward to Christmas in a way that she had not since she was a child. She had even decided that dinner with David's parents and friends would prove to be a joy rather than the trial by fire that he had promised. Eve was ready for anything that the season had to offer.

Eve slowed her pedaling as they approached her drive.

In the dim light that illuminated the porch, she could see someone sitting on her front steps. For a moment, she thought that it was Arty since the man sat slumped in his usual posture. Arty had taken to dropping by at the strangest times. Sometimes he brought little items for Eve to send to Helen. Other times he would arrive empty-handed and sad-eyed. He had not smiled much since Helen left him following their horrible argument. However, as she rode closer, Eve could see that the visitor was not Arty. She could feel David's back straighten protectively as they approached the stranger on the steps.

As they drew closer, the light shone on the waiting figure. The slumped shoulders spoke of a fatigue deeper than a mere night without the proper rest. This was a man who had a heavy weight resting on his shoulders.

Eve's breath caught as the stranger lifted his face. Glancing at David from the corner of her eye, she saw that he had heard her startled exclamation of recognition. The stranger had heard the sound in the quiet night and had smiled. He had heard that catch in Eve's voice many times.

The stranger stood and walked to meet them at the gate. His posture changed from weary to triumphant. Eve had not sent him away or pretended not to recognize him. He had come a long way for that moment. Brad Wilson, Eve's old boyfriend, was not only in Bermuda, he was on her doorstep.

Chapter Twelve

Squaring his shoulders, Brad held the gate opened so that they could enter. He watched silently as Eve and David rested their bikes against a tree near the front steps. Totally ignoring David, whose posture spoke of irritation at the intrusion, he smiled as Eve turned toward him.

Pulling her into his arms, Brad said, "Ah, Eve! It's been too long. You look great! The constant summer breezes have certainly been good to you."

Feeling her heart pounding heavily in her chest, Eve pushed away slightly and replied, "You're looking tired but good. You're early. Helen said that you wouldn't arrive until after Christmas."

"I changed my reservation. I'd had enough of the snow," Brad responded as he studied her beautiful face.

"I don't see your girlfriend. Gina? Helen said that she would be coming with you," Eve said as she eased from his embrace.

"She's planning to join me later. She's a psychiatrist and has a patient in crisis," Brad explained.

Turning to David, Eve said, "Brad Wilson, this is David Scott, my . . . ah . . . significant other. The title 'boyfriend' just doesn't work in this case."

"Glad to meet you," they both lied.

Shaking hands stiffly, the two men gave each other the once-over. They were of almost equal height although David appeared taller due to his lean swimmer's build. Their flashing eyes told Eve that she would have to moderate their time together especially if Brad's girlfriend did not arrive.

Feeling somewhat exhilarated by the obvious enmity that instantaneously developed between the two men, Eve watched as they squared off. She had never introduced a former boyfriend to a current one and was amazed at the speed with which the tension developed. Both men were usually quiet and slow to anger. Now Eve could see the sparks shooting from their eyes as David and Brad continued to assess each other's worth over carefully worded civil conversation.

Deciding that she needed to do something before the dogfight began in earnest, Eve cheerfully said, "Let's go inside. You'll just love my little cottage, Brad. It's nothing like the condo in D.C. The school system set me up in this delightful little place. I couldn't have asked for more."

Eve positioned herself between the two men with David on her right. Although she enjoyed the attention of the obviously competing men, she had dreamed of a pleasant Christmas with David before Brad arrived. Now she would have to deal with their personality and territorial conflicts over the holidays. This was not working out the way she had envisioned.

Once inside the usually comfortable cottage now made too small by the presence of the men, Eve tried to conduct a pleasant conversation. As David and Brad took turns sending darts and barbs at each other, she managed to maintain some degree of civility. Silently, Eve wished that Helen or Brad's girlfriend was there to add one more level head to the mix.

"Brad," Eve asked, "what brings you here on vacation? As long as I've known you, you've never wanted to spend any time at the beach. As much as I love these islands, I have to admit that the main attraction is the pink sand and water sports."

"Helen made it seem too beautiful to pass up," Brad replied, turning his back to David. "She talked about the island and Arty so much that I found myself making the reservations. Gina was sold, too, so we decided that the cold season at home would be the perfect time to visit. Considering all the snow I've left behind, I'd say that this trip will be one of my better ideas."

"Helen fell in love with more than just the island, so you'll need to weigh her comments. However, I think you'll like it here although I'm not exactly impartial in my opinion either," Eve stated with a quick smile at David, who sat like a swollen toad without saying anything. She could almost see the steam rising from his body in the cool air of the house.

"She told me about Arty, his art and him," Brad replied and then added with a touch of sadness, "I think I know Helen pretty well after all these years. She painted a good picture of the islands' natural beauty and the heart-stopping people who live here. I needed to see for myself if the majesty of the islands was working its magic on everyone."

David glared at Brad, knowing that he was making direct reference to Eve. He was behaving better than Eve had expected. Perhaps the week of Brad's visit would not put too much strain on the relationship after all.

Ignoring him, Eve commented, "I fell in love with this place when I first arrived. I found a little spot and sat on the beach looking at the ocean. It was the best moment of my life."

"It's a shame that you didn't have anyone with whom to share it," Brad said gently under David's increasingly hostile stare.

"I did," Eve replied with a huge smile and sweep of her hand in David's direction. "That's where I met David. We sat on the beach, sipping the island specialty tea and munching cookies. That was my first and favorite tea time."

Immediately, David's rigid posture began to relax. Eve's comment had securely placed him at the top of her list. Brad had been dethroned permanently.

Not willing to accept defeat yet, Brad said, "You'll have to take me there. If it's that impressive, I'd like to see it, too."

"That's one of the first places that I'll share with you . . . and Gina," Eve responded with a hint of something akin to sadness creeping into her voice. Both Brad and David heard it despite Eve's big smile, and both men wondered at its meaning.

"Let's hope she'll join us. In the meantime, you're stuck with me. I'm at loose ends and in need of a guide. I hope you don't mind," Brad stated, using the tone of voice that always melted Eve's heart.

Stealing herself against the familiar and immediate reaction, Eve replied, "School's closed, so I'm available. We have plans for Christmas day, but I don't think I have any other obligations. David's free, too, and will be able to join us. He's much better at leading tours than I am. I'm still learning my way around. I have a few favorite places, but he knows all of the best spots."

194   *Courtni Wright*

Ignoring the inclusion of David in the equation, Brad said, "I'm sure you'll do just fine. You've never led me astray before."

Unable to stand the intruder's familiar tone any longer, David interjected, "If what you want is an all-inclusive tour, we should really get an early start tomorrow. We'll see some of the sights that Eve hasn't visited yet. We should call you a cab."

Rising, Brad said, "Don't bother. I biked from the hotel in Hamilton. You have a good point. I'll be here at nine, if that's okay."

Ushering him to the door with a surprised Eve at his side, David stated, "Don't get lost. See you early in the morning."

Standing on the front step, Brad asked, "Aren't you leaving now, too? You'll need your rest for tomorrow."

Easing his arm around Eve's shoulders, David announced, "I'm staying here tonight."

A crooked smile of defeat twisted the lips that Eve had kissed so often. Placing a discreet peck on Eve's cheek, Brad said, "See you good people tomorrow. Sleep well and think of me . . . alone in that lonely hotel room."

"Not likely," David muttered threateningly. His usually composed demeanor was shattered by his first attack of jealousy.

As soon as David closed the door, Eve demanded, "What's wrong with you? I've never known you to behave so rudely."

"That guy was coming on to you right here in front of me. I didn't like it one bit," David replied.

"First, his name is Brad. Second, he was only teasing. You would have known that if you'd given him a chance," Eve scolded, walking toward the stairs.

"I didn't like the way he looked at you or his little

innuendos. He's not over you despite having a new girlfriend. I don't want you to go anywhere alone with him," David insisted.

Standing with her hand on the newel post, Eve demanded, "Are you standing in my home and telling me how to act toward an old friend? I don't believe this is happening."

"Sorry, I said that too strongly, although that's the way I feel," David corrected. "I'm asking you not to go out with him alone. I'll go with you."

"Why? Don't you trust me?" Eve asked as she maintained the barricade of the staircase.

"I trust you but not him," David replied honestly. "He's here without his girlfriend, if one exists. He's already looking you over with thoughts of the old times you shared. It looked to me as if he was anticipating picking up where he left off."

"Let me make something perfectly clear," Eve stated firmly, feeling her temper beginning to boil over. "I broke up with Brad before coming here because there was nothing left in the relationship. There's no animosity between us, and we'll always be friends with a strong bond. Don't make more of his little quips than really exists."

"I love you, Eve, and don't want anything or anyone to come between us," David said in defense of his behavior.

Placing her free hand on David's shoulder, Eve said, "I love you, too, but the fastest way to push a wedge between us is for you not to allow me the freedom to live as I choose. I've missed my old friends, and Brad's one of them. We go way back but that's it."

"I'm sorry. It's just that I've never felt this strongly about any woman. I've never asked any other girlfriend to marry me. I don't want to lose you."

"Brad isn't your competition; the U.S. is. Don't push me at either one of them," Eve said sternly.

"I hear you, and I'll do better tomorrow," David said as he moved toward the step as if to climb the stairs.

"I'm still angry, and, as the song says, 'I just want to be mad for a while.' You can spend the night in the guest room but not in my bed," Eve said without emotion.

Shocked, stunned, and knocked off his pins, David sputtered, "I'll go home. See you in the morning."

"Until tomorrow," Eve replied as she locked the door behind him.

Eve covered her face with her hands and cried tears of tension, anxiety, and anger. She had missed Brad far more than she had suspected, not because she still loved him, but because he represented home and her past. She was angrier with David than she had ever been with anyone. Not even Helen's younger sibling antics had ever made her this furious. David had overstepped the bounds of their relationship. Eve understood that his insecurities had simply been showing, but she had not appreciated the testosterone display. Brad had behaved badly, too, but, free of the constraints of his relationship with Gina, his behavior was to be expected and rather typical of a man whose former girlfriend was in the presence of her present boyfriend. Eve would speak with him the next day about his behavior. She was too angry to handle it now. For the moment, she could only handle one petulant lover at a time.

Climbing the stairs alone for the first time in ages, Eve thought again of the States and home. It was Christmas, and she was far from her family. She loved David, but he was not her folks and her sister. Eve needed to be near them and to share the joy of the season with them. David's mother's generosity was heartwarming, but Mrs. Scott, despite her warm reception, was not her mother. At the holidays, Eve needed and missed her parents and sister.

The holiday season that had started so well now promised to offer heartache rather than happiness. Eve had thought that she would have been able to enjoy a Bermudian Christmas of warm weather and even warmer friends and David's family. Now, with Brad's early solo arrival, the warmth had taken an unfortunate turn and become very frosty without the benefit of a white Christmas.

Slipping into bed, Eve made up her mind that she would not allow the two men in her life to ruin her holiday. She wanted to enjoy all that Bermuda had to offer in every season and for every holiday. If she never lived on the islands again, she would at least have the memories to keep her company.

Besides, Eve could not honestly say that she no longer had feelings for Brad. Seeing him again and being in his arms however briefly had awakened emotions that Eve had thought had died before she left for Bermuda. Instead, Eve discovered that Brad was more handsome, his arms more comforting, and his voice more exciting than she had remembered. He reminded her of home and old times. Their time together normally fit into a warm spot in her heart. Now, however, the memories threatened to expand past their boundaries and push away everything and everyone else.

Pulling up the sheet that usually covered two, Eve found that she did not mind being alone that night. She loved David and the memory of Brad. She needed time to sort out her feelings. Spending time with Brad while not having David in her bed would give her time to decide if Bermuda and its constant summer breezes or the States with its changing seasons would win her heart and devotion.

Eve plumped her pillow again and turned out the light. She had one more piece of unfinished business to settle. Helen. Her conniving little sister had given Brad her address and directions to her house. If Helen had not interfered, Brad would have phoned from his hotel room, giving Eve a chance to compose herself before seeing him again. She would not have been caught off guard by the aroma of his cologne or the width of his shoulders. She could have readied herself to keep the tension from reaching boiling point when Brad and David met for the first time. If Helen had only kept clear of the situation, Eve would not be sleeping alone two nights before Christmas.

Suddenly the phone rang. Rising on her elbow, Eve answered on the second ring. Not surprisingly, Helen's voice bubbled on the other end.

"Well, did you see Brad? His girlfriend couldn't come so he's all yours," Helen said.

"Yeah. He was here when we returned from a student's house. Thanks for giving him my address," Eve replied, allowing a little irritation to surface in her voice.

Chuckling, Helen replied, "You're not really mad at me. He looks good, doesn't he? He says he's been working out and eating right since you left him. I don't think Gina has anything to do with it since she's always so busy with her patients. I think Brad decided to remake himself to get you back."

"That's silly," Eve exclaimed. "My contract is for a year. He wouldn't have started to recreate himself that far in advance. Gina probably told him that he needed to get his stuff in order. Brad's notoriously disorganized and flighty despite his success at the hospital."

"Say whatever you want, but I know the change is because of you," Helen rebutted. "Brad still loves you. In fact, I think he started loving you more after you ended the relationship. He's one of those guys who needs the challenge of the chase. You ran, and he followed."

"I didn't run; I left the States for a new environment. I don't call it following when a guy comes on vacation with another woman," Eve said.

"Gina isn't there yet," Helen stated.

"There you go again, making more of a situation than really exists," Eve said, contradicting her firmly. "I love David and don't want Brad back in my life. I wouldn't have ended the relationship if I'd wanted him. While he's here, I'll have to make sure that David knows that he's the only man on my very short list."

Stepping outside the little sister role, Helen said firmly, "Be honest, Eve, you haven't agreed to marry David despite his repeated offers because something is missing. You say it's because your family's here, but that's not really the reason. If you really loved David, you'd relocate in a minute. Something's holding you back. Maybe there's something about David that isn't quite right. Maybe it's homesickness. I don't know what it is, but I know it's there."

"What makes you such an authority on love and my life?" Eve inquired, more than a little angry at her sister's analysis effort. "I seem to remember that you're still pining over Arty and doing nothing about it." When Helen did not respond, Eve continued a little more calmly, "David's almost perfect. He's occasionally too much into his work, but he's doing better. That's the only complaint I have about him. I can see improvement almost every day. He's much more spontaneous. Besides, Brad's far from perfect; he's too spontaneous. I got tired of being the one to hold the relationship together because he was too irresponsible to take the time from sports and other interests to spend it on us. I'm happy with David and would be happier still if someone would build a bridge between the Carolinas and Bermuda."

"Be honest, big sister. You're looking for a man who combines the best qualities of both David and Brad."

"What makes you say that?"

"Because I'm looking for someone with all of Arty's good qualities mixed with Brad's energy and David's sense of responsibility. When I find him, I'll marry him," Helen said sadly.

"Maybe you're right," Eve conceded reluctantly, "but since I doubt that I'll ever find this superhero, I'll keep the man I love and who loves me."

"And which one is that?" Helen asked mischievously.

Eve sighed. "Good night, Helen. This conversation is going nowhere, and I'm tired."

"Call me tomorrow." Helen laughed heartily. She loved having the upper hand over her big sister.

"Will do."

Turning onto her side, Eve came to the realization that Helen, in her meddling, had only forced the issue and created a situation that would have arisen on its own time anyway. Being honest with herself, Eve thought that this Christmas might turn out to be one of the most exciting she had ever spent. She hoped that Gina would stay in the States with her patients and leave the men to her.

Chapter Thirteen

Gina arrived the next morning to Brad's surprise. She had managed to console her frazzled patient without much difficulty. Rather than phone ahead, she had simply taken a red-eye that delivered her to the islands before dawn of Christmas Eve. She had reached the hotel just as Brad, in stunning white slacks and shirt, descended to the lobby.

"Where are you going? Aren't you happy and surprised to see me?" Gina gushed, linking her arm through Brad's.

"Very," Brad replied with a sick smile. "I was on my way to join Eve and David for a tour of the island."

"Wait for me! I'd love to go. It won't take me but a minute to change," Gina said as she rushed into the elevator with Brad's key dangling from her fingers.

Finding himself with no other choice, Brad rented another bike and waited. True to her word, Gina returned in only five minutes. The sight of her slender, shapely body on any other occasion would have made him smile and think of pleasurable moments that they would share later that night. However, Eve occupied all of Brad's thoughts, leaving no room for any other woman. Brad was genuinely fond of Gina, but his love for Eve had never died. He had come to the island for the purpose of rekindling the old flame within her. Neither Gina nor David would deter him from his mission.

When Brad returned to Eve's, Gina was with him and eager for the tour of the island. She embraced Eve warmly at their introduction and complimented the little cottage excessively. Chatting gaily about her flight and patient, Gina would have made an ideal guest if Eve had not wanted time alone to speak with Brad. Eve had not worked out a plan for being alone with him but knew that the opportunity would arise. David could not possibly stay at her side every minute of the day.

Although Brad looked less than happy to have Gina with him, David was thrilled by her presence. He had brought Eve a basket of her favorite fruits as an apology gift for his crummy behavior. She had accepted it happily and had melted in his arms when he kissed her. Athough Eve had smiled a little too gaily at the sight of Brad wobbling through the garden gate on his bike and frowned too much as she watched Gina skillfully navigate the same obstacle, David felt that everything between them would soon return to normal.

As soon as Eve locked the door, the foursome pedaled off toward the first of the tourist sights. Since they were staying in the glitzy city of Hamilton, David concentrated his tour guide efforts on the quaint surrounding communities. As usual, all tours would end with a sail on their boat for lunch at their favorite cove.

Despite the cool temperature, by the time they reached the dock Brad's shirt clung to his back and dirt spotted his slacks from the numerous falls that he had taken along the way. Gina, of course, looked as fresh as when she first arrived at Eve's little cottage. Not a single hair of her chignon was out of place. No sweat glistened on her forehead and top lip as it did on Eve's. Her apricot slacks and matching shirt still bore laundry creases.

As Brad and Gina stood on the dock, Eve and David rolled their jeans up to their calves and loaded the lunch basket and other supplies. Checking to see that the boat carried the correct number of life jackets, they motioned Brad and Gina aboard. Brad, not being the boating type, hesitated slightly while Gina, raised on Maryland's eastern shore boating community, quickly climbed aboard.

"When did you learn to sail?" Brad asked as he watched Eve handle the sheets. "You wouldn't even set foot in a rowboat before moving here."

"David taught me when we first met," Eve replied while David beamed with pride at her accomplishments. "Boating in all forms is a way of life here. I wanted to sample everything about life on the islands. Boating was part of it."

"You handle the sails as if you were born on the water," Gina said. "I prefer motorboats, but I have a great respect for anyone who's good with the lines."

"Thanks," Eve replied. "It's great fun and not that hard to do once you learn the personality of the boat."

Looking uncomfortable at the camaraderie that seemed to be developing between the two women, Brad asked, "Whose boat is this anyway? Is it yours, David?"

"No, it's Eve's. I gave it to her after she had mastered the techniques on my boat," David commented, proudly.

"It used to be his mother's," Eve added, "but she doesn't sail without her husband anymore."

"Oh," Brad replied without enthusiasm. He could feel the obstacles to winning Eve increasing as he learned more of the depths of David's devotion to her.

"We almost lost it as soon as I gave it to her," David stated without further embellishment.

"We almost lost ourselves that day," Eve added with a little chuckle.

"What happened?" Gina asked as Brad continued to grip the sides of the boat.

"A storm came up and capsized us," Eve explained in a matter-of-fact manner. "If we hadn't been wearing these vests, we would have died. It was just one of those freak storms, but I just knew I'd never see David again."

Gazing at him from across the width of the boat, Eve felt a delicious warmth suddenly spread through her body. She and David had shared much in the short time that they had been together. The affection had grown into love quickly. Smiling into David's eyes, Eve felt torn between her old love and her new one. She hoped that she would never hurt David; he did not deserve that kind of treatment. He had been true and wonderful, all that a woman could want in a man.

Brad looked from Eve's glowing face to David's. Sadly, he saw that they wore the same expression of adoration. She had never looked at him that way although his eyes had devoured her face every time he looked at her then or now. Still, Brad was determined to win her back. If David loved Eve as much as his body language said, he would put up a fight for her, or at the very least, he would set her free to decide for herself.

Eve felt Brad's eyes burning into her skin. As David worked the rudder, she glanced at Brad. For a moment, she thought of all the old times they had shared and the

moments when she had delighted under the weight of
his gaze. She remembered most of them fondly.

Now, with Bermuda's sun on her skin and the waves
lapping at the sides of the boat, Eve was confused.
When she had left home for Bermuda, she knew that
the relationship with Brad had ended long before the
ink had dried on her teaching contract. However, after
months of separation, he looked better than she had remembered. He was more attentive and entertaining. He
even seemed less scattered and random in his behavior
and much more deliberate as if he might have grown
up a bit and become more responsible. Eve wondered
if she would have lost interest in the relationship if
Brad had shown that side of his personality. She wondered if he had changed under Gina's careful direction
or if the modifications had been internally generated
from the need to improve himself. Either way, Brad
was different, and Eve found the modifications to be
unsettling and enticing.

Pushing the disturbing thoughts from her mind, Eve
directed, "We're approaching the cove. We'll sail into
shallow water, and everyone will help pull the boat to
shore."

"What do you mean? There's no dock?" Brad asked
as he continued to clutch the boat's sides. He was not
normally nervous about boating, but his experience
only covered rivers and lakes. The high sea, even just
off the coast of Bermuda, was too deep and bottomless
for his taste. The unseen fish in the dark waters made
Brad put aside his usual bravado.

"No dock," David interjected with a suppressed chuckle at Brad's white knuckles. "We'll ride the waves as
close as we can get to the shore and then pull the boat
onto the sand. With luck, the water will only come up

to your knees. It's an exhilarating experience, feeling a boat bobbing under you as you head toward land. It's a little like riding a horse when the current's strong and like skating when it's calm."

Watching Brad, Eve could see him pale under the baseball cap that shaded his face. He was once so daredevil and bold. She wondered what had changed him. Now he appeared even more conservative than David. Loyally, Eve forced herself to remember that Brad had not spent his childhood on the water and was not a boater. Although he could swim, he had never been really comfortable around deep water and had refused to take a vacation cruise for fear the ship would sink. Smiling at the memory, Eve concluded that Brad had not changed at all but was simply manifesting a fear that she already knew existed. Boats, ocean sailing, and Brad just did not mix.

"Don't worry," Gina chimed in, "we'll all help. It's really very easy. The tide does most of the work. Roll up your pant legs."

Brad hesitated for only a minute. Fearing that further conversation on the subject would dim Eve's opinion of him, he released the sides of the boat, rolled up his pants, and, thinking no one noticed, tightened his life vest. As the boat slowly slid into shallow water, Brad immediately responded to David's call for hands overboard. Gripping the sides, he joined Eve and Gina in guiding the boat to shore while David steered with first the rudder and then pushed from the stern before joining them in the water.

Once the foursome was safely ashore and the boat carefully lashed to the nearest driftwood, they spent a few minutes looking for the perfect picnic spot. Eve and David suggested their second favorite location, wanting to keep the primary one to themselves. Gina and

Brad agreed and immediately began to spread out the blanket and set out the plates and utensils.

Turning to Eve, Gina said, "I don't think I've ever seen a more beautiful location. Thanks for bringing us here."

"Glad to show you our island," Eve replied.

"If you think this is something, wait until you see my parents' home," David stated proudly. "Not only do they have the beach but a fabulous garden and a waterfall. It's paradise."

"I'd love to see it," Gina responded enthusiastically.

"I'll arrange the visit for after Boxing Day. It's second only to Christmas in terms of preparation," David said.

"I've heard that people party nonstop on these islands," Brad interjected.

"Maybe on the Caribbean islands but not here," Eve replied quickly and protectively of her adopted home. "Life is much more conservative here."

Placing his hand on Eve's shoulder affectionately, David said, "We celebrate the same holidays that you do plus Boxing Day and the first official day of the summer season. Our 'stiff upper lip' British heritage makes us a rather reserved people."

"Anyone for a swim?" Eve asked as she stripped off her jeans and T-shirt. Her body, trim and muscular from sailing and swimming, glistened in the sunlight.

"My suit's in my bag," Gina said. "Where can I change?"

"There's a little privacy behind that boulder," David replied, pointing to the farthest rock near the cluster of palms.

"I didn't bring one," Brad stated with a touch of cheer in his voice.

"I always carry an extra in Eve's boat for guests.

Help yourself. It's in a waterproof bag under the seat at the stern," David said, slipping from his clothes to reveal his muscular body.

Pulling off his damp white shirt, Brad strolled toward the boat, showing off the broadness of his shoulders and his muscular form with each step. Knowing him as well as she did, Eve could tell that he was putting on a macho front to impress her and to convince himself that he was not afraid of swimming in something considerably larger than a pool or a lake. She could imagine that he hoped that the swim trunks would not fit him.

Brad watched as Eve, Gina, and David casually walked into the water until it was waist high and then began to skillfully stroke the waves. Sighing and shrugging his shoulders, he felt under the seat for the bag. Finding it, he ducked behind another of the cove's massive rocks and tried on the trunks.

"Damn!" Brad muttered against the crashing of the waves. "They fit."

Searching for the others, Brad saw that they had stopped swimming and were perched atop a massive boulder as they waited for him to join them. Silently, he wished that they had decided not to wait for him. Now, wearing David's extra pair of trunks, he had no choice but to dive in.

Waving to the others, Brad walked resolutely into the water that quickly reached his waist. Trying to look less like a landlubber, he fought to tame the waves. By the time he had reached the others, Brad was exhausted.

"You made it," Eve exclaimed. "It's not at all like our swims at home. The currents are tough. You have to fight every inch of the way."

"I didn't push myself," Brad lied as he pulled himself onto the rock. Every muscle in his body quivered as he added, "The trunks are a little too large, and I didn't want to lose them."

Stifling a chuckle, David said, "Let's swim to the far curve of the cove. It's not much distance, and the coral reefs along the way are spectacular."

Looking from Eve to Gina, Brad asked, "Do you think the ladies can handle a swim of that distance? Eve said that the current's strong out here."

"Don't worry about me," Gina stated. "I'm not at all tired and should be able to keep up without trouble."

"Okay, Let's go," David instructed.

"Wait a minute. What about Eve?" Brad asked, continuing to hope that something would postpone the swim indefinitely.

Looking at Brad as if seeing him for the first time, Eve replied, "I swim this route at least twice each week. We usually race, and I usually win."

"I let you win, you mean," David corrected with a chuckle.

"Oh, yeah? Let's race this time, too. Gina and Brad will declare the winner," Eve replied.

"This is so exciting!" Gina exclaimed. "I'll be the timekeeper."

Setting the rules, David said, "We'll swim to that distant black rock. The first one to touch, turn, and wave wins."

"I'm game if you are," Eve agreed happily.

As Eve and David took their positions, Brad watched sadly. Unless he could think of something that would put him into competition with this math professor/swimming star, he would lose Eve forever. With the water splashing against the rocks, he could only sigh and concede that the task would be monumental on dry

land and almost insurmountable in this watery play-
ground. Brad decided that his moment of triumph
would have to come later onshore.

"On my word, go!" Gina shouted.

Immediately Eve and David turned from humans,
bobbing in the surf, to creatures of the sea, cutting the
water like dolphins. Eve's burst of energy matched
David's strength. At first, they swam side by side, too
close to call. Then slowly, it looked as if Eve might be
pulling away as her head grew smaller and smaller.

"She's waving!" Brad shouted. "She won! Eve beat
him."

"She said she would," Gina stated. "She's a woman
of her word. I like her."

Feeling his pride in Eve swelling, Brad responded,
"She is that. She's a good one."

At that moment, despite the spray of salty water in
her face, Gina studied Brad's expression and recognized the emotions she had suspected since she first
saw him with Eve. Sadly, Gina conceded that Brad was
still in love with Eve. In that instant, Gina realized that
her relationship with him was at best a rebound affair
and would not be anything else until he was over Eve.
In the meantime, she would be the fourth in the party
to prevent the love triangle from appearing too obvious. Some women have all the luck, and Gina decided
that Eve was one of them. To be loved by two men
must do wonderful things for her ego.

Realizing that Gina was looking at him, Brad said
softly, "I think we should join them . . . leisurely. I'm
not a strong enough swimmer for a race."

"Okay," Gina agreed slowly. "But first, tell me something, Brad. Why did you invite me along on this vacation? You're in love with Eve. You certainly don't need
me to run interference for you."

"I don't understand what you mean. That relationship ended a long time ago," Brad sputtered. "Aren't you having a good time?"

Touching his cheek softly, Gina said, "Maybe you're able to fool yourself, but you can't fool me. Your love for her is written all over your face."

Speaking emphatically, Brad stated, "I'm proud of her accomplishments, that's all. Let's not discuss this anymore. We'll only fight. Besides, it's a baseless discussion."

Nodding, Gina agreed. "Okay, I'll agree not to discuss it while we're here, but we will discuss this when we return to the States. I told you when we first started dating that I want a man who's interested in marriage. I don't want to waste time on a relationship that doesn't have a chance of making that progression."

"I told you when we first met that I want that life, too. We're on the same page," Brad said.

"Maybe, but I'm not convinced that we're on that page together. You might have someone else in mind," Gina stated and then added, "They're waving for us to join them. Let's not hold up the tour of the coral reefs. We can finish this discussion when we're not under the spell of the Bermuda breezes."

Lowering herself from the rock into the water, Gina began the long swim. Although she was not as confident as Eve in the deep, open ocean, Gina's trim body glided through the water effortlessly. Each stroke carried her farther away, leaving Brad alone on the rock.

Taking a deep breath both to clear his head and to give himself courage to face the currents of his life and the sea, Brad began his choppy stroke in the cool water. With each movement, Brad promised himself that if he survived this vacation, he would never let Eve out of his sight again. Trying to win her back was too physically and emotionally exhausting. He was a man of few fears, but, unfortunately, most of them resided in the deep seas that surrounded the breathtaking island.

Eve and David had no idea of the conversation that had passed between Gina and Brad. They had been so busy teasing each other about the dubious victory that they barely noticed that they were alone at the rock. It was not until Eve conceded the possibility that David had helped her to win that they noticed Gina and Brad at the starting point. They waved and waited for the two to join them.

Soon the foursome swam together over the shallow water of the coral reef. Periodically they would tread water to admire the fish that fed on the reef. Spotting fish in colors that she had only seen in Baltimore's aquarium, Gina exclaimed as each one brushed boldly against her outstretched hands. No one noticed that Brad was very quiet despite the splendor of the sea creatures.

"Anyone hungry?" Eve asked as they lingered on the flat surface of the rock at the entrance to the coral reef.

"Starving!" Gina replied. "I haven't eaten anything except airplane peanuts."

"I could stand a little something. Did we really swim out that far?" Brad asked, looking back at the distance between them and the picnic spot.

Laughing, David said, "Eve asked the same thing the first time we made this trip. It's really not that far or that deep. It's an optical illusion."

"Isn't this where the storm almost drowned you?" Gina asked as she lightly touched a playful little fish.

"Not here exactly," Eve said, "further out in the ocean near where those fishermen are trawling. I sailed here to safety."

"This is a peaceful little cove," David added before gliding toward the shore.

"You could have fooled me," Brad muttered as he jumped into the water and followed the others back to the beach.

The simple lunch tasted especially good to Brad now that he was once again attired in his white slacks and shirt. He had endured enough of the stressful swim in the deep sea and Gina's scrutiny. Hopefully, the food and conversation would take her mind off his love for Eve.

"What'll we do next?" Eve asked David, whom she still considered the expert on Bermuda.

"If it's okay with you, I'd like to return to the hotel," Gina interjected. "I haven't had much sleep, and the water's made me feel very relaxed."

"It's back to the hotel then," Brad stated, only too happy to get away from the water for a while. "We could meet you somewhere for dinner."

Looking at each other and smiling, David said, "We know just the place. The attire's casual, and the food's phenomenal. We'll bike to your hotel to pick you up around eight o'clock."

The dinner plans settled, the couples cleaned up their spot of beach and shoved off for the trip back to the dock. With the sails rigged, Eve snuggled against David's strong chest while he controlled the rudder. She had enjoyed another wonderful day in Bermuda, a unique Christmas Eve that she would remember for the rest of her life regardless of the turns it might take.

Noticing that Brad and Gina sat apart at the bow, Eve motioned to them and whispered, "Do you think they had an argument?"

"When? We were together the whole day," David replied.

"Maybe during our race. They were alone then," Eve suggested.

"I think she's just tired. Unless, of course, she's noticed it, too," David added slowly.

"Noticed what?" Eve asked, yawning lightly at the gentle rocking of the boat after a satisfying meal.

"Brad's still in love with you," David replied, studying Eve's reaction. "It's written all over his face. I feel sorry for the guy. I know how it feels to love a woman so much that it's not possible to hide it."

"I'm sure he isn't. It's just friendship or old memories," Eve said lightly although she could feel her heart pounding in her chest.

"That's not friendship I see on his face when he looks at you. I'm flattered that another man finds my woman attractive, but I still feel sorry for the guy," David said, tacking the boat skillfully.

"It's a figment of your imagination . . . too much sun and surf," Eve said, trying to keep the tone of her voice light.

"If it is, Gina shares the same figment," David replied.

Eve continued to lean against David's strong shoulder, quietly watching the late afternoon sun play on the water despite the currents that ripped through her body. She hoped that David had not read her as easily as he had Brad. Eve knew that she loved David, but her feelings were strong for Brad, too.

To her surprise, the two men from opposite ends of the continuum had moved closer to the center, each gaining the good qualities of the other and leaving behind the bad. The change had muddied Eve's thinking as both became the kind of man she always knew she would marry. The only problem was to identify the one that fit the image the best. Until she decided, Eve would work hard not to cause either man any pain.

Chapter Fourteen

The holiday season passed quickly with Eve and David spending most of their time with his family, and Brad and Gina acting as tourists on their own to enjoy the big cities. Eve had enjoyed every minute of the time she had spent with David's family. They always treated her as one of their own, and the holiday spirit had made their reception even warmer. However, despite the hospitality or perhaps because of it, Eve missed her family terribly and phoned Helen at least twice each day.

"Did you give Mom and Dad the gift from me? Did they like it?" Eve asked Helen late Christmas evening.

"Sure, who wouldn't like one of Arty's creations?" Helen replied with a touch of melancholy in her voice.

"Any idea how his sales are doing?" Eve asked, hating to hear the sadness in her sister's voice.

Sighing, Helen replied, "The gallery owner penned a note in the holiday greeting she sent me, saying that she had just faxed him more orders. She's even sold but not delivered the sample pieces in the gallery. I'd say that he's doing just fine."

"Every time we see him, Arty's up to his ears in projects. He never has time to hang out with us anymore," Eve said.

"Is he dating anyone?" Helen asked tentatively.

Eve laughed. "Yeah, sure, his pliers, wire cutters, and blowtorch."

Eve could hear Helen exhale as she asked, "How's Brad? Is he behaving himself? Sometimes he can be so energetic that he's annoying."   –

"He's changed or mellowed, I'm not sure which one, and I don't know why. I don't know if it's Gina's influence or the fact that time stops for no one, but he's more conservative and slower to take action than he used to be. It's sort of ironic, but David and Brad have become more similar. David's still very organized and conscientious about his work, but he enjoys having fun now although he used to act as if enjoying life were a sin. Brad doesn't seem quite as irresponsible although he's definitely still fun-loving when on dry land. He's not much for ocean sports. It's amazing . . . and confusing."

"Sounds like Brad's casting his spell on you again," Helen said. "How's Gina taking it?"

Sighing, Eve replied, "She watches his every move. We haven't been alone since she arrived. I think she's even more jealous or suspicious than David, who has told me that he knows that Brad's still in love with me."

"Good for her. You don't need to be alone with him. You have enough confusion in your life already without adding your feelings about Brad to the list."

"Too late. I'm already confused about him, and David isn't helping matters at all. He senses Brad's feelings for me but isn't putting up any opposition or being more attentive, not that he could be . . . he's already the best. Still, it looks like he'd step up his efforts to push Brad out of the picture."

"Maybe David feels as if he has already shown you all he has. He loves you and spends all of his free time with you. There's probably nothing more he could do."

"I guess you're right. In fact, I know you are," Eve conceded. "Anyway, I'm not going to worry about any of this. I'm enjoying my life here with David. When Brad leaves, everything will return to normal."

"We'll see." Helen sounded wary.

"Don't sound so cynical. Seeing Brad caused a ripple on the water of my life, and that's all."

"A ripple? I'd say it's more like a tidal wave. Keep me posted."

Eve did not have to wait long to find out which one of them had the more accurate view of the effect of Brad's visit on her life. Since the couples spent so much time together, it was inevitable that something or someone would break the tension and force the issue. However, Eve had not imagined that it would happen as it did.

The couples had gone sailing so often that Brad had finally overcome his fear of the sea. His stroke had not improved, but he no longer hesitated to take the plunge and often threw himself into the water ahead of them. Although he was less reckless than in the past, Brad also discovered that parasailing satisfied his thirst for adventure. He would spend the early morning hours high above them before joining them for their daily lunch at the cove. He never won the races against Gina, but he tried with determination. On his last day on the island, he almost beat her. The effort had caused him to pull a muscle in his back, giving him an excuse for the last defeat at her hands.

After dinner at Eve and David's favorite restaurant, the couples decided that they would like ice cream for dessert. While David and Gina walked the short distance to the shop in Eve's neighborhood, Eve and Brad stayed behind in her cottage. Brad had settled in the high-back chair with a heating pad on the sore muscle and did not want to go out until it was time to return to the hotel. David had taken his place, looking reluctantly at Eve, who sat working on a beaded purse that Brad would deliver to Helen.

"How's your back?" Eve asked as she loaded the needle with the last of the seed pearls for the topmost clouds in the intricate design.

Flinching a little as he moved to test the area, Brad replied, "I'll live, but I won't be swimming any races for a while."

"Considering the foot of new snow that fell on D.C. last night, I don't think you'll need to worry about that. You might have a little trouble shoveling your car out of the drift though." Eve chuckled without looking up from her beading.

"Have you almost finished the purse?" Brad asked as he watched her nimble fingers ply the needle.

Eve nodded, "Just one last row and I'll be in the homestretch with only the finishing off to do. You're still planning to deliver it to Helen for me, aren't you?"

"I will if the snow's not too bad in her neighborhood," Brad said as he leaned heavily against the heating pad.

"There's no rush," Eve said and added, "Her birthday's not until the middle of January. I just don't want to take the chance that the mail service will ruin it."

Silence fell between the old friends as Eve worked the last of the stitches. As soon as she placed the purse in the gift box and tied the ribbon securely, Brad turned off the pad. Moving gingerly, he joined her on the sofa.

"While the others are away, I'd like to talk with you," Brad said seriously.

Eve eyed him suspiciously. Since their last conversation, she had been careful to avoid being alone with him. If she had not wanted to complete the purse for Helen, she would have joined David in the quest for ice cream instead of Gina. Now she was alone with the man whose closeness managed to make her heart pound and her hands grow moist. She wished the door would open at that moment and put an end to the conversation before it began.

"I'm all ears," she said, trying to keep the atmosphere light despite the serious expression on Brad's face.

"I can't leave here without saying this, so here goes," Brad began after clearing his throat of the dust ball that made his voice come in a whisper. "I love you. I've always loved you, and I probably always will. I know it's not fair to Gina, but I can't help it. Even if I manage to make you part of my past, I'll still continue to love what we had as I make a future with someone else. I messed up by not showing my feelings when we were together. I was too flippant about life and love. I know now that I made the worst mistake of my life in not settling down and becoming more responsible . . . like David."

"You can't help who you are," Eve replied, trying to ease some of Brad's sadness. "We were in different places . . . you were more interested in a good time and fun, and I wanted more, a family, a special someone sitting by the fire with me. That's just the truth of our lives. We loved each other once. That'll have to be enough."

"But I've changed. I know that I have even more work to do to make myself into that man you want, but I'm willing to do it. I love you and will do anything to win you back. Come home with me and let me prove it to you," Brad urged, taking Eve's small hands in his.

Eve felt her heart breaking at the sadness in his voice and on his face. She had loved Brad deeply until the realization that she would never play a prominent role in his life. She had tried to modify her expectations to meet his reality, but she had not been able to put aside her dreams. After many tears and much self-doubt, she had realized that her love for him had changed into a warm friendship and she allowed the relationship to die of natural causes. Watching him spend endless hours at the hospital, drive recklessly as if nothing mattered, and take daredevil chances as if trying to chase away the reality of death, Eve had decided that the end of the relationship was the best thing for both of them. She would never be able to embrace Brad's lifestyle and would do nothing to break his spirit.

"You're asking much more than I can give," Eve replied softly. "I have a contract here that I don't intend to break. I've met an absolutely wonderful man who I love dearly. David wants to get married and make a life together. We would have gotten married by now if I had settled my issues. I can see the changes in you, but I wonder if you aren't still the same guy barely under the surface of a more reserved persona. I still care for you, but I don't know if that's enough."

"Take a chance on me and find out. I know you don't want to break the contract, but it happens all the time. Come home so that I can show you the changes," Brad insisted.

"No, I won't do that to the kids, and I won't turn my back on David. He deserves more," Eve said firmly. She was determined not to allow Brad's sad eyes to sway her resolve.

"Then, come home during your spring break. I'm not happy about having to wait, but I'll do it. Promise that you'll think about it."

"No, I don't trust myself enough to do that. I might not return if I do. I've already purchased my summer return ticket; we'll have to wait until then. I'll come home as soon as school closes. We need time and distance so that we can think clearly," Eve said as she liberated her hands from his.

"You mentioned having issues. Do any of them have to do with us?" Brad asked, hoping for a sign of encouragement.

"Maybe a few of them," Eve replied with a slow smile. "I have to see the States again so that I can make up my mind about accepting a permanent contract and relocating here permanently. I love this island, but my heart's in Maryland. It's a tough decision to make. It's not every day that a woman has to decide between a man and his island and a man with whom she shares a country."

Slightly disappointed that Eve's heart did not belong to him exclusively, Brad asked, "Will David be with you?"

"No, he wants me to decide for myself without any encouragement from him. Besides, he knows that you love me and that I still have feelings for you. He's read the emotions on your face and thinks that I'm hiding mine. He wants to give me the distance I need to be sure of my feelings. He doesn't want me to live here if I can't be one hundred percent with him."

"I'll try to be fair, too, but it'll be hard. It's easier for him since he has you with him every day. I'll only have e-mails and the occasional phone call," Brad said sadly.

"That's more than some nights when we were together," Eve reminded him.

"Med school and internship put a strain on our relationship. So does establishing a practice. But that's over and my practice is doing great."

"If I remember correctly, it wasn't your practice that interfered; it was your interest in doing dangerous things and taking risks," Eve stressed with a touch of irritation in her voice.

Seeing that the moment was taking a turn that he did not like, Brad said, "Let's not argue. We don't have much time left. I've changed; I'm not the wild man I used to be. I'll show you when you come home."

Eve smiled. "Yes, you're right. I'll see when I come home at the end of June."

Rising stiffly and favoring his strained muscles, Brad pulled Eve to her feet and into his arms. "This will have to keep me until I see you again."

Pressing his lips possessively against her, Brad kissed Eve with an overwhelming intensity that spoke of his love for her. His arms enfolded her as if to block out everything except the two of them. In the silence, he could feel her heart pounding against his. He knew that he would have to make every minute, e-mail, and phone call count if he wanted to win her back.

As she melted into his body, Eve knew that she would have a tough decision to make. She loved David and had loved Brad. Even as she returned his kisses, Eve admitted that she still loved him. The distance between the past and the present was insignificant when the smell of his cologne was so intoxicating.

Stepping back abruptly, Eve said as tears glistened in her eyes, "I'm glad you're leaving tomorrow. The temptation is too great, and I don't want to hurt David or Gina."

Realizing that the moment had ended, Brad said, "Someone will have to be hurt if we're to resume our old relationship. We'll do it gently, but we can't stop the pain."

"I know . . . not for us or them. I wish you'd shown this side of yourself earlier. It would have made all the difference and saved a lot of heartbreak," Eve said softly.

"I should have, but I was a fool," Brad replied.

"Either that or you didn't know a good thing until you didn't have it anymore. David's not like that. He appreciates me now."

"I've changed, Eve. You'll see," Brad stated firmly.

Hearing voices in the yard, Eve picked up the box containing the purse for Helen. Holding it between them, she looked into Brad's sad eyes. The moment had ended.

"Don't forget to give this to Helen," Eve said as she walked toward the door.

The warm breezed entered the room as Gina and David returned with the ice cream. Feeling the tension in the little cottage, they looked at each other and then back at Eve and Brad. They sensed that something had happened in their absence that might have an impact on their lives, too.

Seeing Brad's strained face, Gina asked with a touch of sarcasm in her voice, "Did you miss us?"

Linking her arm through David's, Eve replied, "Why? Were you gone long? I was too busy to notice. I finished the purse for Helen."

Taking the box from Brad, who stood silently, Eve carefully opened it to display the exquisitely beaded bag. Although David showed genuine interest in the purse, Gina only gave it a quick, superficial going-over. She sensed that Brad's sore back was not the real reason for his pained expression. David might be blinded by his love for Eve, but Gina saw everything. She wondered if Eve had managed to elude Brad's charm. Past experience might have hardened her resolve. She would be one of the few who had been able to resist him if she did. Perhaps that explained Brad's downcast expression.

Taking the bag containing the ice cream carton from David, Eve asked, "Ice cream, anyone?"

The couples took their cones onto the front porch and watched the sparkling stars in the clear sky. Gina and Brad were quiet, caught up in their independent thoughts. David and Eve chatted gaily about their plans for the coming weekend, the last before the second semester began. Neither David nor Gina mentioned the way Brad's eyes followed Eve's every movement. After they finished eating, Gina and Brad departed with a promise to keep in touch and kisses all around.

The next day, Eve and David took their breakfast onto the beach behind the house. Although this was not their favorite spot, they often ate their meals on the small stretch of beach near the cottage. For Eve, who normally would have been dressed in heavy wools at this time of year, the beach in late December was a real treat. David, until Eve's arrival, would have thought nothing of wearing shorts and sandals on New Year's Eve. Now that he was seeing his world through her eyes, he, too, was thrilled by the experience.

As they sipped their tea, a jet flew overhead. Shading her eyes, Eve watched it disappear into the clouds. She turned toward David in time to see a smile playing at the corners of his lips.

"Do you think that was their flight?" Eve asked.

"I don't know, but I'm glad they've gone. Brad and Gina are nice people, but I don't like sharing you with anyone," David said, kissing her gently on the lips.

"That's so strange, considering you share me with my students every day," Eve replied, sliding closer on the drift bench.

"That's different," David declared.

"Why?"

"It's a job. You can walk away from the classroom at any time. It's harder to remove friends from your life," David said gently.

"Students get under your skin, too," Eve said, hoping to deflect his thoughts from Brad and Gina.

"True, but not as much," David continued, studying Eve's face for signs of the affection he knew she held for Brad.

"I don't know. I can still remember the faces of kids that I would have loved to adopt to save them from their home life," Eve mused, forcing her face to remain passive.

"You've got me there, but I still think it's different from removing an old love from your life when he still loves you," David said, looking into the depths of Eve's eyes.

Not wanting to spoil a wonderful day with further discussion about Brad, Eve replied, "Not when you've closed that chapter of your life."

"Have you?" David studied Eve's face.

"With as much assurance as you feel about your past loves," Eve answered in a tone that sounded much more assured than she felt.

Smiling gently and knowing that he had lost the argument, David let the subject drop. Although he suspected that a flame still burned in Eve's heart for Brad, he did not want to pursue it any further. Now that Brad had left the island, the physical distance between them would quiet any romantic stirrings. At least, David hoped that would happen.

"What'll we do today?" he asked.

"Let's go cheer up Arty," Eve suggested happily.

"That's a big task," David replied with a chuckle.

"I know, but I feel that I have to spend a little time with him. After all, Helen, the heartbreaker, is my sister," Eve said as she gathered her plate for the return to the house.

Once in the kitchen, David took Eve into his arms. Looking deeply into her beautiful eyes, he said, "I love you, but I know that something very important existed between you and Brad. I also know that you were faithful to our love while he was here despite his very obvious display of affection for you. If you ever need to resolve questions about your feelings for him, let me know. I won't hold you. I don't want anything, not Bermuda or the States, or anyone to stand between us when we take our vows."

Her eyes filling with tears at his sweetness, Eve replied, "I love you. You're the most understanding person I've ever known."

Kissing her lightly, David said, "No, not understanding, selfish. When you're mine, I won't have anything or anyone in bed with us. I won't have you dreaming of another man or pining for your home country. When we take out vows, we'll make our own world. Nothing else will matter. Okay?"

"Sounds perfect to me," Eve said.

As they exited the little cottage, the warm breezes caressed their faces. Eve smiled at the Bermuda landscape that she loved so well and the man who made her heart sing. One day, she would embrace all that the island and David promised.

Linking arms, they started for Arty's house. He needed cheering up more than anyone either of them had ever known. Helping him would make Eve forget about the flight that carried one of the two men she loved far away from her. David, too, needed to take his mind off his own worries. He had read the expression on Brad's face whenever he was near Eve, and he knew that Brad still loved her. Brad had been a fool to let her go; David did not plan to follow in his footsteps. He would do everything in his power to keep Eve at his side. He did not intend to allow Eve to leave and take the sunshine with her. Yet, he knew that he did not want to join their lives until she was sure of her heart's wishes. He could not imagine life without her. She had reopened his island world with all of its possibilities and beauty. All he could do was to love her and wait.

Chapter Fifteen

As the months passed, David watched Eve become increasingly restless. Although she remained dedicated to her students, her mind often seemed far away. He especially noticed the change after the increasingly frequent conversations with her sister and friends in the States. Although Eve never complained, he knew that her homesickness had increased. David could sense that the constant summer breezes could not take the place of the fresh scent of early spring and the sound of blue jays quarreling in the trees. He worked extra hard to make her love of Bermuda carry her through the rough transition, but David feared that all of his efforts amounted to nothing.

Eve missed home. In the dead of winter, she had not missed the snowfall that crippled the city or the hills of dirty snow melting on the side of the road and in every parking lot. When Helen phoned to complain about the cost of the heating bill or the thickness of the ice on her car windshield, Eve only smiled and gazed out the window at the flowers in full bloom. When her mother whined that she had not been able to leave her house in over a week and that Eve's father was driving her crazy, she could only suggest that, perhaps, her parents should move to a warmer climate so that her dad could play golf every day. After those calls, Eve felt very smug about her decision to teach in Bermuda for the year.

Now that spring had pushed winter's cold down the Potomac River and summer was promising to appear at any moment, Eve missed seeing the cherry blossoms on the Mall and the forsythia in her parents' yard. She longed for the return of the birds that made the Washington, D.C., area home in the warm months and the sight of the flowering trees in full bloom. She missed the tinkling of the ice cream truck's bell and the squeals of the happy children as they tasted the first of the warm weather's traditions.

After Brad's calls, a feeling of loneliness immediately encompassed Eve. She missed their conversations more than she did the returning birds. He spoke of the plays he had seen, the patients he had treated, and the plans he would make if Eve would only return. He missed her and told her often. He loved her and began and ended every call by reminding her of his affection. Part of Eve wanted to believe that he had become more responsible, but part of him knew that he never would. Eve needed to see for herself if the transformations she had seen during his Christmas vacation visit to the islands were permanent.

At the same time, Eve wanted the calls to end. She loved David and hated being pulled from him. It was over with Brad, or should have been. She had left the past behind only for it to follow her into her present and play havoc with her happy future.

The school year dragged as it often did in the late spring. Despite the idyllic weather, the kids were ready for a break from the drudgery of textbooks and tests. Eve had grown tired of grading papers and preparing lesson plans and could use a break, too. The last week of June would not arrive soon enough.

David could feel the restlessness in his adult students also. Although they were older than Eve's high school kids, they had grown tired of attending classes and writing research papers. They longed to be outside in the sunshine, too. Now that David had learned to enjoy his island home more fully with Eve's help, he discovered that he longed for the outside activities that he had long abandoned. Teaching prevented him from enjoying the sun and surf during the week, leaving him with only the weekend and a few stolen moments in the evening for the pursuit of his hobbies. Summer break would not come soon enough for him either. He had decided not to teach during the summer months and envisioned lying on the sand with Eve at his side. Long, lazy afternoons sipping tea were a pleasant dream that would soon become a reality.

Eve had told him that she planned to return home for break but not about seeing Brad. Every time she tried to bring up the subject, something else would draw her attention away. The moment soon passed. Although she was aware of the need to tell David, Eve just had not found the time.

"Eve, have you made your reservations?" Helen asked during one of their phone conversations.

"Of course, I'm leaving here as soon as school ends for break. My flight lands at BWI at ten P.M. I'm almost packed. Nothing can stop me now."

"Do you realize that this is the longest we've been separated since your college freshman year? I can't wait until you come home," Helen breathed excitedly.

"Have you moved all of your extra stuff from my

bedroom?" Eve asked, knowing her sister's tendency to absorb every available space for her business activities.

"Uh, no, not yet, but I will. When I had an office in a firm, I didn't bring as much stuff home with me or have as many supplies to inventory. Now that I'm self-employed, I have to keep brochures, stationery, and everything else in stock. I'm afraid that I'm fighting the tendency to turn into another Arty," Helen said, groaning.

"Maybe we need a bigger condo," Eve suggested.

"There'll be plenty of time to discuss that later. If you decide to live in Bermuda permanently, which selfishly I hope you don't, I'll convert your room into an office. I'd rather have you here than have more space. For the time being, I've resorted to carefully labeled boxes that I can push under the bed. By the way, they're under yours, too," Helen confided, laughing.

"That's okay as long as I don't have to stumble over them." Eve chuckled. "Have you thought about opening an office here? Your Web site is very impressive and could serve as your introduction to the people here and in other countries."

Helen laughed. "Every day that I have to slop through the snow, clear ice from my windshield, or fight an overturned umbrella, I think about it."

"Well, why don't you?" Eve asked again.

After a lengthy pause, Helen replied, "Before meeting Arty, I would have said that I would buy a ticket for the next flight to Bermuda. Now I'm not so sure that I want to move there. I know that if I were to move, your relocation worries would be over, and we could convince Mom and Dad to join us. They talk about relocating almost daily as if they're trying to convince me to join you, but they don't mention their plans. You could marry David without any concern for continued isolation from us. But the island is small, and I'd run into Arty sooner or later."

"Would that be so awful? You know he'll never act like that again. He was just nervous," Eve counseled, ignoring the part about her marriage to David.

"I know, but it's more than that. I don't know if I want to be with a man who's as needy as Arty. That artistic temperament stuff might become tiring after a while."

"You liked it when you two were together. That's not what drove you away. His behavior at the exhibit did it."

"His behavior that night was simply an amplification of his needy tendency," Helen argued. "Arty needed to be made much of. He needed to be the center of attention rather than letting his art speak for him. He needed to be babied and pampered and didn't understand the importance of selling himself through his work."

"But he's learned," Eve replied, defending the devastated Arty. "You should see him. Despite working incredible hours to finish all the work that's coming his way, he's keeping his house and studio in pristine order. He's even weeding the flower beds you planted. He's a changed man."

"I don't know if I can bear to go through a relationship with him again," Helen said softly.

Eve could tell that Helen was crying by the sound in her voice. She knew that the breakup had been difficult for Helen even though she and Arty had been together for a very short time. Something had made them soul mates immediately. Perhaps she had fallen in love with him through his sensitive creations. Whatever the cause, both Helen and Arty had continued to mourn the loss of the relationship and both were pouring themselves into their work in search of consolation. Arty was producing incredible art, and Helen was making impressive amounts of money and gaining clients daily during the early stages of her self-employment when most people have to supplement from their savings. In fact, Helen was doing so well that she had told Eve not to send her half of the mortgage payment; she did not need the help.

Not wanting to inflict any more pain on her sister, Eve said gently, "Don't think about this anymore. We can talk about it when I come home or not at all. I know you'll do what's right. Don't beat yourself up about him."

"But there's a complication," Helen said, sniffing. "I still love him."

"I know, but you have to be true to yourself and your needs first."

"And to think that, when we were kids, I could hardly wait to be a grown-up. This love stuff sucks!" Helen complained with a tearful chuckle.

"Tell me about it."

Later that night, determined to broach the subject of summer break, Eve carefully prepared dinner and set the table. She decanted David's favorite wine and added cut flowers from the garden to the vase on the dining room table. After making sure that the house was perfectly clean and neat, Eve showered with a fragrant body scrub and dressed in a soft cotton dress that David had recently purchased for her. Adding a necklace of Arty's creation, she checked her reflection and decided that she looked especially fetching and presented the perfect image for the discussion of a potentially unpleasant topic.

They chatted gaily over steak, coleslaw, and French fries. David repeatedly complimented not only Eve's appearance but her cooking. Knowing that their customary dessert of ice cream would come later, they loaded the dishwasher and headed outside for a stroll on the beach.

"Summer break starts in a couple of days," Eve began.

"I can hardly wait. We'll have time alone before you sign a permanent contract and another school year begins," David exclaimed.

"David, I haven't made up my mind about that yet. I need to go home before I sign anything. I'm going home for a while before deciding on my contract issues," Eve said quickly, almost as if she had taken a deep breath and now exhaled all at once.

The lapping of the waves on the shore filled the silence between them. Eve could feel David's reaction from the sudden clamminess of his hand. However, he said nothing, only walked along the shore looking at the expanse of ocean.

Finally unable to stand the pregnant pause any longer, Eve said, "Do you want me to bring you back anything? Have you been able to find that CD that you wanted?"

Turning and placing his hands on her shoulders, David replied, "I want nothing except for you to come back to me. Not back to your teaching commitment, but to me."

"You know that I have to go, don't you? It's not that I don't love you, it's—" Eve tried to explain.

Silencing her with a kiss, David said, "I've known since Christmas that I wasn't the only man in your heart. I saw the way you and Brad looked at each other. I feared that, when he left, you would, too. You've been very considerate about the phone calls, but I've known that he phones you at least once a week. I've seen the pain and struggle on your face. I know that you love me, but you still love him, too. Do what you have to do. I'll be here when you return. But do me a favor and don't come back if you can't be with me a hundred percent. The school board will offer the contract to another person for the next school year. I'm being selfish, but I don't want to be another Arty. I don't want to live on the dream that you'll change your mind one day."

"Fair enough. I hope the school board will understand," Eve said, genuinely surprised that the conversation had gone so well and so terribly at the same time.

"The members are human, and they'll understand. I'm sure it happens all the time," David replied with profound sadness in his voice.

Reaching the end of their customary path, Eve and David turned and walked the distance back to the little cottage. It had always looked so inviting, but now it seemed small and lonely on the deserted beach. David watched silently as Eve unlocked the door. Pulling her into his arms one last time, he kissed her and then walked toward his bike. Both of them would sleep alone until Eve resolved her conflicts.

For the next two days, Eve's students were almost impossible to motivate. Their minds were on summer break and nothing else. Realizing the futility of engaging them in serious literature analysis, Eve decided to use the time for theatrical productions. Assigning them to groups and distributing scenes from famous plays, she gave them one day in which to prepare their scene and another in which to present it. To her delight, the physical activity gave the students a release for their energy and vacation anticipation. Surprisingly, watching them interpret and enact the scenes focused her attention on something other than the sadness of the divide that separated her from David.

Immediately after school closed, Eve caught a cab

to the airport. She had not heard from David since the night she told him of her plans for summer break, and she could not bring herself to phone him. Deciding that some things needed time and space, Eve spent lonely nights in the little cottage that no longer felt like home.

BWI Airport was packed as usual with people on the move. Eve had told Helen not to pick her up, preferring to take a cab home. It was an expensive decision but one that saved both sisters from the anxiety of not finding each other in the prearranged place. Flights and passengers were often delayed and luggage retrieval was even slower since the events of 9/11. Besides, Helen was so busy these days that she had little time to pick her up. Although she had told Brad of her plans, Eve did not expect to see him until the next day. His work schedule kept him tied to the hospital.

Eve had forgotten the craziness of traffic in the Washington-Baltimore corridor. However, the memory quickly returned as the cab squeezed between cars at the airport, often making its own lane, and zipped down Route 95 on the way to the condo she shared with her sister. Gripping the dirty upholstery, Eve prayed that she would survive the short trip aboard the speeding yellow cab.

Breathing a sigh of relief, Eve paid the driver and quickly vanished inside the lobby of the condo building. Now, instead of ocean and stars, she saw mailboxes and banks of elevators. Pressing the button that would take her to the eleventh floor, she rode up in silence. Smiling, she thought that the building still contained its familiar fragrance of trapped perfume, fragments of meals, and hurried people.

Eve only had to wait a few moments for Helen to throw open the door and pull her inside. The two sisters hugged happily as jazz played in the background. With Helen following, Eve walked through the condo lovingly looking at everything like one returning from a long absence, which she was. Throwing her bags onto the bed, Eve smiled; she was home.

"How was your flight? Are you hungry? How's David? Did he see you off?" Helen asked in rapid succession.

Eve laughed. "The flight was on time and the weather was clear. It was good. Of course, I'm hungry. They don't serve anything on flights except in first class, and I didn't pack a meal. I left from school and haven't eaten since lunch. David's okay, I guess. I haven't heard from him in two days. He says he understands, but it hurt his heart for me to confirm what he already knew about Brad."

"Speaking of Brad," Helen interjected, "he phoned thirty minutes ago to say that he won't be able to come over tonight; he's stuck at the hospital until late. He said that he'll pick you up early tomorrow . . . around nine."

Hiding her disappointment, Eve said, "That's fine. I'm tired and hungry and in need of a bath. After I grab something, I plan to take a shower and go to bed."

"Do you think we could talk a little first?" Helen asked, sounding like the little sister Eve remembered from college days.

"Sure. About what?" Eve asked as she hastily made a sandwich for each of them from the tuna salad Helen had prepared earlier.

"You know . . . Arty," Helen replied almost shyly.

"I saw him last night," Eve replied. "He came over with this."

Eve reached into the pocket of her jacket and extracted a carefully wrapped box. Handing it to Helen, she waited patiently for her sister to open it. Instead, Helen turned it over several times and placed the unopened box on the table.

"Aren't you going to open it?" Eve asked, puzzled by Helen's reaction.

"No. Not yet. I can tell from the size of the box that it's a ring," Helen replied as she nibbled her sandwich.

"You think it's an engagement ring?" Eve asked as she fingered the tape that sealed the delicate paper.

"His latest e-mail would lead me to believe that."

"Wow! I had no idea that Arty could be that direct or persistent."

"I told you that he phoned and e-mailed, too. He regularly calls on Sunday."

"You didn't say that marriage was his topic of discussion," Eve said.

"It isn't usually. He usually tells me about the contracts he's received. I think he's trying to impress me with his new sense of purpose and organization," Helen stated.

"And has he?" Eve asked, studying Helen's face.

"A little. Okay, more than a little," Helen confessed. "I'm overwhelmed with the amount of work he's put out lately. Even the gallery owner he insulted with his artistic temperament says that she's making money hand over fist selling his work. I sent you the newspaper reviews. He's the talk of the town."

"You still haven't opened the box," Eve reminded her.

"I know. I don't know how to react to Arty. He's gentle, kind, sweet, and loving, but he's also a brat, a pain, irritable, rude, sullen, and unpredictable. Do I need to add more?" Helen sighed.

"Only that you still love him."

"Yes, I don't know why, but I do. First impression

through his art was incredible. Meeting him was a delight. He has sparked my attention and awakened my heart in a way that no man ever has. Yes, I love him, but is that enough?"

"You're asking me? I'm the girl who left a perfectly wonderful man, who I love, on a paradise island to return to the congestion and hurry of the States to be with a man who is less than perfect but whom I might still love. I don't think that I'm the right person to ask."

Helen groaned. "What a pair we are! Our parents are so normal. How did we turn out like this?"

Waxing philosophical, Eve replied, "I think we're the product of too many romantic television programs and movies in which the people meet and live happily ever after with little or no conflict in their lives. The biggest problem in their relationship is usually which pair of shoes to wear for the first date and sexual compatibility. Life is more than that."

"Maybe you're right," Helen agreed. "I certainly lived off those shows. I never expected to fall for Arty; he's just not my type. I'm the stockbroker/investment banker/neurosurgeon type of girl. I've never been attracted to an artist. When I fell in love with Arty's work, I never thought that I'd meet the man and love him immediately. I thought I'd react like most lovesick women and swoon at the sight of the man with such tender, creative insights, have a good time with him, and then leave, taking with me great memories of even better sex. I never in my wildest dreams thought that I'd want to pig out on chocolate because I'm miserably unhappy over loving an artist."

Pointing to the gift from Arty, Eve said, "Open the box."

"I can't," Helen replied, pushing the box toward her sister. "You open it, and don't let me see it."

As Helen watched, Eve slowly lifted the lid of the tiny carefully wrapped box. Inside nestled on a pillow of black velvet sat a huge diamond surrounded by colored precious gems of infinite beauty. The style was pure Arty.

"Well?" Helen asked impatiently.

"It's stunning. It's the most beautiful ring I've ever seen," Eve gushed.

"Do you think it's an engagement ring or is it one of his jewelry creations?" Helen asked, trying to peer into the box.

"It could be either, but, from the size and nature of the center stone, I'd say that this ring is Arty's way of asking you to marry him," Eve replied, not showing the ring to Helen.

"How can you be sure? Is there a note?" Helen asked without moving even a fraction of an inch in her chair.

Lifting the ring from the holder, Eve carefully extracted the thin piece of paper attached to the narrow portion of the band. Without opening it, she handed the sliver to Helen, who jumped back as if burned. Holding up both hands, Helen made it clear that she did not intend to touch it.

Opening the sliver carefully so as not to tear it, Eve unfolded a note in Arty's familiar scrawl. Without glancing at Helen's immobile face, she read, "Marry me. I can't live without you any longer."

Helen's eyes filled with tears that quickly began to flow down her cheeks. Covering her face with her hands, she sobbed, "I can't take this stress. He's not the right man for me, but I love him so much."

Immediately, Eve threw her arms around her baby sister. She hated to see Helen cry. Memories of their childhood bumps and bruises ran through Eve's mind as she cradled Helen against her breast. She had always tried to shelter her sister from hurt, but this was one time that Helen had to bear the pain alone. Eve knew that, until Helen came to terms with the discrepancy between her expectations for herself and her reality, her sister would not be able to embrace the love that pulled at her heart.

Knowing her own confusion, Eve could think of nothing wise or comforting to say. She had left behind the man she loved and a solid future as a professor's wife to follow old memories. Considering the turmoil in her life, she could think of nothing to help Helen.

"This is silly," Helen said as she pulled herself together. "I can't cry every time I think of Arty."

"What about the ring?" Eve asked, offering the box.

Taking it gingerly as if it contained a poisonous snake rather than a ring from her lover, Helen said, "I'll wear it to keep it safe. I certainly can't leave it here while I'm away."

Eve watched as Helen slipped the stunning creation onto the third finger of her left hand. It fit perfectly as if Arty had recently measured her finger. Although the ring looked large and overwhelming in the box, once on Helen's long, tapered fingers, it wrapped around her knuckle and complemented her hand perfectly.

"I guess I should call Arty," Helen said as she walked toward her bedroom.

"He said that he'd phone you at eleven," Eve stated, watching Helen blink back more tears.

"That's only three minutes!" Helen said in a new panic. "I look terrible. I have to do something with my face. My eyes are puffy and bloodshot."

Thinking that her sister had snapped, Eve advised softly and slowly, "Helen, he won't see you. You don't have a video phone."

Briefly turning to Eve, Helen replied, "I know you think I've gone mad, but I haven't. I know he can't see me, but I'll feel more confident if I don't look as if I've been crying for hours."

Eve watched as Helen darted into the bathroom for something to clear her eyes and then headed into her bedroom, closing the door behind her. As the grand-father clock in the hall chimed eleven, she heard the phone ring and Helen pick up on the first ring. After that, she heard only a muffled voice and sniffling.

"I hope I'm not that pathetic," Eve muttered as she cleaned up the dishes, grabbed her bag, and headed to her room. The second shower of the day would wait. She was too tired to care.

Sliding between the fresh sheets, Eve thought about the bed she had left behind. She had become accus-tomed to the sounds of the little cottage at night and wondered if she would be able to sleep. If she listened carefully, Eve could hear the sound of traffic on the street below and the opening and closing of condo doors.

Eve had thought of phoning David since she knew that David would not call her. Looking at the idle phone, she decided that she would not make the first gesture until she had something definitive to say. She had seen the heartbreak on his face and did not need to hear it in his voice, too.

As she relaxed and started to fall asleep, Eve re-membered that she would see Brad the next morning. Not seeing him that night had been a disappointment, but she had survived. With luck, the pieces of her ro-mantic puzzle would begin to come together as soon as she saw him. One way or the other, this trip had to give her the answers she needed

Chapter Sixteen

The next morning Eve was up early. Surprisingly, she had slept soundly despite the feeling of anticipation that made her stomach flutter every time she thought of Brad. Being in her own home in her own bed was so comforting that she could put aside all thoughts of Brad and David and rest without trouble.

Now, however, as the grandfather clock struck nine o'clock, her stomach did a back flip. She had not seen him since his Christmas vacation in Bermuda although he phoned or e-mailed regularly. As the excitement built, Eve reminded herself that she should be angry with him for not arranging his schedule so that they might spend some time together on the night of her return to the States. She would have gone the extra mile for him simply because she wanted to see him. However, Eve sighed with the realization that some men were different when it came to relationships, and Brad was one of them. David, however, never would have kept her waiting without phoning to explain the delay.

Eve knew that she was unfairly judging Brad by

constantly comparing him to David, but she could not break the habit. They both occupied spots in her heart, making it difficult to separate their actions. Eve found that she regularly weighed the actions of one against those of the other. Often, Brad fell short of David's standards. However, she still thought she loved him, making the trip home very necessary.

Hearing Helen closing drawers in her room, Eve decide to check on her while she waited for Brad to arrive. He was already a few minutes late, but she knew he would appear shortly. She looked forward to seeing him so much that she overlooked his irritating habit of being late. One time he had kept her waiting without a call for over two hours. She was starving by the time they arrived at the restaurant for which they had originally had reservations. Without them, they had to wait over an hour to be seated. By the time their order arrived, Eve was so hungry that she could have eaten the menu.

"Helen, are you up?" Eve asked at the door.

"Up and dressed. I'll be right there," Helen replied.

"What did Arty have to say last night?" Eve shouted through a crack in the door.

Opening the door, Helen mused, "Was it last night? We only ended the call an hour ago."

"What? You were on the phone the entire night?" Eve asked incredulously.

"Yup," Helen said as she dragged herself to the kitchen.

Eve followed her. "I've already made coffee."

"Good. I hope it's strong. I need strong coffee this morning if I'm to get any work done," Helen stated, pouring a cup

"Tell me about the conversation," Eve urged, sitting at the table opposite her sister.

"Why are you still here?" Helen asked sleepily. "I thought Brad would have swished you away by now."

"I did, too, but you know Brad. Time is definitely not his friend," Eve replied with a limp smile in an effort to appear unaffected by Brad's tardiness.

"I bet David wouldn't keep you waiting like this. Even Arty has a better sense of time than Brad, and Arty's the artistic forgetful type," Helen mused, sipping the hot brew.

"Let's not talk about either Brad or David right now. Tell me about Arty's call," Eve insisted. As the minutes ticked away, she needed something to take her mind off the tardy Brad.

"This is an engagement ring." Helen pointed to the ornament on her left hand. "He must have asked me one hundred times to marry him over the course of our marathon conversation. He apologized repeatedly for his childish behavior, his insensitivity, and his rudeness. Although we've had this conversation many times, he blamed his insecurities as the cause. He talked about the love he feels for me, the wonderful life we could have together, and the success he would be with me at his side."

"That's soo sweet!" Eve gushed.

"Anyway," Helen continued after stifling a yawn, "I reminded Arty that he's quite a success now without me, to which he replied that he was working to give himself purpose . . . something he doesn't have without me. With me, he's constantly inspired. It sounded corny, but I think he meant it. We were both crying most of the time."

"So? What will you do?" Eve asked, tossing more sugar into the strong coffee.

"I don't know yet," Helen replied, pouring another

cup of black coffee. "If you stay here to marry Brad, I don't want to live in Bermuda without you and our parents. I'd be in the same situation that you've been in this year. Being with the man I love but missing family and home just doesn't do it for me."

Eve stared at her sister's tormented face. "You wouldn't turn down Arty's proposal if I married Brad, would you?"

"Not if he'd move here. If he wouldn't, we'd be at odds just as you and David are."

"It wouldn't be exactly the same. I have the inconvenient obstacle of old memories of a tardy lover, making my decision to marry David and remain on the island even more complicated," Eve retorted, irritated at Brad for being so late.

"Arty's willing to give me time to think. He wants to live in Bermuda but would live here if necessary. He said last night that he'll live wherever I am," Helen stated with a tired little smile.

"David said the same thing even though it would mean starting over at a new university for him," Eve said.

"I think we have two wonderful men," Helen said through a yawn.

"You have one; I have two. Brad's a neat guy, too, don't forget."

"Brad's an hour late. I don't think that this particular leopard has changed his spots. Has he offered to practice medicine in Bermuda so that you could stay on the island that you love?"

"No, but that's not really an issue. If I were to marry Brad, I'd gladly give up the island for a life together. I'd teach here again."

"And you'd fight the snowdrifts and the bone-chilling cold again?"

"The weather in Bermuda is perfect. It would be difficult to leave a paradise, but I would. I'll do it just to be closer to you and our folks because I missed you so much. I don't see the difference in doing it for Brad."

"If you married David and I married Arty, you wouldn't have to leave the island. I think Mom and Dad would relocate to be with us. They're pretty tired of the winters here," Helen said, rising unsteadily.

"Yes, but they'd do it reluctantly. They love it here. Anyway, the issue of marriage and husbands is the topic I plan to resolve if I ever see the late Brad Wilson," Eve said as the doorbell sounded.

"Saved by the bell," Helen declared and returned to her room. "I'll give you two some privacy."

"Sorry I'm late. I just could not get out of bed this morning," Brad said as Eve opened the door. Pulling her into his arms, he added, "It's so good having you back home where you belong."

"I see that having me here made you hurry over last night and this morning," Eve replied sarcastically as she continued to resist his charm. "It doesn't look to me as if anything's changed. You were always late for every date."

"That's true, but we always have fun once I arrive." Brad chuckled as a smile that could melt the sternest disciplinarian spread across his handsome face.

"What's on the agenda today?" Eve asked as her resolve faded under the force of his charm.

Beaming like a little boy offering a handmade gift, Brad replied, "I know how much you like flowers, so we'll head to the botanical gardens. There's a good exhibit at the National Art Gallery, too. That should take up most of the day. If there's time, I thought we could go boating at Great Falls . . . either rafting or canoeing. We'll have an early dinner since I have to work tomorrow. I think that's about it."

"I don't understand it. Why didn't you take off this week so that we could spend leisurely time together? You knew I was coming home. Couldn't someone have covered for you?" Eve asked angrily as the impact of Brad's charm faded.

"I didn't ask. I didn't want to use up all of my leave. We'll need it for the honeymoon," Brad stated as they stepped from the elevator into the lobby.

Snapping between closed teeth to keep her voice down, Eve said, "I thought you understood the nature of my visit. There won't be a honeymoon with you unless you show that you've made considerable changes to your lifestyle."

Pulling her into his arms as they stood on the sidewalk, Brad said formally, "The simple fact that you're here signals your intention to consider accepting my repeated proposals of marriage. Even if you can't see it from my tardy arrival, I've changed. I'm much more responsible although the same fun-loving guy."

Smiling despite her irritation, Eve said, "The jury's still out on that one. It might be in your best interest not to assume that you're the chosen one. David's a formidable opponent. By the way, when did you take up rafting? You didn't exactly look like a water baby in Bermuda."

"I decided that rafting was safer than bungee jumping. Once I gave it up, I needed something to take its place," Brad joked and then added, "A friend took me white-water rafting, and I loved it. I like the thrill of shooting the rapids. It's not swimming, something I don't do especially well. I'm happy in the boat with my little life vest and helmet. I enjoy watching the scenery and fighting the force of the water."

"I'm not surprised that you'd like the challenge of the sport, but I am surprised that you'd choose a water sport. It's not just your lack of swimming skill either. I didn't think you enjoyed being on or near deep water."

"A guy's got to have fun. Besides, this is a river sport. I'm okay as long as I'm not on the bay or the ocean. If we rent a boat today, we'll stay away from the swift currents. As a matter of fact, I think we'll simply go for a leisurely paddle. Anyway, you're the last one to question my interest in water sports. I remember that you had a near-death experience that overshadows any of my pranks," Brad said, feeling Eve draw back at the thought of engaging in a hair-raising activity.

"That boating accident was not my idea of fun. David and I could have drowned. I definitely didn't go out looking for something dangerous to do with my afternoon. The storm came up, and we got sucked into it," Eve explained.

"Didn't you find the experience in the least exhilarating?"

"No. It was the worst horror that I've ever experienced. Having David go under and not come up tore out my heart. Having to leave the area in which he disappeared caused me incredible pain, but I had no choice. I had waited as long as I could, and the boat was taking in water. When he never grabbed the tow line, I knew I'd lost him."

"Well, don't worry about our trip on the Potomac. Nothing frightening will happen. We'll take it nice and slow," Brad said, choosing to ignore the sound of affection that colored Eve's voice every time she said David's name and the way she connected her feelings with his existence.

Eve's annoyance at Brad's tardiness and lack of consideration did not lessen as they turned the car toward the downtown section of D.C. The congestion on the Maryland roads on the way into the city only added to

Eve's annoyance. She wondered what could have made her leave the island and David for Washington traffic and a man who would not even take time off to be with her. She did not accept the honeymoon excuse. Knowing Brad as she did, Eve suspected that he simply did not anticipate the need to be available during her week at home. He had probably reasoned that she would be happy with whatever time he offered. David would not have entertained that thought. He always put Eve's feelings before his own.

Looking at Brad's profile as he navigated the crush of cars, Eve could feel her resistance weakening and her irritation lessening. Brad was handsome and so much fun to be with despite his irresponsible behavior about relationship issues. He was a wonderful physician who was gaining local celebrity for his caring and professionalism. The traits he lacked in relationship management, he had in triplicate in his profession.

Waiting for him one day in the emergency room's anteroom, Eve had observed David in action with young children. He was a natural at making them relax. They would settle down as soon as he spoke to them. As a result, he had entered a pediatric field that treated critically and sometimes fatally ill children. Eve had known from the first that he would be a star, and he was.

"Let's go," Brad said as he parked the car. "This trip's for you, but I'd like to be able to spend a little time on the river, if possible."

"Okay, we'll see the exhibit and then leave. I'd enjoy a trip down the Potomac, too."

"It's larger than I remember from our last trip here," Brad commented as the overhead sprinkler misted the flowers and them.

"Yes, but the blooms just aren't as pretty as the ones

on the island," Eve said. "I guess the greenhouse environment can't compete with nature."

"Look, we haven't begun to see the exhibits. I vote for getting out of here and heading to Great Falls. The water's calling us," Brad stated, looking at yet another specimen moth orchid.

"Let's go," Eve agreed as they quickly found the door and escaped into the sunshine.

Although the season for boating on the Potomac would not officially open for weeks with the traditional regattas, people already dotted the river. The hot summer weather and clear sky had brought them out in force. Finally finding a parking space, Brad and Eve joined them.

"This is wonderful," Eve said as Brad paddled the boat away from the pier.

"The best," Brad replied. "And this time I don't have to swim out to a rock in the ocean."

"You really didn't like that, did you? It's just something we do. I guess it just comes naturally after living there for a while. All water games and activities just seem to fit our lifestyle," Eve said with a smile.

"Gina liked it, but it wasn't for me. I'm not a secure swimmer," Brad said, tightening his life vest.

"Now that you've mentioned Gina, what happened to your relationship with her? You said that you'd explain when we were together again," Eve said as she trailed her fingers in the water.

Speaking earnestly, Brad said, "Gina knew as soon as she saw us together on the islands that I still loved you. She said that she suspected it even before our vacation because I talk about you all the time; however, seeing us together confirmed it. Anyway, she ended the relationship, saying that we could get together again if

I ever got you out of my heart. Since that's not possible, I wished her a happy life."

"Did she say anything about David?" Eve inquired.

"Not much. She just said that he's formidable competition and that, if I really wanted to win, I'd have to show you that I can be better than he is in every way," Brad replied with a slow smile.

Joking, Eve asked, "Does that mean punctuality, too?"

Brad laughed. "Fortunately not. I guess you'll just have to face the reality that I have no sense of time. I spend too much time on each appointment, or so the nursing staff tells me. I'm always behind schedule."

"If the nurses don't mind, I think that your desire to spend time with a patient rather than punching a clock is a praiseworthy aspect of your personality," Eve said with a smile.

"Ah, so it's just keeping you waiting that's the negative. I'll remember that." Brad chuckled.

They spent the rest of the afternoon floating on the Potomac. Occasionally, Brad would reach for her hand, but, usually, he simply paddled the boat, told jokes, and sang. Eve did not mind the corny jokes, but she could not wait until he exhausted his repertoire of songs and stopped the off-key singing. Brad avoided boulders and logs skillfully, steering a course to an area in which the park service had set up a concession stand on the shore. Hitching the boat to the post, he led Eve to a table while he purchased sodas and hot dogs. Smiling as she watched him go about the simple task of purchasing food, Eve decided that she was happy with Brad. The picnic table was not a corner table in her favorite Bermudian restaurant and the cuisine was not five stars, but the company was definitely worth doing battle with the marauding ants.

"Do you come here often?" Eve asked, enjoying the beauty of the river.

"Not as often as I'd like. It's so tranquil here," Brad replied.

"The lazy river reminds me of Bermuda's tranquillity," Eve commented. "It's hard to imagine that the bustle of D.C.'s traffic is only a few miles from here."

"This is our little bit of paradise," Brad said, leaning forward and kissing Eve gently.

"I guess that's what makes it so special," Eve said with a smile.

The currents were stiffer on the return trip, and Eve had to help paddle the boat. After the long days of sailing in Bermuda, she found boating on the Potomac to be an easy task. Even the late afternoon currents could not compare to the fury of the Atlantic Ocean and its bays.

On the drive home, Eve and Brad chatted more like old friends than lovers. She wished that they could have spent more time together but she had to settle for Brad's promise to phone. Unfortunately, they would not be able to see each other for two days during which Eve planned to visit her parents and friends from her former teaching assignment. As unfortunate as Brad's absence would be, it gave her time to herself to think.

"What'll you do while I'm at work?" Brad asked as he walked her to her door with his arm securely around her waist.

Kissing him lightly on the cheek, Eve replied, "I have more than enough to keep me busy, thank you. Remember, I haven't gone shopping since June, because everything's too expensive on the island. I might just take Helen with me and shop until we drop."

"Good thing you're not Helen." Brad laughed. "I

don't think she could go a week without shopping. Months would be too much for her."

"If she decides to move to Bermuda, she'll have to give up that pastime. Clothing is too expensive there," Eve said, unlocking the door and walking into the quiet apartment.

"Move to Bermuda? Why would she want to do that?" Brad asked as he flopped onto the sofa with his customary familiarity.

"There's more to Bermuda than pink sand beaches," Eve said, sitting next to him.

"You mean that Helen's fallen in love with one of your new friends?"

"Actually, he's David's friend Arty. She's in love with his art and with him."

"Do you think she'll marry him and move there? Not having you here has been a real downer for her. Do you think she'd live on the islands without you?"

"If she loves him enough and if it's not feasible for him to move here she would. Besides, you're making the assumption that our marriage is a done deal. I'm still deciding between you and David."

After a long pause in the conversation, Brad said, "I need you and I love you. We're a unit. Your teaching assignment in the islands is only a temporary intrusion in our lives. We'll weather this and come out stronger for it."

"You forget that we had broken off our love relationship and returned to being friends before I left. That's one of the reasons that I accepted the assignment. I never would have left you alone if we'd still been dating," Eve explained.

"I haven't forgotten anything," Brad replied softly. "I remember everything that ever happened between us. I remember the wonderful times we shared, the arguments over my reckless behavior, and the incredible silences that we didn't need to fill with words. I know that we had changed course before you left, but that was only a blip on our radar. Even before you ended our relationship, I had planned to launch a campaign to change your mind about me by showing you that I could change my ways and make a good husband. It would have been successful, too. I have changed, maybe not everything, but I'm not as wild as I used to be. I know that a lot rides on this week. Just give me a chance, and I'll show you the new me."

"That won't be easy with you working twelve-plus-hour shifts," Eve stated bluntly.

"That was a tactical error that I intend to rectify. After tonight, we'll be inseparable. I'll ask one of my buddies to cover for me," Brad replied with confidence.

Eve laughed. "I suppose I can wait that long,"

"I promise that I'll make it up to you. I know I have a long way to go, especially after this mistake," Brad said, kissing Eve gently.

"You're doing okay so far."

"I can't promise that I'll call, but, if I get the chance, I'll phone between patients," Brad said as he kissed Eve good night.

She watched as he drove away. He was a good man. If she had not met David, Eve would have found the changes in Brad remarkable. Although he still had work to do, Eve could see that Brad had tried to improve himself. Because of that, she was determined to give the visit a chance. She had to know which man really held the key to her heart. Until she was sure, she could not consider a future with either of them.

"How was your day with Brad?" Helen asked, appearing from her bedroom.

"Good. It's been a while since we've been together

without either Gina or David. It was nice being with him again," Eve replied, tossing her bag onto the sofa.

"You sound as if you're discussing the reunion of two old friends rather than lovers," Helen said.

"Maybe that's what we are. I don't know. It's very confusing. That's what I came home to learn, but it's not happening the way I thought. I can't stop comparing David and Brad. I know that's not fair, but I can't help it. I'll never be able to make up my mind if I can't see Brad as an individual rather than a shadow of David," Eve replied.

"Do you ever wonder about David in the same way that you do about Brad?"

"No, he's my rock. He's made my relocation to the islands a wonderful experience. He fills my life with warmth. I never question David's love for me," Eve said honestly.

"So who exactly are you testing?" Helen asked.

Without hesitation, Eve replied, "Myself. I have doubts about my total and complete devotion to David. I can't marry him until I know for sure. I still feel more than simply friendship for Brad."

Shaking her head, Helen said, "Well, at least one of us knows who to question. I blame Arty for behaving the way he did, but I know that he couldn't help it. He was nervous and scared. He couldn't control his behavior at the show. Instead of doubting his affection, I should question my devotion to him for wanting to change him into someone that he isn't. I loved him from afar for being different but tried to change him as soon as I met him. That's messed up. I need to turn the mirror on myself. I'm trying, but it's not an easy task."

Hugging her sister, Eve commented, "I don't think we're the only women who can see the flaws in our men rather than in ourselves. I think that shipwreck made me appreciate David in a way that I wouldn't have if it hadn't happened. Being that close to losing someone special is a real eye-opener. I suppose that's one of the reasons that I want to make sure that I love him unconditionally. I don't want to put him through any unnecessary heartache. The other part of the equation is that I'll have to leave you, Mom, and Dad here if I marry David. That's a lot to give up."

With sadness in her tired eyes, Helen said, "Your reality could become mine, too, if I decide to marry Arty. He says that he'll move here, but what'll happen to his art if he does? His environment and his love of the island shout from every piece. I don't know if I can allow him to make that sacrifice for me."

"Regardless of what course of action we follow, we can't solve all the problems of our lives immediately. That'll take a little time. I'm hungry. Have you eaten?" Eve asked with a sigh.

"No. Let's go out for a pizza. I need to get away from here for a while. Arty said that he won't phone again. The next one's on me. I've been so close to picking up the phone so many times. I really don't know what I'd say. I just want to hear his voice. Let's get out of here before I do something that I might regret. I don't want the responsibility for two lives on my shoulders," Helen said.

"What would you say if you called him?" Eve asked, collecting her purse.

"I don't know. I'm not ready to accept his proposal, and I don't want to turn him down either. I told you that my life's a mess right now," Helen stated as an air of dejection settled on her shoulders.

"Well, at least you didn't have to work today. That's the advantage of being your own boss," Eve said as she locked the door.

Yawning, Helen said, "I guess that's one small advantage. I can't even think straight. There's no way that I'd be able to work."

The sisters walked the short distance to their favorite pizza place. Slipping into their regular table, they ordered their customary pizza with salad. Engulfed in a silence that neither felt the need to fill, they reflected on their dilemmas. One day they would work out a solution to their problems but not immediately. For the moment, the solution was beyond their grasp.

Chapter Seventeen

True to his word, Brad appeared at their door the next day. He looked tired from working more than a twelve-hour shift, but his smiling eyes glistened at the sight of Eve as she opened the door. He had kept his promise and hoped that she would see the change in him.

"Here I am," he announced, handing Eve a beautiful bouquet of flowers and a bag of chocolate-covered raisins. The top of the bag was heavily crumpled as a child's gift would have been. Eve was moved by the simplicity of his attention.

"What do you want to do today? There are some really good movies in the theaters these days if you're interested," Brad suggested as he slumped into the sofa. Fatigue had carved deep lines in his handsome face.

"Great! I'll make us something to eat and then we can go. It's your pick," Eve replied, but too late.

Brad's eyes had closed and a soft snore escaped his lips. The long, hard hours proved too much for him. Smiling, Eve covered him with the light afghan that decorated the back of the sofa. She knew from experience that he would awaken refreshed after a few hours of sleep. In the meantime, she would occupy herself with phone calls to her friends. Now that she was home, Eve wanted to share her photos and get caught up as soon as possible.

Stretching, Helen emerged from her room in cutoff jeans and a T-shirt. She looked somewhat refreshed by the long rest, although the lines still lingered at the corners of her mouth. Anyone seeing her would have realized that she was not a happy woman.

"He came straight here from the hospital," Eve said, with a nod toward Brad who was sleeping soundly.

"Just like the old days. I'm glad I didn't give away that afghan," Helen said, walking toward the kitchen. "What time is it? I got up, showered, and dressed early, but fell asleep again. I only got up because I heard voices out here."

"You needed the rest after yesterday's marathon call from Arty. It's almost noon," Eve replied as she made omelets for both of them.

"I hate to sleep away my weekend. I have so little time to myself these days. No one told me that I'd work longer hours as a self-employed person than I did as a corporate slave."

"Sometimes that happens, but at least your time belongs to you and you don't have to punch a clock."

The phone rang as soon as Eve set the plates on the table. She had almost decided not to answer it when she read the caller ID. Eyes wide, she pressed the button and waited as the familiar voice caused goose bumps to appear on her arms.

"I said that I wouldn't phone, but I couldn't help myself. I miss you," David stated simply.

"I'm glad you called. I miss you, too, but I'm really glad to be home," Eve replied.

"I have some news to share with you, if you have time," David said almost shyly.

"I'm all ears," Eve said, taking a peek at the sleeping Brad and her cooling omelet. The sound of David's voice had pushed aside the hunger pangs.

Slowly, David said, "I've been offered a tenure-track position at Georgetown University. The pay's much better than what I'm making here, and, of course, the university carries more prestige. I don't have to let them know my decision immediately, but it would mean that we'd live in the States. You wouldn't have to leave your family."

"That's great! Wonderful even, but you'd have to leave your island home. It's still not a perfect solution," Eve replied, as Helen watched with her fork in midair.

"That doesn't matter," David said. "I discovered that my home is wherever you are. I don't care where we live as long as we're together."

Eve couldn't speak for the hard knot in her throat. David was willing to leave his home for her. No one had ever loved her that much, not even the sleeping Brad.

"Did you hear what I said, Eve?" David asked when the silence lengthened.

"I heard. I just don't know what to say," Eve said softly. The tears behind her lids would not allow her to say more.

"Say you'll marry me, and I'll tell the university that I'll be there at the end of the week to sign the contract," David responded with hope in his voice.

"I need time to think about this," Eve replied thickly. "There are so many complications. I had thought that to have you I'd have to abandon my homeland and leave my family. Now you're giving me an incredible gift that should solve some of my problems, but it doesn't. There's still Brad, but, even more, I feel guilty that you've had to do this. You're well established in your career. If I hadn't taken that teaching job, you would never have thought about leaving. I don't know if I can let you do that for me."

"Before you came to this island, my life was, at best, flat," David stated without hesitation. "As soon as I met you, you added excitement to my little world. Yes, I was content to live here for the rest of my life, like my parents, who returned from the States dissatisfied with life there, and my grandparents, but I'm not anymore. You've given me a world that I never knew existed. I love you and want to live with you wherever we can find happiness."

"You'll have to give me time to think about this. I can't commit to anything until I sort through the layers of confusion," Eve said, sniffling.

"That's fine. I just wanted you to know about the teaching offer. Keep in mind that this is a great opportunity for me as well as a solution to your relocation problem. I'll phone again in a week or two."

"Are you terribly disappointed that your sacrifice didn't solve my problem?" Eve asked, wiping the tears from her cheeks.

"No, not really. At least you didn't turn me down. I know from your reaction that Brad hasn't worked his magic on you, and that I still have a chance. I was almost afraid that the university's offer had come too late. I know now that you're still my girl," David replied with a smile in his voice.

"Oh, David, what have I done to deserve you?" Eve asked softly as a tearful Helen looked on.

"You've opened my life to a world of happiness and love. It's I who don't deserve you. Take care of yourself. I love you."

Eve covered her face and cried as she had not since she feared that she had lost David in the storm. She was angry with herself for not being able to accept his proposal. He was a wonderful man and would make an ideal husband. He had made the ultimate sacrifice of taking steps to leave his homeland for her without her having to ask him. He loved her that much.

"What's the matter?" Brad demanded sleepily from the sofa. "Has someone died?"

"No, nothing's wrong. I'm just tired. Give me a minute to wash my face," Eve replied as she rushed from the room.

"Will someone tell me what happened? Are your parents okay?" Brad inquired again.

"Everyone's just fine." Helen sniffled, wiping tears from her eyes.

"Then, why are you two sobbing like this?" a totally bewildered Brad asked.

"David called," Helen said.

"That son of a . . . He's not playing fair. This is my time with Eve," Brad said, jumping to his feet. At the mention of his competition's name, he was completely awake.

"You phoned Eve while she was on the island with him. He's not doing anything that you didn't do," Helen said, defending David.

Brad sulked. "My case is different. I'm the underdog."

"Eve's on your home turf with you at her side. I don't understand in what way this isn't an even fight," Helen stated.

"It's hard enough to fight the summer breezes, sun,

sea, and sand of Bermuda; she doesn't need to hear from him now. I only have myself and summer humidity to offer," Brad argued.

"As a totally impartial observer, let me remind you that you have years of fond memories on your side," Helen suggested firmly.

"Yeah, and years of being a jerk, too," Brad complained.

"And whose fault was that? You had every opportunity to mend your ways," Helen stated, covering Eve's untouched plate with plastic and storing it in the refrigerator.

"I thought you were impartial," Brad said angrily.

"I am," Helen said. "I've pointed out the negatives of both relationships to Eve. I'm just trying to show you that you're on even ground with David. He's not really your competition. Your behavior is what got you into this 'underdog' situation. Remember that. I'm going to check on Eve."

"I always knew that having a little sister around would eventually cause trouble," Brad said with a crooked smile. "I'm going home. Tell her that I'll call later about going to a movie and dinner. I don't think this is the best time for me to be here. Besides, I'm so tired I can't keep my eyes open."

"Good idea," Helen agreed without hesitation.

"Do you think I have a chance with Eve?" Brad asked at the door. "I've loved her for a long time and don't want to mess it up again."

Kissing Brad lightly on the cheek, Helen replied, "I told you that I'm impartial. I can't say one way or the other. The only thing I can suggest is that you need to make sure that Eve understands that you love her more than you do yourself, and the idea of making a life together more than you love even her. She has to know that you're with her every inch of the way and then some."

"Thanks, Helen." Brad smiled. "I guess little sisters aren't really all that bad after all."

As Brad walked slowly toward the elevator, Helen closed the door. Brad, David, and Arty. One thing for certain with those three men adding complications to their lives, the sisters were never bored. Rounding the corner to check on Eve, Helen sighed with the realization that she and her sister would eventually resolve the dilemma. At this moment, however, she did not know exactly how it would end.

Later, after collecting her emotions, Eve headed to her parents' home for a visit. She always enjoyed returning to the house in which she grew up. She knew that her unresolved issues would still exist when she left, but, for a few minutes, her parents would make her feel like a beloved, pampered child again. Somehow, her issues seemed more manageable after being with them for a while.

Eve's mother had been watching from the front window and threw the door open as soon as her daughter started up the walk. Pulling Eve into her arms, Mrs. Turner stood on her tiptoes to kiss her daughter's cheek. Eve towered over her mother, who appeared to have shrunk in the months that Eve had been away. Her father, too, looked shorter but no less strong as he hugged her tightly.

Leaving her troubles at the front door, Eve followed them into the kitchen that had been her favorite room since she was a little girl. As always, her mother had a freshly baked cake and recently brewed coffee waiting for her. Sitting in the offered chair with her back to the door, Eve breathed deeply for the first time since she had realized that she loved two men.

"You look great although your eyes are a bit red," her mother stated after carefully examining every aspect of her face and body.

"I think she looks tired," her father said, "almost as if she's been staying up too long and not getting enough sleep."

"I'm sleeping fine, Daddy, at least on the island," Eve replied with a big smile, "but I'm having trouble getting used to the sounds of the city again. Sirens and traffic are not as tranquil as the sound of the sea lapping against the shore."

"How's David?" her mother asked with a knowing smile.

"He's fine. As a matter of fact, he phoned to tell me that he's been offered a professorship here," Eve said.

"That's nice, dear," her mother commented warmly. "Both of you could live here. Bermuda's so far away."

Interrupting, her father stated, "I told you, Sara, that it's only a short flight from here. It's a great place to live as a retiree."

Turning to Eve, her mother said, "Your father's been making those not too subtle comments since you sent the first pictures from there. He might like the constant summer breezes and the golf, but I like the seasons."

"You'd love it," Eve said without flourish. "The people are warm and welcoming, the kids are great students, and the weather is perfect. Daddy could golf every day, and you could garden to your heart's content. It's a terrific place to live."

"You like being locked in here all winter?" her father demanded, scowling at his wife.

"No, but this winter was especially bad," Mrs. Turner said. "You know that we don't usually have any trouble with cabin fever. I still like seeing the seasons. I'd miss that on a tropical island."

Turning to Eve, her father said, "Because of my love for this woman, I have to give up a chance to live in paradise on earth."

"From the way you carry on, you'd think that moving to Bermuda would be your only chance for an idyllic life. There's still the afterlife," her mother explained.

"How can a man argue with this?" her father stated as he lifted his hands in defeat.

Seeing her father roll his eyes in annoyance, Eve could tell that this had been the subject of many conversations. Just the same, even with him as an ally, she knew that it would take much more than one of her father's arguments about flexibility and adaptability to convince her mother to change her mind. Her mother might visit the island, but she would never live on it.

"Mom, everyone I know who has relocated to the islands loves it. You would, too," Eve interjected on her father's behalf. Even as a child, she often took his side in arguments with Helen taking their mother's.

"Then why are you here, trying to adjust to the city sounds, rather than enjoying your life there?" her mother demanded.

Never able to keep anything from her mother, who seemed to be able to read her thoughts, Eve said, "I'm trying to decide if I like it enough in Bermuda to move there permanently."

"Is that all?" her father asked, studying her face.

"No. I've fallen in love with a college professor, but I don't know if I'm ready for the commitment," Eve acknowledged frankly.

"Why not, dear? You've been alone long enough," her mother suggested.

"That's not all, is it, Eve?" her father probed.

"I'm not sure if I'm really over Brad. I thought I was

until he visited at Christmas. Now I'm not sure," Eve replied honestly.

"Brad? Oh, gracious!" Her mother sighed. "He's not the man for you. I don't care if he is on his way to being a rich and famous physician. He's too wild. Even his mother says that he's heading for disaster one day. His hobbies are enough to make my hair turn gray just thinking about them. I didn't want to be the interfering mother when you two were together, so I kept my reservations to myself. I was glad that you ended that relationship. Don't resurrect it."

"That's just it," Eve said. "I'm not really sure that it ended or if I simply needed a change. Until I know that for certain, I can't decide about David and the islands. To make matters worse, David needs to know my decision so that he can notify the college of his plans."

Her dad sniffed and said, "I don't often agree with your mother, but I do this time. Brad's a good man, but he's not for you. He and that Gina he was dating while you were away were always on the go and doing reckless things. His latest is white-water rafting. His father thinks the boy's a daredevil."

"David's certainly the opposite." Eve smiled warmly. "When I first met him, he was all work. The most adventurous thing he'd do was eating lunch by the water. Now, however, he enjoys parasailing. One part of me thinks that life with him would be wonderful; the other side is uncertain about the future with him."

"You'll get over that uncertainty with time. He sounds perfect for you and you seem to be good for each other. That's the way it should be. You should complement each other," her mother said.

"That's what's kept us going all these years," Eve's father said. "Your mother takes up the slack when I don't do as I should."

Smiling lovingly at her husband, Eve's mother replied, "And he's my rock. You learn to overlook the flaws. They still make you crazy, but you overlook the surface cracks and only see the solid structure underneath."

"As much as I love you two and appreciate your advice, I'm still not sure. I'll have to think about it," Eve stated as she hugged her parents.

"That's fine," her father said. "It's your life, and we can't live it for you. Sleep on it many times. Go out with Brad. Weigh him against David. I'm sure that one of them will emerge the stronger candidate. If not, maybe neither of them is right for you. You're still young. Look around more before making a decision."

"But don't take too long, Eve," her mother interjected. "I want to be a grandmother before I'm too old to play with my grandchild."

Eve smiled at her loving parents, who only had her best interest at heart. Being with them again had soothed her soul but, unfortunately, further complicated the decision she needed to make. She wanted a relationship like theirs and wondered if she would ever have one. She loved being at home in the States, yet she did not want to allow the longing for home she felt while away to influence her decision. She knew that David would relocate to this area to be with her; he had shown his flexibility and determination by applying for a position here without telling her. She would not have asked him to make that sacrifice. She did not want him to feel as homesick as she had over the last school year.

Kissing her parents good-bye, Eve drove home. One thing she knew with certainty was that she had not missed the traffic and the hassle of getting around in the area. The rude, harried drivers and the stop-and-go traffic were a far cry from her leisurely rides around the island. However, she wondered if she would one day become discontent in paradise. The lifestyle was wonderfully laid-back, but she wondered if it was slow to the extreme. Maybe it was the perfect getaway place for a big city girl rather than a permanent home. Adding D.C.'s traffic and the island's lifestyle to the factors for consideration on her list, Eve inched home.

When she finally arrived, she saw Brad's car in the parking lot. Pulling into her space in the underground lot, Eve rode the elevator to her floor. Inside the apartment, Helen and Brad sat watching television. Snacks covered the coffee table, and the smell of freshly popped popcorn met her at the door.

"What's this? It looks like you guys are having a good time without me," Eve announced as she locked the door behind her.

"We are. A lot of really good movies are on the tube today," Helen replied without looking away from the screen.

"Come join us. This one is almost over. A good musical starts after this," Brad said, gobbling another handful of popcorn.

Smiling, Eve tossed her purse into the closet and joined them. Brad handed her the popcorn and Helen moved the bowl of jellybeans closer. Sitting between them, Eve felt at home. Maybe her father was right. Maybe she had not found the perfect man yet because she enjoyed being herself more than she relished the idea of being a couple. Watching television with Brad and Helen was like enjoying the afternoon with two siblings instead of one. He made no demands except that she pass the popcorn and keep the jellybeans coming. Maybe this was the happiness she wanted most.

Noticing that Helen dabbed freely at tears that glistened on her cheeks, Eve turned her attention to the movie. It was one of the famous old ones in which the characters had almost lost each other in a freak accident. They had been reunited after each felt that the other no longer cared. In the closing scenes, they cleared up the confusion and agreed never to part again.

"That's so beautiful," Helen said, sobbing freely.

"Has she been like this through the entire movie?" Eve asked Brad.

"The whole time," Brad said, munching on jellybeans. "As soon as the movie started, so did the waterworks. She's seen this movie so many times that she knows the dialogue and the flow of the plot. She started crying as soon as the characters met on the boat."

Helen looked at Eve with wet eyes and smiled. "It's so like Arty and me," she sniffed.

"Oh, brother!" Brad exclaimed. "I'm going to the kitchen. Soda, anyone?"

Before Eve could reply, Helen said as the tears began again, "I'm separated from Arty by an entire ocean. I miss him!"

"Helen, you're in no frame of mind to watch movies like this," Eve said, handing her sister the box of tissues.

"I know, but a purging cry feels so good. Is anyone else hungry?" Helen asked.

"It's not as if she hasn't eaten all afternoon. She's done her share with the popcorn, too," Brad shouted from the kitchen.

"Crying takes a lot out of me and makes me hungry," Helen replied with a pout.

Looking at her emotional sister, Eve decided that she had to make a decision about her own life quickly. Summer was the time for relaxation, not the stress of a confusing love life and Helen bursting into tears whenever she watched a romantic movie. She did not need Helen's melodrama added to her own confusion.

"Let's go out for pizza," Eve suggested as Helen and Brad joined her at the door.

"Fine with me as long as they don't show old movies," Brad commented, chuckling. "I've had enough for one day."

"You're so mean to me," Helen said, giving him a nasty look.

The trio slipped into the foot traffic on the sidewalk. Almost immediately, Eve had the sense that their little group was destined to change. A new reality was only a phone call away.

Chapter Eighteen

The weeks of summer vacation passed quickly. Eve had seen more of Brad than she had in the months before their breakup. She enjoyed his company tremendously, perhaps more as a member of their trio than as a couple. He made the perfect sibling; the verdict was still out on his ability to be an ideal husband.

Unable to make up her mind about David and the island, Eve had asked the school board for an extension and received it. However, even that time was running out. Soon, she would have to sign the contract. Despite the looming decisions, Eve felt happier than she had in months because she was at home.

To take Helen's mind off Arty and the decision with which she struggled, Eve and Brad took her with them often. Despite her loneliness without Arty, her business was growing; she had cultivated clients as far away as the Caribbean islands and Bermuda. Arty phoned often, but he did not put pressure on her to make up her mind. Since she liked the ring, Helen wore it daily on the third finger of her left hand even though she had not formulated her response to the marriage proposal. Arty had said that she would not need to return it if she decided not to marry him. However, Helen knew that she would. She would not want any memories, not even gorgeous jewelry, if she did not decide to marry him.

One morning rather than fighting the traffic to the Chesapeake Bay or to downtown D.C. and the monuments, Eve decided that it was time for her to return to Bermuda. She had made the arrangement, knowing that the fare was nonrefundable. She needed to visit the island one more time to clear her mind and to see David. After that, she would give her answer to the school board and to the men in her life.

"I don't know why you want to do this. It'll only confuse you more to see the island again," Helen stated as she watched Eve pack her bag.

"Probably, but I have to do it. I don't want to make the mistake of my life," Eve explained.

"Maybe I should go with you. I could use a break," Helen mused.

"You'd be able to see Arty again, too," Eve said.

"That's a good idea, but I probably can't get a seat on the flight."

"Look on my dresser."

Helen laughed. "You booked a seat for me? You know me too well."

"No, I wouldn't say that. I just don't want to go alone," Eve said, hugging her sister.

"I'd better throw a few things into a bag," Helen said as she walked toward her room.

"I packed your stuff first. Your bag's in the hall. Let's go."

"Pushy! Pushy!" Helen giggled and added, "Did you tell Brad?"

"Last night."

"What did he say?" Helen demanded in wonder.

"He wasn't thrilled, but there's not much he can do about it."

"Once you've made up your mind, it's a done deal," Helen agreed.

"That's the problem; I haven't. All I know is that I have to see Bermuda and David again. It's time to tie up the loose ends. Both school systems need my response and so do both men. I've got to do it."

"Me too. I can't drag my feet about Arty any longer. I have to decide," Helen said as they settled into the cab.

The ride to the airport in the cab had a different feel from the last time Eve had made the trip. This time instead of Brad's sad face to see her off, she paid an impersonal driver. A lot had changed in almost a year since she made her first trip to the island, and just as much had remained the same. This time, rather than being a stranger, she knew where to look for her friends and happiness. Besides, it was time for the summer breezes to blow in a new beginning.

The flight was perfect, the landing smooth, and Bermuda as lush and beautiful as Eve remembered. Taking a taxi to the little cottage, Eve and Helen enjoyed the familiar scenery. Eve felt as if she was returning to a place of wonderful memories and infinite possibilities. She felt at peace. Helen, however, grew more restless with every mile they traveled from the airport. She fidgeted with the ring constantly and looked out the window as if she expected to find Arty standing on the roadside. Although both sisters registered their inner turmoil differently, they fought with the same desire to make a life-changing decision and the same uneasiness about taking the step.

"Stop at the university for a minute, please," Eve instructed the driver.

"Why?" Helen asked.

"I'd like to see David. He's usually here," Eve replied with a calm demeanor that was too composed for the circumstances.

Helen waited as Eve ran into the math department building. When she returned in only a few minutes, Helen knew that she had not found David hard at work at his desk. However, instead of being disappointed, Eve simply thanked the driver and asked him to continue the trip to the cottage.

As they approached a familiar stretch of beach, Eve asked the driver to pull into the first available parking space. Although the owner had closed the shack for the evening, she wanted to take a look at the place at which she had first met David. Finding their favorite spot deserted, she returned to the cab, said a few words to the driver, and eased into the seat.

Helen frowned at her sister and demanded, "What are you doing?"

"Nothing," Eve replied with a smile. "I just wanted to see the old spot."

Once again the cab pulled away. Eve looked smug and content. Helen, however, was becoming very concerned about her sister's sanity. She could not figure out Eve's reason for wanting to make the frequent stops. They would have days to revisit their favorite locations.

The next stop was at Eve's favorite restaurant. Jumping out, she left Helen to wonder at her motives, considering that they had not discussed arrangements for dinner. Eve returned a short time later with a huge bag from which the most wonderful aroma filled the car. After she handed the driver his food order, the cab pulled away.

"Are you looking for David? We could have stopped

at his condo," Helen said as the cab moved through the quiet evening.

"No, I phoned, but he's not there. I'm hungry, and we needed dinner. The driver wanted something, too. I left the refrigerator in the cottage empty and turned off," Eve replied calmly.

"That bag's huge. Are you planning to feed an army?" Helen demanded.

Eve smiled. "No, just us."

Helen's anxiety increased. It was not like Eve to act in such a random, unplanned way. Helen could not understand the reason for the change in her sister's behavior. Eve was usually so predictable but not now.

Traveling in the most indirect manner for a return trip to the little cottage, the driver pulled into the driveway of a very familiar house. Helen's eyes grew large as she recognized it, and the impeccably clean yard. She slumped slightly in her seat as if trying to hide from someone. She was not ready to face Arty.

Although all of the lights were off, Eve walked quickly to the studio and knocked. Receiving no answer, she returned to the car. As they continued their journey, she hummed merrily.

"Have you lost your mind?" Helen asked, studying her sister's face and straightening her clothing.

"No," Eve replied simply and handed Helen an envelope. "It's for you. I found it on Arty's door."

Helen gazed from her sister's smiling face to the envelope in her hand. She had never been so confused in her life. Instead of feeling relief at being on the island again, Helen only felt incredibly bewildered by Eve's strange behavior and the circuitous trip to the cottage.

"Why would Arty have left a note for me on this shop door?" Helen asked. "He didn't know I was coming with you."

"I don't know. You know as well as I do that there's no explaining the things he does," Eve replied.

Even in the dimming light of twilight, Helen could see that Eve was smiling. Her sister actually looked happy. Helen made up her mind that, if Eve's strange behavior increased, she would ask the cabbie to take a detour to the hospital. Eve must have been experiencing a psychotic episode. Her behavior bordered on bizarre considering the decisions that weighed on her mind.

Finally, the cab stopped in front of the picket fence that surrounded the little cottage. Paying the cabbie, Eve and Helen collected the bags that he had unloaded onto the walk. The food bag was so huge that Helen had to carry both travel bags.

Stopping on the walk, Eve inhaled deeply of the sweet ocean air. Listening carefully, she could hear the waves lapping on the sandy beach behind her house. A few seabirds called from the darkening sky, and the lights of her neighbors glowed in the distant windows. The quiet of the island summer evening offered a delightful break from the noise of the Washington suburbs.

"Are we going in or are we simply planning to stand out here all night?" Helen asked, staring into Eve's upturned face.

"Sorry. I was just enjoying the blissfully quiet evening. I had forgotten how comforting the silence can be," Eve replied as she resumed the walk to the cottage's front door.

"It is lovely here," Helen commented, "but it's not realistic for people like us. It's a place to come during the winter to get away from the snow. As much as I love it here, I know now that I can't live here. I need the bustle of a big city."

"We have to reach our individual conclusions, but

this is my favorite time of day on the island," Eve confided.

"That's nice, Eve, but do you think we could enter the house? My arms are breaking under the weight of these bags," Helen complained gently.

"No problem. Watch your step," Eve said as she unlocked the front door that she had locked ages ago.

The darkened living room came to life at the click of the turning key. Instantly, the lights came on to illuminate the little room that looked just as Eve had left it. The school board had not begun the redecorating process, probably hoping that Eve would return. And they had been right to wait.

"I'm home," Eve said to the little house.

"You've really missed it here, haven't you?" Helen asked, watching Eve's enraptured face.

"More than you'll ever know," Eve replied as tears sparkled on her lashes.

Sadly, Helen commented, "I guess this means that I'll have to find a new roommate."

Hugging her sister, Eve said, "That's easier than you think."

Helen frowned and said, "You're doing it to me again, aren't you? You used to do this when we were kids. I hated it then, and I hate it now. Stop talking between the lines and say what you mean."

Eve laughed from the kitchen where she busily placed the different entrées on platters. "I was wondering when you'd figure out that I was doing it to you. Now all you have to do is decode it."

"I hate this." Helen sulked, placing the heavy bags on the stairs.

"I know." Eve laughed happily. She glowed from the pure joy of being on the island again and being able to tease her sister like in the days when life was simpler.

"You bought enough food for an army," Helen commented, looking at the overloaded dining room table.

"You know that restaurant never serves small portions," Eve replied and added, "Have you opened the letter yet?"

"No, I'll wait until after dinner. I need food to buoy my courage," Helen said, picking at the curry chicken.

"If you wait too much longer, you will have waited too long," Eve said cryptically.

"There you go again," Helen grumbled.

Suddenly the sound of male voices resounded from the front yard. Immediately, two tall figures filled the door that Eve had not locked. The little house felt even smaller with the resonating happiness.

Running toward the tallest one, Eve threw herself into his arms. The warmth of his body enfolded her as their bodies melted together as if they had never been apart. The summer breeze filled the living room with the heady aroma of flowers.

"Eve, I love you. It's been so long," David muttered into her neck.

"A lifetime," Eve replied softly.

"Will you marry me?" David asked quickly, seizing the splendor of the moment.

"Yes, I'll marry you. I love you so." Eve sighed.

"Promise me that you'll never leave me again?" David asked, searching Eve's face and finding the answer clearly written there.

"Never. We'll be inseparable from this day until forever," Eve replied, laughing happily.

Rooted to the spot on which she stood, Helen could only watch the reunion between her sister and David. Equally unsure of his actions, Arty stood and waited. The next move was Helen's.

Eve and David left the cottage for a walk on the

beach, leaving Arty and Helen alone. Neither moved or spoke for what felt like an eternity. The delicious breeze caressed their faces and invited them to join the others on the beach.

Breaking the silence, Arty asked, "Did you read my letter?"

"No, not yet," Helen replied through dry lips.

"You don't need to now," Arty said and added, "I'm here until you send me away."

"Is that what you wrote in your letter?" Helen asked, clinging to the dining room chair to keep from falling at the sight and nearness of the man she loved so dearly.

"That's only part of it," Arty said, taking one step forward in the small cottage.

"What was the rest of it?"

"I wrote that I love you more than my own life and dream of growing old with you," Arty said, moving another step closer.

Still holding on to the chair, Helen said softly, "Regardless of my feelings, why would I want to marry you and give up all that I have at home?"

His voice choking with emotion, Arty replied, "Because my life is empty without you. Because yours has a void without me that work can't fill. Because the life that we would make together would make us happier than living apart ever could."

"But, Arty—" Helen began as his lips silenced any objection that she might have.

The summer breeze embraced them and blew away any further objections. Sinking onto the sofa with their hands locked, Helen and Arty sat side by side saying nothing and not regretting the silence. Their life together would contain many of those overflowing moments during which they would remember that night.

The sound of laughter at the door only added to the

happiness in the little cottage. Opening the door that she would not lock again, Eve and David entered holding hands and sharing little jokes. Their eyes never left each other's face as they took their seats at the table. A great meal and wonderful company added to the magic of the evening.

"When and how did you arrange all of this?" Helen asked Eve, still bewildered by the events of the evening.

"I had some help," Eve replied, motioning to David and Arty.

Helen moaned. "I'm so confused."

Patting Helen's hand, Eve explained, "I know you, little sister. You're determined, stubborn, devoted, and loving. I knew that you weren't really wearing that ring because of its beauty. You love Arty as much as he loves you. The only thing keeping you from running to him was me. You didn't want to leave me alone in D.C. without David."

"You would have been so lonely," Helen said softly.

"I won't be alone," Eve responded with a smile at David.

"I didn't know that," Helen said. "I couldn't tell which way you were leaning."

Eve continued, "I could tell that you really championed his cause and not Brad's. You were right; time has passed for that relationship. He and I are two entirely different people now. We'll always be friends, but that's all. He's fine with my decision."

Smiling tearfully, Helen said, "Brad's a good guy, but I really like David. He has always felt like a brother to me."

"I've always wanted a little sister," David replied, moved by Helen's tears.

"I phoned David and Arty, made the reservations, packed our stuff, and here we are," Eve finished.

"What a mess!" Helen sobbed.

"Now what's the problem?" Arty asked, looking toward Eve for help.

"I don't want to live here either. It's beautiful here, but it's not home. I'll miss Eve too much. I almost died without her this year. Eve and David will live in the States, but I'll be stuck here in paradise," Helen wailed into Arty's shirt.

"If you had opened my letter, you would have read that we're not going to live here. We're moving to the States, too. I'm the new artist-in-residence at Georgetown University. I had an interview on the same day as David. They already knew my work and wanted me to join them. I'll have plenty of time to create plus a regular check. That'll take some of the stress off me. I won't have to mass-produce my creations. I can be more selective," Arty said, patting her shoulder and kissing away her tears.

Immediately, the sobbing stopped. Looking up, Helen asked incredulously, "What? Why didn't anyone tell me?"

"I told you to read Arty's letter," Eve reminded her.

"I can't believe it!" a revived Helen squealed. "We'll all live in the States! What'll happen to your house?"

"It's a family house, so I can't sell it, but a cousin will rent it from me. We'll be able to come here for vacations to check on it whenever we want," Arty replied, hugging Helen close.

David added, "I'll keep my condo as long as it's profitable as a rental to vacationers. I've already signed a contract with a management firm."

"How long have you known about all this?" Helen demanded of her sister.

Smiling, Eve replied, "David shared his plans with me the day he phoned about the university interview. I didn't say anything because I wasn't sure about my decision. He was gentle and kind and not at all pressuring. I guess I didn't see any reason to mention it since you hadn't led me to think that you might be interested in moving here."

"I wasn't and I'm not, but someone should have told me. I may be the little sister, but I'm not a baby," Helen said, sulking.

"I'm sorry," Eve said as she patted Helen's shoulder. "Next time you'll know everything I do. I guess we need to sell our condo and start looking for places that accommodate two old married people."

"Well, actually, I've already started looking for a new condo and have found one that I really like. Our place is too small now that I've opened my own business. I can't function properly out of boxes under the bed. I need an office desperately and so do you for your crafts and paper grading," Helen stated sheepishly.

"Really? When did you plan to tell me? Were you simply going to move out?" Eve inquired with hands on hips.

"Sorry," Helen mumbled. "I guess we're even. I had planned to tell you this week but this trip came up."

"Where is this new condo of yours?" Eve asked, laughing at her sister's embarrassment.

"That's the good part," Helen explained. "It's in our building and on the same floor. It's that big two-bedroom with a family room and a sunroom that the Parkers own. They're moving, so it'll be available. You can buy my interest in our condo. The furniture's yours; it only makes sense that I should be the one to move."

Turning to David, Eve asked, "Is that okay with you?"

"I don't care where we live as long as we're together," he replied, giving Eve's hand a gentle kiss.

"Well, this calls for a celebration," Arty announced. "Let's go for ice cream."

The foursome walked from the cottage into the evening that still smelled of summer breezes off the sea. All of their problems suddenly seemed so small as they linked arms happily. The magic of Bermuda had brought them together; the wonder of love had set them free.

David smiled at Eve as they walked down the road to the restaurant at the foot of the hill. Even if they lived in the States and only visited Bermuda, she was an island woman now. For the first time since Eve had moved to the island, she had not locked the door.

ABOUT THE AUTHOR

Born in 1950 in Washington, D.C., Courtni Wright graduated from Trinity College (D.C.) in 1972 with a major in English and a minor in history. In 1980, she earned a master's degree in education from John Hopkins University in Baltimore, Maryland. She was a fellow of the Council for Basic Education National Endowment for the Humanities in 1990. She has served as a consultant on National Geographic Society educational films on the practice and history of Kwanzaa, the history of the black cowboys, the story of Harriet Tubman, and the African American heritage in the West.

Ms. Wright's writing career covers several genres. Her first romance novel, *Blush,* was published under the Arabesque imprint in September 1997. Since then, eleven other titles have followed. Holiday House published her children's books: *Jumping the Broom,* selected for the Society of School Librarians International's list of "Best Books of 1994"; *Journey to Freedom,* named a "Teacher's Choice" book by the International Reading Association; and *Wagon Train,* an acclaimed favorite. Her venture into Shakespearean analysis, *The Women of Shakespeare's Plays,* was published by University Press of America.

Courtni Wright lives in Maryland with her husband, two Pomeranians, a cat, and a parrot named Max.

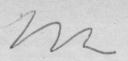

Enter the Arabesque 10th Anniversary Contest!

GRAND PRIZE: 1 Winner will receive:
- $10,000 Prize Package

FIRST PRIZE: 5 Winners will receive:
- Special 10th Anniversary limited edition gift
- 1 Year Arabesque Bookclub subscription

SECOND PRIZE: 10 Winners will receive:
- Special 10th Anniversary prize packs

ARABESQUE 10TH ANNIVERSARY CONTEST RULES:

- Contest open January 1–April 30, 2004.
- Mail-In Entries Only (postmarked by 4/30/04 and received by 5/7/04).
- On letter-size paper: Name your favorite Arabesque novel or author and why in 50 words or less.
- Include proof of purchase of an Arabesque novel (send ISBN).
- Include photograph/head shot (4x6 photo preferred, no larger than 5x7).
- Name, address, city, state, zip, daytime phone number and e-mail address.
- Contest entrants must be 21 years of age or older and live in the U.S.
- Only one entry allowed per person.
- Must be able to travel on dates specified: July 30-Aug 1, 2004.
- Send your entry to:

BET Books—10th Anniversary Contest
One BET Plaza
1235 W Street, NE
Washington, DC   20018